PATH
OF
GODS

Also by Snorri Kristjansson

Swords of Good Men
Blood Will Follow

PATH OF GODS

SNORRI KRISTJANSSON

The Valhalla Saga Book III

Jo Fletcher

BOOKS

First published in Great Britain in 2015 by

Jo Fletcher Books
an imprint of
Quercus Publishing Ltd
Carmelite House
50 Victoria Embankment
London EC4Y 0DZ

An Hachette UK company

HB ISBN 978 1 78206 340 7
TPB ISBN 978 1 78206 339 1
EBOOK ISBN 978 1 78429 046 7

This book is a work of fiction. Names, characters,
places and events are
either the product of the author's imagination
or are used fictitiously. Any resemblance to
actual persons, living or dead, events or
localities is entirely coincidental.

Printed and bound in Great Britain by Clays Ltd, St Ives plc

For Geraldine Cooke.
Defender, believer, campaigner.

Prologue

The clouds parted, and just for a moment, the winter sun shone down on the smooth snow. What might have been tracks were now no more than ridges on a blue-white surface. A depression suggested that there might be a cave in the hillside, but it had long since been snowed in. The hills, solid and silent, looked down on houses that had once stood in defiance of nature; havens of warmth and safety in the unforgiving land.

Now they were just empty.

A strong gust rolled down into the valley, lifting white flakes from the ground and up, up, into whirling clouds of crisp, sparkling specks.

They settled on roofs already covered in sheets of ice.

They danced around black, barren branches.

They covered frozen purple and grey fingers of dead men strewn about between the houses with arms stuck out at odd angles. Severed limbs draped in tendrils of black, frozen blood poked out of drifts. Where there were faces, they were carved in frost and horror.

The silence was broken by a sharp, painful creak as the door to the longhouse inched open, screaming on bent hinges.

A tall man stepped out onto the front step. His grey robes swirled about him, but he did not look touched by the cold. A wide-brimmed hat hung down to cover his right eye, but the left one gleamed as he took in the surroundings. Under a scraggly white beard, dried and cracked skin moved as his stony face broke into a smile.

'So that's how you want it to be,' he said to the wind.

High up in the sky to the south, two black dots appeared, growing bigger by the moment, spreading their wings and swooping down towards the man on the steps. Cawing loudly, the ravens landed with smooth grace at the man's feet. He looked at them and raised an eyebrow. The big birds hopped towards him then flapped their wings and rose until they had settled, one on each shoulder. Behind him, the door creaked again as two big dogs padded out of the longhouse.

'Then that's how it is,' the old man said, and started walking, following six pairs of footprints, heading to the South.

For a moment everything stood still, etched in grey on black: dark forms looming in the shadows, hovering on the edge between moonlight and darkness. At the head of the half-visible army Sven and Sigurd Aegisson stood over the deer carcase, looking at the two travellers. The chieftain and his right-hand man looked leaner, somehow, and older, but more alive.

Frozen halfway through drawing his sword, Ulfar could do nothing but stare. As his brain caught up, he started recognising other faces from Stenvik. He could see at least fifty of them, and there were obviously more in the shadows. Sven, front and centre, turned to Sigurd. 'See? I told you the boy would turn out well. That's the best impression of an idiot I've seen in a long time.'

Sigurd spared him a faint smile, then, nodding to Audun, he walked towards the fire and sat down. Behind him, the silent warriors started moving with purpose. A handful, still eerily quiet, drifted back into the forest. Sven directed two men towards the deer. Knives flashed, and the scent of blood soon drifted towards the fire.

Easing as gracefully as he could out of his fighting stance, Ulfar finally managed, 'What – what news of Stenvik?' Sliding his blade back into the scabbard, he sat down by the fire.

'King Olav took the town as his own,' Sven said as he sat down too. 'He spared our lives, no thanks to Harald, but he demanded that we bend the knee to him and the White Christ. The boys were all smart enough to nod and smile.'

'He couldn't let us walk around because he thought we'd stir up trouble,' Sigurd said.

'Which, to be fair, was correct,' Sven added.

'And he didn't have the stomach for the work. So he kept us locked up,' Sigurd said.

'And great fun it was, too,' Sven said. 'If I get the choice next time and the other option is a cage with a wolf, I'm taking the wolf.' He gestured to another silent, bearded man who stepped into the circle, added some more kindling and blew gently until he was rewarded with a small but sturdy flame. As he moved away the flame disappeared for a moment, then the glow returned and quickly doubled in size, growing even more as warriors continued bringing firewood from the forest.

'Then why are you here?' Audun said.

'Valgard poisoned us,' Sigurd said.

Audun and Ulfar exchanged glances, then looked at Sven. The old man's eyes told them all they needed to know.

'How—?' Audun asked. By the other fire in the clearing, something sizzled and soon the smell of roast meat filled Ulfar's nostrils.

'He brought us our food. We ate it. Laced with shadowroot – well masked, too. I did taste it, but too late. The next we knew, we were being dug up.'

Audun shivered and looked over his shoulder. 'Who dug you up?'

'A traveller,' Sigurd said, and Ulfar mouthed the words as they came out of the old chieftain's mouth: 'Tall, grey hair, beard. Big hat.' He had to stop as he was handed a dagger with a chunk of roast deer on the point. Sven continued, 'He said he'd been passing through when he heard these two men talk about getting rid of some bodies. I'm not clear on the details, but there's no doubt in my mind that he saved our lives.'

'I bet he did,' Ulfar muttered. He glanced at Audun, who looked similarly suspicious. 'Then what?'

'We had some debts to pay,' Sigurd said. Suddenly the silence in the glade deepened. 'So we did. Then we left to find Forkbeard, and now we're here.'

'Forkbeard?' Audun said. 'Why?'

'Because Olav has gone north,' Sven said. 'He's in Trondheim now. If he digs in up there he'll double his army in no time and then we're stuck with him. Hakon was happy to sit on his peasants up north, but I doubt that the kinglet will be as pleasant. We need to convince Sweyn Forkbeard that he'll be better off facing King Olav now, before he goes out west again to collect. If he doesn't, he'll be defending the shores of Denmark from cross-bearing Norse madmen in two years, maybe less.'

'So all roads lead north, then,' Ulfar said as another man handed him a chunk of roasted meat.

'They always do, son,' Sven said. 'They always do.'

Morning brought thick grey skies and a bitter wind. Sigurd's men kept talking to a minimum; they were up and ready at daybreak.

'Here, take this,' Sven said as Ulfar and Audun clambered to their feet. In the old man's outstretched hand were thick-spun woollen trousers and tunics. 'You look like the runts of a litter of runts.'

Looking at Audun and himself, Ulfar had to concede the point. Travelling had taken a lot out of the both of them; their clothes were torn and bloody, and they both looked years older than they had only four short months ago.

'Thank you,' he said.

'It's not for your benefit,' Sven said. 'You're harder to fatten up if you're cold, and we need something to throw at Forkbeard if he's hungry.'

'And your bony old arse won't do,' Ulfar replied as he struggled into the new clothes.

'My bony old arse will do more than yours does,' Sven batted back. 'I've got a hundred hard bastards behind me. You've just got a mopey blacksmith.'

Ulfar smiled. 'That's about right. But don't worry – you'll pick up more men soon and then we'll be even. I'd say about seventy more sounds fair.'

Sven chortled and grinned at Audun, who shrugged.

Soon enough they were dressed and ready, and Ulfar asked, 'Where are you looking for Forkbeard?'

'I reckon we'll do what we've been doing: find the nearest burned-out farm and track him from there,' Sven said. There was nothing more to say, so they headed off, threading their way through the tall birch trees.

The grey sky turned from wool to milk to dirty ice but the sun kept resolutely out of sight. When they cleared the forest they saw fields dusted with white stretching far into the distance, rising and rolling gently away from them. A single-track dirt road cut across the landscape like a scar.

The sun was straight above them when Ulfar spoke. 'I don't like this quiet.'

'It was fine until you ruined it,' Audun said.

'Where there's roads there's people, but we haven't seen a single soul all morning,' Ulfar muttered. 'We might as well be alone in the world.'

'Don't worry, son. Trouble will find us,' Sven said from the front of the line. 'It usually does.' They walked on in silence as the clouds above thickened into a dark grey mass. 'Any time now,' the old rogue muttered darkly, and sure enough, the first flakes of snow soon fluttered down from above. 'Bloody snow,' he added. 'Just like you, Ulfar: pretty but useless.'

'You say that, but at least I can— No, you're right. You forgot annoying, though,' Ulfar said.

'Sven,' Sigurd said. The tone of his voice made the men around him snap to attention immediately.

Two hundred yards ahead of them a fox had wandered out of a thicket and was standing stock-still, sniffing at the air. It ignored the group of men and stared around; it looked almost as if it was listening to a silent tune.

The eagle struck almost too fast for the eye to see. The fox yelped and fought, but it was no use. Powerful wings beat about its head, a strong beak tore at its ears, finger-thick talons dug into its back and clamped down on its spine. The eagle strained, and slowly the fox's paws lifted off the ground. A screech tore the air as another eagle approached and also latched on to the terrified fox.

The Stenvik raiders watched, stunned, blood dripping onto the snow from above as the two huge birds flew away, tearing at the screeching animal caught between them.

'Get moving! *Now!*' Sigurd shouted, and behind him the group of hardened warriors snapped to and trudged on. Around them, Ulfar could hear snatches of muttered conversation.

'—never seen anything like that—'

'—eagles hunting a *fox*? And *two* of them?'

'—the stars ain't right, I'm telling you—'

The talk died down as they walked, but Ulfar couldn't help but notice that every one of the old warriors kept their guard up.

*

A while after midday they came to a farm. Fields stretched out in every direction but tucked in a copse of trees in the distance stood a building.

'Go for it?' Sven said.

Sigurd shrugged. 'Might as well. See about news.' A half-smile played on his lips as he glanced at Ulfar. 'We'll send in our local man.'

'Told you he'd be useful,' Sven said gleefully.

Ulfar rolled his eyes and started preparing to explain why he was showing up at someone's doorstep with a hundred hardened Northmen at his back. When they'd halved the distance, Sigurd motioned for a halt. 'We'll stop here, I think,' he said.

'Right. In you go, son,' Sven said. Around him, the men put down their bags and set about finding a place to rest comfortably, dusting the snow off the ground where possible. 'Take the ox with you if you want. Try to look friendly, though.'

Ulfar unhooked his sword-belt and looked at Audun, who moved to his side without a word. They put the Northmen at their backs and walked down a worn road of sorts that was covered lightly with fresh snow.

It looked good from afar, but up close the farm was very quiet indeed. The barren branches of the trees cast long shadows and the fading light did nothing to make the surroundings more pleasant.

'Not much going on, is there?' Ulfar said.

'No,' Audun replied.

They looked around for evidence of battle but nothing was broken. The farm gate was open, but didn't look like it had been moved for some time. The yard was empty, the stables to their left looked shadowy and lifeless and the barn door was slightly ajar. The house itself looked in reasonably good repair, but there was no flicker of flame anywhere to tell of life or warmth.

'Hello?' Ulfar shouted in a way that he hoped would communicate an absolute lack of intent to kill anyone. No one answered. He tried again, but again his voice echoed off the walls. He was about to move when Audun's heavy hand landed on his forearm and held him back.

'Wait and watch, Thormodsson,' he mumbled. The hairs on Ulfar's neck rose.

Something moved in the farmhouse. Sounds of scuffling, something toppling over and a muted curse drifted out into the yard. A shape appeared in the doorway.

'Strangers,' it said in a thick voice. 'Greetings.'

'Greetings!' Ulfar replied. 'We come in peace, and would like to—'

'No, you don't,' a voice said from inside the cabin. The shape in the shadowy doorway was joined by another.

Wrong-footed, Ulfar stumbled on his words. 'What do you mean? We wish you no harm.'

'I know *that*,' the second man said as he came out into the yard to meet them. He was Ulfar's height and Audun's width, but he looked oddly grey, like he'd been ill for some time. The first man followed him out into the yard: younger, maybe in his teens, sandy-haired and friendly, but with the same big frame and square features. The men were clad in farmer's clothes and unarmed, but they were a little . . . *faded*, somehow. 'But you do not come in peace.'

Beside him Audun tensed, but Ulfar smiled his best and tried to relax. 'I am afraid I do not follow, my friend.'

The big farmer's eyes lit up. 'This is not a time of peace. This is a time of war.'

Familiar territory. Ulfar smiled a rueful smile and shook his head. 'I know. Forkbeard is running wild around these parts, I hear.'

Confusion flitted across their faces. 'Forkbeard?'

'Forkbeard. Danish King. Sweyn Forkbeard. Has a . . . big beard . . .'

'. . . which he braids in a fork,' Audun added.

The big farmer smiled. 'Oh, *him.*' Beside him, the boy laughed. Caught up, Audun and Ulfar both laughed with them. 'He doesn't matter,' the big man said, dismissively.

'. . . oh? I mean, I agree, Forkbeard is not as important as he thinks he is—'

'You're not wrong there!' the youth chimed in, and the big farmer ruffled his hair like a father would.

'—but as far as we know he's been running around the country-side here, burning and killing,' Ulfar added. This was not going the way he had expected.

The big farmer shrugged. 'Way of the world. It all fits.'

'All fits,' the youth repeated.

'How?' Audun said, his face screwed up in concentration.

'It's the Rising,' the youth said. His father nodded.

'What is the Rising?' Ulfar said.

The big man looked at him as if Ulfar had asked him to explain water. 'What is the Rising? Did you hear that, boy?'

'I did!' the boy said.

'The Rising!' the big man said, face lit up in fervour, 'the Rising is when – when *he* has . . . risen!'

'And who is he?' Ulfar asked.

'The – the—' He blinked and winced, as if to shake off a bad headache. 'He is – um – he has risen! *He has risen!*'

'All right, he has risen. I understand,' Ulfar said, glancing at the gate.

'I don't think you do, traveller,' the youth said. 'I think you are one of his enemies, and I think you'll do great harm.'

Audun rolled his shoulders.

'We're not your enemies,' Ulfar said hurriedly. 'We understand. We'll just go now.'

'You can still help him,' the big farmer said. 'You want to help, don't you?'

Audun gestured for Ulfar to be calm. 'No,' he said quietly. 'No, we don't.'

The big farmer homed in on the blacksmith, his eyes ablaze, like someone hearing a familiar song. 'You,' he said. 'There is something inside you . . . that he wants.'

'Come and get it then,' Audun said.

Without warning the big farmer went for Audun, growling, thick arms outstretched, aiming to catch him in a crunching bear-hug.

A moment later, Ulfar's reflexes sent him spinning away from a vicious hook thrown by the youth, but three steps back was not enough; the boy was upon him, raining blows with glee. 'He rises!' he shrieked.

'Who is "he"?' Ulfar shouted back, blocking and retreating. He could just glimpse Audun and the big farmer locked in a wrestler's hold, neither giving an inch.

'He is the cold in the North! He is death in winter! He is the life-blood of the Viking! The path to Valhalla!' the youth spat, kicking, gouging and clawing.

'Where in the North?' Ulfar shouted, landing a blow of his own, but the youth didn't appear to feel it.

'He rises!' the youth screamed, pointing to the heavens.

'So that's all you know. Fine,' Ulfar said. He stepped into the boy's reach, swung his elbow as hard as he could and felt the nose give way. Blood welled out and as the boy fell to the ground, writhing in pain, Ulfar stepped over him and walked towards Audun, who was standing over the body of the big farmer.

'Is he dead?' Ulfar asked.

'No,' Audun said. 'Knocked him out.'

'Hm,' Ulfar said. 'So what do you make of this?'

'I don't know,' Audun said. 'I honestly don't know.'

'There's more and more that we don't know, my friend,' Ulfar said. He turned to look at the two men on the ground. 'But with what I've seen recently, I am pretty certain,' he said, 'that if we leave them like this they will not have a good life.' He looked around until his eyes fastened on a wrist-thick wooden bar resting up against a wall.

'What did they say?' Sven asked as Audun and Ulfar returned to Sigurd's camp. 'We heard some screaming.'

'They weren't best pleased to see us,' Ulfar said. 'Two men, both absolutely mad. Thought we were Forkbeard's men and attacked us on sight.'

'Shame,' Sven said. 'So they didn't even point you in the right direction?'

'No,' Audun said. 'I don't think they knew much.'

'Well,' Sven said, 'worth a try. Do you think they'll follow?'

Ulfar pushed aside the image of legs spasming as the wooden bar smashed the farmers' skulls and ended their lives. It had felt uncomfortably like an act of kindness. 'No, they won't,' he said.

Sven turned to the seated men. 'Right. Come on, you old grannies! Up we get.' The men protested as they rose, but within moments they were ready to move. The snow continued to fall around them as they marched on, following the road.

'You ran with Forkbeard's men,' Sigurd said to Audun. 'What do you know?'

'Not much,' Audun said. 'He's apparently eight foot tall, three arms and so on.'

'How is he set up?' Sven said.

'Groups of twelve or so roam around, sacking and burning everything they can find,' Ulfar chimed in.

'See? Told you,' Sven said, a glint in his eye.

'What?' Ulfar said.

'Oh, nothing,' Sven said. 'Nothing at all. I've just been thinking, that's all.' There was a spring in the old man's step as he bounded to Sigurd's side. 'Just thinking,' he said, to no one in particular.

Behind them, an unnaturally large black fox slunk away from the farm and into the shadow of the nearby trees.

Feeling every one of his advanced years twice over, Thormund huddled further into his furs and wished, not for the first time, that he could go back to the simple joys of risking his life stealing horses. Since he'd been rounded up by Forkbeard's army and grouped with the mad Norseman, his life had gone from bad to worse. After the berserker got injured and half his men disappeared in the middle of the night, his war-band had been down to himself, Mouthpiece and six others. They'd met another of Forkbeard's groups, headed up by a big Eastman bastard called Oskarl; the mercenary, a full head taller than Thormund, had assumed command immediately. He walked with a limp, but the cane he used was as thick as a forearm and splattered with reddish-brown stains of many hues near the end. Thormund knew better than to question the authority of such men.

So now there were twenty of them, and they were all cold, wet and hungry. 'Fuck this,' he muttered. 'All of it, twice, with a pine cone.' He wasn't in charge any more, though, so that was probably a good thing.

They'd made a camp of sorts when the sun set. Oskarl, optimistically, had sent out a couple of men to hunt, and against all odds they'd come back with a brace of pheasants. There wasn't enough for everyone, of course, and the biggest fighters got to the meat first, but Thormund had got his long, bony fingers on two carcases and he shared them with Mouthpiece as they huddled on the far edge of the fire, behind Oskarl's men.

'War is not as heroic as I thought,' Mouthpiece mumbled. His jaw had mostly healed now, but it had set a little off and the young man now looked like his mouth was stuck in a sceptical scowl.

'Most things aren't,' Thormund replied. 'They really aren't.'

They sat in silence for a while, listening to the conversation of the men around the campfire, until a deep, rasping voice cut through the night.

'Good evening!'

Oskarl was up in a flash, moving remarkably quickly for a man of his size. 'Who's there?' he shouted. He peered into the darkness, half-blinded by the firelight.

'Relax, son,' another voice said. 'Don't worry. Just two old men here, looking for some warmth.' Two greybeards stepped into the very edge of the firelight, on Oskarl's side, and Thormund's heart stopped for a moment.

Mouthpiece was almost on his feet when the old horse thief caught the hem of his shirt and pulled him down. 'No,' he hissed, as quietly as he could.

'Why?' Mouthpiece said, but Thormund just shook his head.

'Are you the leader?' the first man asked.

'Who's asking?' Oskarl said, taking a short step back.

'I am Sigurd Aegisson,' the old man said. 'I am seeking Fork-beard, and you're going to help me.'

'Fuck you, old man,' Oskarl said, smirking. 'Are you going to make me?'

'No,' the old man said, 'but they are.'

Almost too late, Thormund noticed movement right by him and looked up – into a familiar face: the Norse berserker, standing quietly beside a tall young man. The light from the fire danced on their faces. Very subtly, the Norseman motioned, palm flat to the ground: *stay down, stay quiet*. Thormund looked around. The campfire was surrounded by silent, still figures with a variety of unpleasant-looking weapons at the ready.

Oskarl turned to face the two old men. 'What do you want?'

'These are now my men. So are you. Understood?' the man who called himself Sigurd said.

The Eastman moved incredibly fast, whipping up his cane and swinging it at the old man's head. In a blur, the handle of a great-axe was up to meet it.

'That's enough, son,' the other greybeard said. A bony hand was holding Oskarl's belt and a dagger was pointing straight at his groin. The shorter man with the beard was standing really close to the Eastman. Looking up into his face, he said, 'You're a big lad, right enough, but you've left your weak side open and I've floored bigger. If I even cough now, you're either dead or singing real pretty.'

The big Eastman looked down. 'Had to try,' he said in his heavily accented Norse. 'You understand.'

'I do,' the bushy-bearded man said.

Audun knelt down. 'That's Sven,' he whispered, 'from my home-town. Sigurd's the chieftain.'

'I thought I'd seen them before,' Thormund said. 'This day just gets better and better.'

'Stay down,' Oskarl barked at his men. 'Sigurd's in charge now. Any problems?' None of the men seemed inclined to dis-agree. Across the fire, Thormund watched the old chieftain quietly giving orders, then the fighters parted for him and the man with the bushy beard as they moved through them and sat down. Behind him, the standing men went to work dispensing the cooked meat.

'So I'm guessing this is the Swede, then?' Thormund said, pointing at Ulfar.

'It is,' Audun said.

The tall man sat down next to them. 'Ulfar,' he said by way of greeting.

'I'm Thormund, and this is—'

Mouthpiece went to speak but Sven's voice, loud and strong, rang out across the fire: 'Now listen up, boys. Sigurd and I are searching for Forkbeard. When we've found him and told him what we need to, he'll want to move north for some serious fighting. There will be blood, and it won't get any warmer, but there will be food to eat and things to steal. I'm an old man with a failing memory and bad eyesight' – Oskarl smirked next to him – 'and I've not done a head-count yet. I figure I will, though, in the next little while. If you're here when I do, you stay. Understood?'

Two of Thormund's party left the circle without words and disappeared into the shadows. Another two of Oskarl's men walked off in a different direction. No one paid them any mind and no one else moved.

'Right. So: sixteen, from the looks of it. Well met, boys. As I said, my name is Sven and this is Sigurd Aegisson. We're from a town called Stenvik. Have any of you heard of it? No? Well, let me tell you a story.'

The Swede sat down next to them. 'We'll do introductions later,' he said to Mouthpiece. 'Old Sven knows how to spin a tale.'

Dots of light shone in the sky above them and Thormund wondered whether his life could get any worse.

*

In the next four days they rounded up another three of Forkbeard's war bands. More than a hundred and fifty men now trailed Sigurd and Sven, kept in check by the men of Stenvik; just two days in and Ulfar found himself struggling to tell the newcomers apart. Sigurd's raiders made it simple to follow and hard to step out of line. Cold and hunger helped the men to find the easiest path.

Around them, winter was strengthening its grip. Snow fell in the morning and blew away in the afternoon, but there was always a little left the next day and gradually, the world turned white.

At midday on the fourth day, Sven motioned to Sigurd, who brought the column to a halt. Plains stretched away on both sides, but a big forest of pine up ahead drew a black smudge across the shades of white and grey.

'What's going on?' Thormund said.

'I don't know . . .' Ulfar's voice trailed off as he strained to see what Sven and Sigurd were looking at. Then, '. . . but I think it's—'

'Over there.' Mouthpiece mumbled and pointed to the border of the forest up ahead. 'Soldiers. Lots of 'em.'

'You're right,' Thormund said, 'more'n a few, that.' Thick clouds in shades of greyish white were forming above them. The pine forest was maybe a mile away, and armed men just kept emerging. 'Over a hundred, I'd say.'

'Form up,' Sven's voice rasped over their heads, 'ten abreast. If you've got a shield you're up front.' The men of Stenvik organised the newcomers and soon Sven and Sigurd were standing at the forefront of a shield square. 'Audun! Ulfar!' Sven barked. 'Come here, you useless tits!'

Audun sighed, reached for his pack, got out his hammers and hooked them on his belt. The weight felt reassuring on his hips. Ulfar, already up ahead of him, was conversing with Sigurd.

'—no idea,' he was saying. 'I would think it highly unlikely.'

'Well,' Sven said, 'you're wrong. I'd smell Alfgeir Bjorne from much further away. We might have a use for you two. Audun: look scary.'

Ulfar snorted. 'He doesn't need to try that hard.'

Audun suddenly became aware of the sheer weight of souls that the men around him had sent to Valhalla, and he realised that now he was finally one of them. *You can run all you want, Blacksmith, but you can't run away from yourself*, he thought. *This is where you belong.*

'They've seen us,' Sigurd said.

'I should hope so,' Sven said. 'I wouldn't give much for their future if a hundred men could sneak up on them.'

Audun could hear the snickering among the soldiers. The old rogue had always had a knack for lifting men's spirits.

Sigurd gestured in the direction of the forest and started walking.

'Come on,' Sven barked, 'hold your place. We want to talk, but we're not rolling over for a belly-scratch.'

Behind them, the square held nicely. Audun could hear Oskarl growling commands, stepping smoothly into the role of sheepdog.

The group at the other end of the field had grown a lot bigger. The men in front were just about distinguishable: a slim, tall man next to a bear-like figure.

'You're right. That's Jolawer and Alfgeir,' Ulfar said. Next to them, standing out in a background of leather and wool, a tall man dressed head to toe in white. He swallowed and took a deep breath. 'And . . . Karle. The king's second cousin. Says that makes him a prince. He also tried to kill me on the way south.'

'Noted,' Sigurd said. 'Keep it to yourself and don't start anything for a couple of days.'

'I—'

'Not up for a fucking vote,' Sven snapped. 'Sigurd, then me, then Oskarl. No one else makes any kind of decision on anything. We're making friends now. Other things for later. Understood?'

'Understood,' Ulfar said.

'On my command,' Sigurd said, louder. 'March.'

Audun felt the men behind him fall in step, moving with rhythm and purpose. Snow drifted gently down to the ground, settling in the footsteps of the hundred and fifty soldiers emboldened by common purpose and leadership.

When they were no more than a hundred yards distant, Sigurd raised his arm and as one, the fighters stopped.

Audun looked at the men facing them. There were maybe seven or eight hundred now, give or take. Thick woollen shifts down to mid-leg, glimpses of chain mail here and there, spears, axes, and the odd sword, big round shields and small bucklers. Some of the armour looked recently used; some of it looked like it had been sitting in a farmer's shed for a while.

The men up front looked different.

Audun's eye was drawn to the tall man in white. His face was narrow, framed by long blond hair. His clothes were the white of new-fallen snow: a thick, fur-lined coat that had to have been taken in Rus, and expensive-looking white boots. He carried a proper-sized longbow and looked like he knew how to use it.

Next to him stood a bear of a man, nearly as tall and twice as wide. Audun had to assume this was Alfgeir Bjorne, father of Geiri.

The thin, wiry youth by Alfgeir's side looked like a twig next to a tree. Blond hair pulled back from the sides framed a birdlike face, an angular nose and quick, darting eyes. His slight shoulders held a bearskin cape, fastened around the neck with a silver chain. He favoured simple travelling clothes in shades of brown and grey.

On his head he bore a simple metal band, but despite looking like he could be swept off by a changing wind, he carried himself with the bearing of a king.

'King Jolawer Scot of Svealand demands to know what you are doing on his land!' Alfgeir boomed.

Without a word, Sigurd knelt, and behind him a hundred men did the same. A half-step slow, Audun realised that they should also be kneeling.

Head down, he muttered to Ulfar, 'What's this?'

'Sigurd, doing it right,' Ulfar muttered. 'Follow his lead.'

'We are travellers from the west, wishing an audience with the king,' Sigurd said, eyes downcast.

There was a long silence. Audun chanced a glance, and saw the three men conferring.

A couple of moments later, Alfgeir's voice boomed across the field. 'Meet us in the middle.'

Sigurd and Sven rose. 'Audun, Ulfar, Oskarl. With us,' Sven said. 'The rest of you – stand up and try to look less frightening, lads. I can smell them pissing themselves from here.'

A few of the men laughed, and chatter broke out.

'Ulfar, anything you've forgotten to tell us?' Sven said under his breath as they walked to the mid-point between the two groups.

Ulfar chose his words. 'He's young, but don't underestimate the king,' he muttered at last.

'Fine,' Sven said, 'so we'll not stick our arm in Fenrir's mouth.'

'I thought he was older,' Oskarl said.

'That was Erik,' Ulfar answered automatically. 'His father.'

'They're often older. You're right,' Oskarl said.

'That's enough,' Sven said under his breath. 'From now on, you speak when spoken to.'

Sigurd stopped; they stepped up and stood in line next to him.

Alfgeir, Jolawer and Karle lined up in front of them.

The big man clocked Ulfar, and Audun was sure he smiled.

'Well met, travellers,' Jolawer Scot said. 'I see you walk with our cousin Ulfar.'

'He honours us with his presence,' Sigurd said.

'Which is funny, considering you don't have a skirt,' Karle snapped.

'Hah! Mouth on 'im!' Sven barked, grinning. He nodded towards Sigurd. 'I could see if Old Scruffy here will wear one, if you want.'

Jolawer Scot looked flustered. 'That will not be needed,' he said.

'Are you sure? Once in a lifetime offer. Some mighty fine legs under there,' Sven cackled. Next to the king, Karle looked to be somewhere between amused and disgusted; Alfgeir Bjorne was grinning happily.

'That's enough,' Sigurd said, almost gently. 'I take it you know what happened in Stenvik.' Suddenly Audun didn't recognise his gruff, surly chieftain – this man knew how to talk to kings.

'We do,' the young king said.

'We seek to raise or join an army to march on King Olav,' Sigurd said. 'We have rounded up some of Forkbeard's war bands—'

'—and we're going to go give 'em back,' Sven said, with ill-disguised glee.

The king's head snapped to the side and he muttered something to Alfgeir, who rumbled something in return.

After a brief pause for thought, he turned back to Sigurd. 'Who do you consider more dangerous – Forkbeard or Olav?'

'Olav,' Sigurd replied without hesitation. 'Forkbeard bangs his shield louder, but there's much more blood beneath the cross.'

'Do you think Forkbeard will agree?'

'Well,' Sven said, all mirth vanished from his voice, 'between us I think we can argue the case fairly well.'

There was a silence then, broken only when Jolawer Scot took three steps forward and stuck out his hand to Sigurd. Behind him, Audun saw Alfgeir Bjorne tense up for just a blink of an eye, then breathe out.

'Sigurd Aegisson of Stenvik, join us and we will go north to find King Olav.'

Sigurd clasped the young man's hand, and Audun was impressed to see that the king did not waver.

'That's that then,' Sven said. 'Good to see you again, old bear,' he added as he saluted Alfgeir, who raised his hand in return.

When Audun looked at the man called Karle, he had already turned and started walking towards the camp.

'He's a one, that one,' Oskarl said.

'Can't argue there,' Ulfar said.

Sigurd and Sven were silent until they got back to their men, who fell quiet when Sigurd turned to them. 'That is Jolawer Scot,' he said. 'He has around eight hundred men to his name, and he will make a fine king one day. I would suggest that whoever wants to have a future in this country joins us, because we are joining his army.'

'What about Forkbeard?' Thormund said.

'We're going to find Forkbeard,' Sven said, 'and then we're joining up with him too.' This set a number of the men to talking, until he said, 'Oh shut up, you old chickens. We're all fighting for the same thing, really.'

'And what's that?' someone shouted.

'We're going north.'

NORTH DENMARK
EARLY DECEMBER, AD 996

Far away, across hills, forest and blue-grey, white-capped ocean, Streak tossed her head and snorted. Helga from Ovregard pulled her thick travelling cloak closer and tightened her hood. Leaning over the horse's neck, she muttered into her ear, 'Come on now, girl. It's going to be all right. I know you don't like it, but we have to.'

She spurred her horse on towards cold, death and danger.

Every last inch of the benches in Hakon Jarl's great hall was filled. The fire roared and the fur-lined jackets had come off long ago. The best and bravest of King Olav's holy army were busy making short work of their unwilling host's winter supplies. Down by the end of the hall an old raider with a thin, wispy beard was leading a handful of his friends in an enthusiastically filthy song. The soft moans of creaking wood belied the strength of the wind outside.

When the snowstorm hit, they'd barred the vents. A day later they'd barred the big doors and now the longhouse was almost completely sealed off, accessible only through thick skin flaps strung over a small door on the leeside of the building. King Olav's men were trapped inside, snowed in like everyone else in Trondheim, warming their outsides with fire and their insides with mead.

In the high seat, the king shifted and wiped the sweat off his brow. 'Stop it,' he muttered.

Hjalti leaned in from the seat next to him. His new right-hand man was gaunt and scraggly-bearded, and he had a habit of rapid blinking that made him look like an anxious hawk. 'What, my King? Stop what?' he said.

'No more peat on the fire,' Olav said. 'It's too hot in here.' He rose, grabbing the armrest for balance, then made his way down off the dais as Hjalti started to shout at the boy in charge of fanning the flames. 'Too hot,' he mumbled as he staggered out, picking his way past warm, sweaty bodies. The flap lifted before he touched it, and he sighed. One of his men was making himself useful in his mission to bring Christ to this God-forsaken place by standing by the furs and waiting until the king needed to take a piss.

The cold blast of wind and snow hit him in the face and wiped away his problems. This was more like it: fresh air that didn't smell of unwashed men and a hot fire under a sodden roof. He took a deep breath, filled his lungs with it and released it slowly, letting the worries escape at the same time. Before him was Trondheim, a spread-out collection of snow-covered houses that seemed to be huddling together for warmth under the dancing flurries. He could smell salt on the air and feel the tiny needles of frost on his face.

'. . . my King?' Hjalti had appeared by the door but was reluctant to go out into the cold. 'You do remember Gunnthor, Jarl of the Deep Dales.'

Silence.

'He'll be here by evening.'

Olav sighed. 'Of course he will. They're all coming, every last one of them.' He turned and walked reluctantly back into the long-house, the wind roaring at his back.

'We need men. And corn. Our babes cry in the night,' Gunnthor Jarl said, elbows on the table. Thick grey hair flowed over sloping shoulders, blue eyes sparkled in a face that was weathered but open and honest. Olav had to fight back a sneer. Why should he care? Last year every single one of the mighty Jarls of the North would have happily speared him for his beliefs. Now here was Gunnthor, begging in Hakon's back room, and the rest of them would soon descend like bears on honey, rats on meat. *Flies on a corpse . . .*

He pushed the thoughts away. *This is not a time for making new enemies.* He needed friends.

'We'll see what we can do. I cannot spare the men, but we might be able to help you with the corn. We can't have the children crying,' he said.

Gunnthor Jarl smiled. 'All hail King Olav! I knew I shouldn't believe the stories.'

Hjalti, on the king's right, stiffened and frowned. 'What stories?' he snarled.

The greybeard at least had the grace to look embarrassed. 'Surely you've heard what they talk about? The burnings – the sacrifices. The king's . . . appetite?'

'What appetite? What are you talking about? I'll—' Hjalti sputtered and reached for the sword at his hip, but the king raised a hand to stop him. 'No. Gunnthor, you were right: you shouldn't believe the stories.' He smiled at the old man. 'I thank you for your wisdom.'

'And I thank you for your generous spirit, in the name of the White Christ.' The words sounded uncomfortable in the old chieftain's mouth. 'If there's anything I can do . . .'

'There is one thing,' he said. 'Talk to your people. Tell them what you've seen here. Do it when they hold the bread in their hands, not before, nor after. I know that what I am doing is not going to gain me the love of the people, but I don't want to win their hearts.' He leaned forward. 'I want to win their immortal souls.' He noted with some satisfaction that Gunnthor did not back down, nor did he wince this time.

'I will, my Lord.'

After the jarl had said his goodbyes and scurried away, Hjalti hawked and spat. 'Lord of sheep and ruler of mud,' the gaunt man said with a sneer. 'He'll get a few extra bags of grain for being sneaky enough to arrive before the others, but give him a sword and he'll try to plough with it.'

'Maybe so,' the king said, 'but have you ever had your foot run over by a plough?'

Hjalti checked for signs of a joke, found none and swallowed. 'No,' he muttered. 'No, I haven't.'

'We shall keep it that way. You are from around here, Hjalti, are you not?'

'I left young, to go raiding, but my father's farm is about six days further south in a small valley by the coast.'

'I see. All right, so who's next?'

'Hakon Jarl wants to talk to you.'

King Olav didn't even try to hide his displeasure. 'Send him in,' he said. 'I'll receive him in his hall.'

Hjalti disappeared and the king made his way out into the big hall. The men were singing louder now – another group, Southern boys by the look of them, had taken up the challenge; they were braying out a horrible old rhyme about Loki and the goat.

Olav was the only one to see Hakon enter. Since he'd landed his fleet on Hakon's doorstep and taken over his house, the former Jarl of Trondheim had almost faded. Now, framed by the doorway he must once have filled, he looked less like an iron-fisted ruler and more like a tired old man. He shuffled in and sat down at the long table, opposite the king. Hjalti appeared beside him and made his way to his seat at King Olav's right side.

'Your Majesty,' Hakon began, slow and heavy, and Olav had to resist the urge to leap down and slap the words out of him. 'You haven't – I mean, your men haven't— I need more food. And peat for my fire. My bones are cold.'

'Your bones are cold because it's winter and you're old. Tell me about Gunnthor,' Olav said. Colour flashed in Hakon's cheeks, and his hands balled into fists at his sides.

Good, he thought. *That'll keep him warm for a spell.*

'Gunnthor is a good man,' the old man said. 'He looks after his people.'

'Can he be trusted?' Hjalti said.

Hakon flashed a look at Olav. The king smirked, and the old chieftain smirked back and for a moment the two men shared an understanding.

'Oh, yes,' Hakon said, 'good man. That's what I said. Trust him. Definitely.'

Hjalti leaned back, satisfied.

He had a lot to learn, Olav thought. *You don't ask the enemy who you should trust.* 'Stew for the Jarl,' he shouted and within moments one of the local boys had arrived with a generously filled bowl.

As he watched Hakon tuck into his food, Olav leaned over to Hjalti. 'Go out and check on the weather, will you. I have a feeling in my bones.'

Hjalti rose without question and moved towards the flaps of skin. King Olav watched him go, then waved Einar over. The tall boy had been put in charge of the hunters, despite his tender age – the men said he could shoot the beak off a blackbird at a hundred paces; he'd been personally responsible for a good half the contents of the stew. He was quiet, effective and loyal, and not for the first time, King Olav prayed silently that the Lord would send him a few more such men.

'Any word from the travellers?' he asked.

Einar thought this over before he answered, 'No, your Majesty, still no word. My boys saw Storrek Jarl's party at a distance a couple of days ago, but they didn't see us.' He paused, then added, 'Cold out there.'

'No sign of Valgard?'

'No sign,' the hunter said.

The king waved Einar off as Hjalti returned and reported, 'The wind is dying down, my Lord.'

'Hakon!' King Olav said just as the old Jarl finished his last spoonful of stew. 'Tell me more about the guests we are about to receive.'

The sky was the crisp colour of bluebells in spring and the sun's rays bounced off the pristine snow, frozen in a hard, sparkling shell. The column, men and horses both, inched forward.

At the front, a broad-shouldered youth leading a dappled horse dug his walking stick into the snow and picked his way huffily through the crusty edges of the white carpet. 'I hate him. I hate him, I hate him, I hate him,' he muttered.

'Shut up, Heimir,' the rider growled. Udal Jarl was a block of a man, with a bushy red beard to go with a thick, red braid of hair that had only a few streaks of white in it. 'Shut up and watch your mouth.'

'But Father, why are we going? You said yourself that he was—'

'I know what I said,' Udal rumbled, 'and if you repeat it I'll break your nose again. Do you remember your uncle's dog?'

'The one that started biting?'

'Yes.'

'Of course I do. Why?'

Up ahead the bright blue winter sky was now smeared with heavy grey clouds. Udal Jarl cleared his throat and spat, a long arc into the snow.

'You can't go straight at a dog like that. You have to feed it first: feed it, and maybe scratch it behind the ear, until it's close and it trusts you. And then—?'

Heimir Udalsson turned around to look at his father, who rewarded him with a smile full of jagged, yellowing teeth.

'—then you take care of the problem. Understood?'

The boy smiled back. 'Understood,' he said, and he turned around and waded through the snow with renewed vigour. 'Here, doggie! Here, boy!' he shouted, thrashing at the snow with his stick.

Behind him, Udal Jarl grinned. This was going to be a good trip.

Two valleys over, Storrek Jarl scratched himself and farted loudly. 'I'm tired of this!' he shouted. 'Fucking Southern twig king-child, summoning us like – like what? Like we're his fucking sheepdogs?'

The five men in his convoy knew better than to answer; they just kept trudging along in the footsteps of their fat chieftain.

'He comes up here, pushes poor old Hakon around – and for what? Does he think we'll bend the knee? Fenrir can piss in his eye,' he mumbled into his bushy beard.

Behind him, one of his men shouted and pointed up at a huge flock of gannets flying overhead, heading south.

'The birds are coming his way too,' Storrek Jarl muttered. 'Hope they shit on him. Let's move!' Still grumbling to no one in particular, he waddled on through the snow.

The night was cold and crisp and starless, with oppressive grey clouds covering the village. Astride his white horse, King Olav Tryggvason, rightful ruler of Norway and champion of the White Christ, leaned back and waited, savouring the smell of burning pitch on the torches that circled the small settlement.

Finn's voice rang out in the night. 'Who is your chieftain?'

The man had a good voice on him, the king mused. Finn Trueheart: good old dependable Finn. Sharp as an old hammer, but equally useful.

Voices carried on the wind and a patch of darkness moved beneath him.

'They're ready, my Lord,' a disembodied voice said by his knee.

Olav didn't reply but adjusted the metal band he wore in place of a crown – the damn thing was still not quite comfortable – and touched the reins lightly. The horse started walking towards the fires. He'd taken pains to train this one properly himself; the men needed to see that he was the master of his surroundings. You could hardly expect to rule a kingdom if you couldn't control your own horse.

The men parted before him like the sea before Moses and light spilled out from behind the massed bodies.

The place was much as he had come to expect. He rode towards the centre, towards the shrine, where Finn had lined up their elders all in a row. He reined in and dismounted swiftly. Aware of the eyes on him, he walked around the shrine. The cross at his breast felt heavy, and he was glad that he could still feel the burn of conviction. He would judge them according to their behaviour.

Turning to the farmers, he fixed the leader of the council with the coldest stare he could muster. 'Who is your god?'

The man looked at him and smirked. 'Now that . . . that is a tricky question,' he said.

Olav felt a pang of jealousy. He was not a vain man, but he had to admit that he wished he had the council leader's height, almost a head taller than his future king. The man was handsome, with long black hair flowing to his shoulders, sparkling, green eyes and a fox-like smirk that was fast becoming a full-blown smile. 'A tricky question indeed.'

Finn punched him in the mouth. 'You will respect the king,' he growled.

The man didn't flinch. A thick blue liquid seeped out of his burst lip, drying up almost immediately.

Finn was stunned. 'You little—' He swung at the man again, then froze in mid-movement and coughed. The farmer's hand returned to his side, a wooden sliver dripping with black blood in his hand. Finn collapsed, sputtering and clutching his throat.

Olav grabbed for his sword, but it wasn't there any more. 'Attack!' he screamed, but no one in the circle moved.

The council leader wiped his mouth with the back of his hand. 'It is very rude, wouldn't you say, to march into someone's home and presume to order them around, to tell them what they should do. How they should stand, and walk, and believe. Don't you think?'

Olav screamed at his body to move, but it didn't – *couldn't*. 'I – I – bring the word—'

'—of the White Christ. Yes, yes. I know. We've seen you before, you know. Different name, different face, but we've all seen you before.' The tall man's appearance was somehow . . . changing. His clothes were no longer a simple farmer's garb. In the firelight, he was slowly turning more colourful: a rich purple was seeping into his cape, and his shirt had turned a most sumptuous green. 'And we need to have a word about that.'

The man kicked Finn's dead body, looked down at him and smiled. 'Poor Finn. He really tried, didn't he?' Then he looked back at King Olav. 'There is nothing here for you,' he said, and his face was suddenly hard. He took a step closer.

Olav sensed the presence behind him, but too late. Huge hands clasped his shoulders and pulled his arms painfully upwards, exposing his chest. He kicked out and hit something, but it felt thick; unresponsive. Pain lashed through him as he was pulled roughly upwards. His heart thumped in his chest and he could hear a heavy, scraping sound behind him. He tried to look, but hands were on his head, several strong, heavy hands, holding him steady, suspended a good four feet above the ground.

A shadow crept up from behind him and fell over his shoulder. The familiar shape of the wooden cross did not give him any relief.

He looked back at the leader of the village, who now held a wooden mallet in his hand.

'You know what they say, though,' he said, smiling. 'When all you have is a hammer, every problem becomes a nail.'

The stench of death overwhelmed Olav then, the cold of blue-frozen bodies, and he saw the soldiers in the circle. They were all big, all quiet, and blue, like the mountains.

He fought them as they dragged him to the cross, and he screamed when the tall man touched the sharp point of a wooden sliver to his palm and lifted the hammer—

King Olav woke with a start, drenched in sweat under his furs. The room was stuffy, and stank of sweat and fear. Half-mad, the king fumbled for the cross on his necklace, grasped it and started muttering, '*Pater noster, qui es in caelis . . .*'

Outside his window, the northern winds picked up again. All over Trondheim animals cowered in corners, huddling together for warmth and safety.

Forty miles further north, the sun rose on a farmer clambering awkwardly through a snowdrift half his height to get to a barn. The animals bleated at him the moment he opened the door and the stocky, coarse-featured, red-haired man waved them off. 'Calm down,' he said, walking over the boards to the fenced-off hay enclosure. 'Easy now. You'll be fed, soon enough. Just like yesterday, and the day before.'

The sheep bleated in response, nudging their heads through the wooden fence to get closer. The farmer wrapped his coat tighter around him. 'I should shear a couple more of you,' he said to the nearest ones as he grabbed his pitchfork. 'Make me another shift. It's sharp out there, all right.' The temperature had been dropping steadily for a week; even for the season, it was unusually cold. He stabbed the hay with a vengeance and shovelled the first load in the trough. 'There you go,' he said.

The barn had gone dead quiet.

The sheep were all standing stock-still and staring in the same direction: towards the north corner of the room. The farmer banged his pitchfork on the feeder, but none of them responded; they just stood there, eyes trained on the corner of the barn, nostrils flaring.

Then the first one started to bleat and move backwards, away from the corner.

The second one followed.

The farmer felt time slow down around him as he thought back over a lifetime of working the land. He had seen and cared for more sheep than he ever could count, and he remembered a couple of times when wolves had got in among his herd, but the animals had never sounded like this; they'd never taken on this bad.

Half the flock was now bleating wildly, with more joining in with every breath, and the barn was bursting with the noise. The sheep were pushing at each other to get away from the north corner, but none of them seemed to dare look anywhere else. Out of the corner of his eye he saw a fat ewe bite half an ear off another just because it was in the way, and the blood shocked the farmer out of his stupor. The wooden fence that kept the sheep penned in their square enclosures was creaking now, and all the animals were bleating, all of them, constantly.

A stench of shit, piss and hot air flooded the barn as bowels started voiding and the bleating grew louder still. On his left, one animal charged head-first into the south wall, as if trying to smash its way out, and the smell of blood started to drive the animals further into madness.

Something in the back of the farmer's brain told him *move get out now now now* and he sprinted towards the door, and behind him he heard the sound of snapping wood and the panicked scrabbling of hooves on planks as a hundred and ten animals all clamoured to get out after him, into the arms of cold and certain death. He punched the doors open, launched himself out and slammed them shut again, dragging the bar in place just as the first sheep thudded into the door. Pushing himself away, the farmer looked on in horror as the bleating grew louder, accompanied by thuds as the walls shook with the impact of animals smashing into the walls, over and over again, pushing to get out.

On the other side of the barn, a mile away, six men crested the hill and walked south.

The sun set early, but the army marched on for as long as they thought they could. When the last dim light started to fade, Alfgeir looked at Jolawer and shouted, 'Stop!' The command travelled down through the lines and slowly a thousand men came to a halt.

'Camp!' the big man cried, and the men split into small groups and started erecting lean-tos and tents. Ulfar watched Sigurd and Sven set to rounding up their troops and setting up a tight camp off to the side with a perimeter, paths and a space for a fire in the middle.

'The bear's gone soft, hasn't he?' Sven muttered.

'He was never one for this kind of discipline,' Sigurd replied.

'True,' Sven said. 'Still, one would think he'd try to teach the young king good habits.'

'Habits grow where they will,' Sigurd said slowly. 'Maybe Alfgeir Bjorne is training the king just right.'

Ulfar followed his eye to where King Jolawer Scot was standing, observing their little side camp from afar with a watchful eye.

Sven grinned and turned to salute. 'My king! Come on over, why won't you?'

The king moved closer, head swivelling to take it all in. When he was fully within their camp, he spoke, surprising Ulfar again with his steady voice. 'This is very impressive,' he said.

'We've done it a couple of times,' Sven said, with enough false modesty to force Ulfar to suppress a laugh.

'We wish you to come sit with us at our fire. We could use all the knowledge you have on King Olav,' Jolawer said.

'Lead the way,' Sven said.

As Jolawer turned and walked off Sigurd followed, while Sven darted off in the other direction. He reappeared moments later and found Ulfar. 'Oskarl is in charge. Son, you're not coming to this one. Understood?'

'Yes.'

Sven looked him up and down, frowning. 'And don't go doing anything stupid while I'm not looking after your bony arse, either.'

'I will follow your shining example in all things,' Ulfar said.

'That's what I'm worried about,' Sven said, shooting him one last dirty look before turning to catch up with Sigurd.

He doesn't have to worry, Ulfar thought. There were other and more important things to do. He found Audun sitting close to the fire with a bucket of snow and a metal rod, sharpening knives. 'So they found out, then?'

'Yep,' Audun said. 'One of the Stenvik boys said the blades went to shit after I left, then one of Jolawer's asked if I'd been a smith and now I'm stuck with this.' He gestured to his feet. A cloth held two blades that glistened wetly in the firelight. Next to it, fourteen knives were laid out, waiting to be sharpened.

'We need to talk,' Ulfar said.

'We do,' Audun said.

'Hasn't been much time,' Ulfar said.

'There hasn't,' Audun said.

'I died in Uppsala,' Ulfar said.

Audun was quiet for a while, then, to the backdrop of camp noise and the steady scraping of steel on iron. 'So that's it, then,' he said eventually. 'Both of us.'

'Seems to be,' Ulfar said. The truth hung in the air between them.

'Saw you when the old guys said they'd been dug up,' Audun said. 'Did you meet . . . *him?*'

'I think I did, yes.'

'Me too. He called himself Fjolnir—'

'—Gestumblindi—'

'—and he gave me a gift. A belt.'

This time Ulfar fell quiet.

Audun looked up from the knife's edge. 'You too?'

Ulfar nodded.

'What was it?'

'He saved my life. Scared off Karle in the forest.'

'Hm. What does he want?'

'I think I know, but I'm not talking about that here,' Ulfar said quietly.

'What are you two lovers whispering about?' Thormund said from the darkness. Moments later his face appeared across the fire.

'How Audun's leaving me for you and your lovely beard,' Ulfar said.

The old horse thief chortled and shuffled around the fire until he stood next to them. 'You're funny, Swede.'

'Ulfar,' Ulfar said. 'And thank you.'

Thormund looked the tall young man up and down in the fire-light. 'Was it a woman?'

Audun suppressed a smile and continued sharpening the blades.

'What do you mean?' Ulfar said.

'You pissed off their archer, what's his name . . . ?'

'Karle,' Ulfar said.

'Yeah, him. You got on his wrong side: if he could kill you with a look your limbs would be in seven countries by now. Was it a woman?'

'You could say that. I caught him with a young girl – he was about to take what he wanted, and she didn't want him to. We had a discussion.'

'Broke his arm,' Audun said.

Thormund's expression softened somewhat. 'Knew we'd get along,' he murmured. 'Suspect you might want to tread lightly in this camp, though. Heard some mutterings.'

Ulfar looked around, at the lean-tos and tents in the dark, at the heart of the black shadows in between.

'Oh, they won't come here. They don't care for us much on account of us going with Forkbeard, but they're staying five steps south of the Stenvik boys. They have a reputation,' the old horse thief added.

'Do they?' Ulfar said.

'Sure do,' Thormund said. 'Sigurd Aegisson? Sven? Oh, youth. You really do not know who you're running with?'

'Assume that we don't,' Ulfar said.

Beside him, Audun's sharpening iron moved a lot slower.

'As young men they would raid up and down the coast of Anglia. Aegir, Sigurd's father, was a hard bastard and no lie. He was involved in the wars of the kings, about seventy summers ago, maybe. He taught the boys, Sigurd and Sven, everything there was to know about sailing a boat. They went south, as far south as anyone's been, right down to the kingdom of the Turk. For the first forty years of their lives they must have spent four days at sea for every one on land. Their reputation grew steadily, until mothers in coastal towns everywhere within reach were sending kids to sleep saying Sigurd Sea-Wolf would get them if they weren't good.' Thormund's eyes sparkled in the firelight. 'When they came back, a great war was afoot – they'd started collecting the Danegeld, and there was room for hard men to get very rich indeed. So they signed on to sail with a terrifying crew.' The old horse thief looked into the middle distance, as if he could spot the sail on the horizon. 'One ship – just one ship – but every single one of those bastards was worth ten, fifteen normal men. It was a proper drake, too. It was called *Njordur's Mercy*. Their captain was the hardest of them all, a big bull of a man. Legend had it he was from the Far North and his mother was a Finn-witch. When she saw the child, she carved a scar on his neck.'

'Why?' Audun said.

The old man cleared his throat. 'There was a rhyme . . . I can't remember it now, but it said that since he'd been carved by someone who loved him, he couldn't be harmed by the ones who hated him. It wasn't true – he got hurt plenty – but he believed it at first, and once he grew up to be big and strong he realised that other people believed it too and it became the mark of his trade. So when the time came, he carved a scar in his son's neck, and another in his own. He was the captain, and he was called—'

'—Skargrim,' Ulfar said.

'And from the very first day, our boatsman was called Thormund,' a voice said in the darkness, and Sigurd emerged from the shadows. 'Well, not back then. We called him Cutter, because whenever there was fighting to be done he'd disappear. Then we'd do the counting and quite a lot of throats would have just got . . . cut. Sometimes, if the men had been a bit hard on the women in the place, they'd be our own.'

'I – I—' the old horse thief stammered.

'Let me guess. You were going to slink away just as soon as you'd said goodbye to the boys?' Sigurd said. 'Some things never change, do they?'

Thormund's shoulders slumped. 'No. They don't.'

'But you said you hated boats,' Audun said.

'Didn't always,' Thormund said.

Sigurd came closer, a half-smile on his lips. 'Good to see you, old friend. I thought I recognised you, but it's been a while.'

'Thirty years.'

'I know the dark is calling you, and if I know you at all, I don't think anything about this little party of ours is to your liking. But I am afraid there may not be any running away from this one.'

Suddenly, Ulfar felt the chill in the air. 'Why not?'

'Jolawer has agreed. We're going to find Forkbeard. Apparently King Olav is gathering chieftains in the north, so we're going up there to kick him in the teeth.'

None of the men spoke. Behind them, snowflakes drifted to the ground and hissed as they hit the flames.

In the king's tent, Alfgeir Bjorne watched Jolawer Scot. The young king sat silently, just staring into the mug he held in both hands.

'I still don't understand why we need to have these old farts along with us,' Karle said. 'They're nothing but trouble. And they have no respect. They just like to talk shit and pull faces and they won't be able to back it up. I mean, half of their little army is Forkbeard's, for fuck's sake! What's to stop them from turning on us when we meet Forkbeard himself, hm? What's to stop them from squeezing us between them and him, falling on our backs? They get paid for getting you, Forkbeard is King of Sweden and the Dane-lands. Forkbeard wins. You die.'

'Shut up, Karle,' the young king said calmly, not taking his eyes off the mug. Alfgeir Bjorne had to swallow a laugh as Karle turned beetroot-red. The king didn't notice. 'Tomorrow you're going to organise our camp. We need to be like they are.'

'What?' Karle sputtered. 'What are you *on* about?'

Jolawer turned to face his cousin. 'There are two camps here,' he said, his voice calm and strong. 'One is set by men of war. It is put together by men who are used to travelling, men who are ready to go at a moment's notice. It is set with minimum effort, blades within reach, and you can bet—' The king stopped, looked around again, then continued, 'I'll bet everything will be packed and ready to go at sun-up. The other camp – the other is a hodgepodge of tents, thrown up by farmers, followers and old men in rusted mail, grouped by allegiances and families, spread out over half again the space they really need. In an attack, it would crumble. Men would run out of their tents and into each other. It says, loud and clear, that whoever runs it is not ready for a stern exchange of words, let alone a war.'

Stunned, Karle could do nothing but stare at King Jolawer Scot.

Unmoved, the king took a long sip of mead. 'Now, which one is ours?'

Karle swallowed. 'I think—'

'Which one is ours?'

'You can't compare—'

'I can, and I will. Next to Sigurd we look like children with sticks, Karle. And I don't want to sit down opposite Forkbeard with a crowd of children at my back. Tomorrow, start making soldiers for me.' He looked up and his eyes found the hulking figure of Alfgeir Bjorne. 'You will help.' Then he turned and kept his gaze steady on Karle. 'And you will not tell me again what I can and cannot do. Understood?'

Karle stared at the king. '. . . Understood,' he mumbled. 'I will go to rest now, then.'

'You do that,' King Jolawer Scot said.

When the white cloak had swished out of view, Jolawer turned to Alfgeir again. 'Was that . . . too much?'

'Not at all, your Majesty,' the old soldier rumbled, trying and failing to hide the grin on his face. 'Not at all.'

'This is not daylight,' Audun grumbled, massaging a sore back. 'This is just slightly less dark.'

Ulfar mumbled something unintelligible at him. Sigurd and Sven had been very insistent on the men being up before the crack of dawn, and Oskarl had gone one further and had some very calm but uncomfortable suggestions involving blades and armpits for those who felt they should be allowed to rise when they wanted to.

Around them the men of Stenvik worked quickly and quietly, folding up tents and shelters, packing up the camp. Audun thought of a pack of wolves as he watched Forkbeard's newcomers fall into the rhythm without needing any instructions. Nobody howled, but there was an unspoken understanding that if you stepped out, you'd get bitten.

Sven moved up to their station. 'Well done, boys,' he said. 'You're on track.'

Ulfar leaned over to the old man. 'Why are we doing this?' he muttered. 'None of the others are up.'

'Which is exactly why we're doing it,' Thormund said from two tents over. 'We want the young king and all of his men to see us, sitting and waiting for them. Makes us look serious, and if they've got any sense or shame they'll tighten up some.'

Sven grinned. 'See? The old boy still knows his stuff.'

'So we gather,' Ulfar said.

'Step to it,' Sven said. On some invisible signal he turned and shouted 'Ready!' across their camp, and soon Oskarl shouted back from the far end.

'Go!' Sigurd bellowed from the centre and in a sudden flurry of activity tents and shelters simply melted away as they shrank into their component parts.

Audun had to elbow Ulfar, who was gazing at the spectacle. 'Move,' he hissed.

Ulfar shook his head a couple of times, then kneeled down to help Audun bundle the sticks into the sheet and wrap it up tight. 'That's as sharp as anything I've seen,' he said as they worked.

'I only knew them from Stenvik,' Audun said. 'It's like I only saw a very small part of what they were.'

'You're not wrong there,' Thormund chimed in as he tossed his tent-pack, neatly trussed up, on the ground. 'Ready to go?'

Audun gritted his teeth and forced his cold hands to work faster. There! He yanked the string and the knot slid into place. 'Yes.'

'Well, then you'd better be ready to sit and wait for a while. To be fair, though, Sigurd's got what he wanted.'

The old horse thief glanced over at Jolawer Scot's camp. Farmers, pot boys and soldiers alike were working hard to escape the attentions of Alfgeir Bjorne, who waded through the disorganised groups of tents cursing and shouting at anything that moved and shouting more at anything that didn't. A flurry of activity followed in his path. 'And look,' Thormund added, 'there's your friend.'

Karle stood at the edge of the camp, glowering and pointing, yelling commands.

'Looks like someone didn't get all the sleep they wanted,' Ulfar said. 'Thank you. I feel better now.'

Soon a column of tired and grumpy men was marching through new-fallen snow. Audun cleared his mind. *Left, right. Left, right.* Marching was all right, once you fell into the rhythm – you could let your legs walk and your mind wander.

'Listen,' Ulfar said, coming up beside him, 'tonight, we'll go somewhere quiet and have a talk about . . .'

'. . . our friend,' Audun replied.

'Yes,' Ulfar said.

Audun nodded. 'Anything else you want to tell me?'

Ulfar frowned. 'Not really. Why?'

'Because those two' – he glanced towards the middle of the column – 'have been turning around from time to time and staring straight at you.'

Ulfar scanned the line. When he found the people Audun had mentioned, he let loose a string of curses under his breath. When he'd composed himself he said, 'I might need you to watch my back when we camp.'

Audun shrugged. 'If I must,' he said with a hint of a grin.

They marched on.

The world was nothing but white, grey and black. The treeline to the left of the marching column towered over them like a fortress wall, and giant wolf-shaped clouds chased across the grey sky. To the right the trees were starting to thicken, forming a corridor of white between the shadowy pines.

'Who are they?' Audun glanced at the couple over Ulfar's shoulder as they walked.

'He is Ivar, and her name is Greta,' Ulfar said wearily. 'They are brother and sister. He stabbed me in the leg in Uppsala. I am pretty sure Karle put them up to it. Shortly after that I was poisoned.'

'What did you do to her?' Audun asked.

Ulfar threw his hands in the air. 'Why is it always sure to be *my* fault? Why is everyone so certain that I—?' He caught sight of Audun's face. 'Fine. I promised her I'd wed her, shagged her and left.'

'I see. No wonder the brother is upset.'

'A bit too upset, if you ask me,' Ulfar mumbled.

Snow drifted gently down, melting on their faces and settling on their shoulders. They marched in silence for a while, settling into a rhythm that cost as little energy as possible.

'Hey!'

Ulfar was jarred out of his walking half-dream by running into the man in front of him, who had stopped. Behind, the line was slowly doing the same.

'Listen up!' Alfgeir Bjorne's voice rang out. 'Men of the Dales! Northlanders! To me!'

Beside him, Karle shouted. 'Southern boys! Lakefolk! To me!' The two men then strode in opposite directions.

The men of Stenvik waited to be told where to go, but no instructions came. Instead, as Jolawer Scot's men drifted to either side, grumbling under their breaths, a thin line of cold and tired warriors was left in the middle.

'Now what?' Audun mumbled.

'I've got a bad feeling about this,' Thormund mumbled.

'I'm beginning to think you have a bad feeling about everything,' Ulfar said.

'And what of it?' Thormund said. 'I am old and alive, which is rare. Shut up.'

Up ahead, Sven barked out orders. 'Right, boys: we're going for a little meeting. We're going up front with the king, as we figure if we show 'im the ugliest bastards first he'll laugh so hard it might soften him some.'

'Who the hell are we meeting?' Mouthpiece whispered behind them.

Ulfar frowned, then caught Thormund's eye.

'Told you,' the old man mouthed. Beside them, Alfgeir and Karle led their groups to the sides, off the road and into the woods.

'Square UP!' Oskarl shouted up ahead.

*

The line spread all the way across the road and ran at least ten deep. Men clad in furs over chain mail and leather armour; lines of spears, lines of shields.

'Old boy's looking good,' Sven said.

'He always did,' Sigurd said. 'Took great care to make sure. Win the battle first—'

'—then fight it,' Sven added.

Jolawer Scot stood between them, staring at Sweyn Forkbeard's army. 'That's at least, what . . . ?'

'Fifteen hundred, I'd guess,' Sven said.

Sigurd nodded beside him.

'So what do we do now?' Jolawer Scot said.

'We do to him exactly what we did to you, and hope our surprise works,' Sven said. 'I'll make sure the men behind us line up right.'

At that, a hint of a smile crept up on the king's face.

'Let's go.'

The men of Stenvik moved into formation, making a square behind Jolawer, Sigurd and Sven. In the middle, standing half a head taller than most, Oskarl shouted orders and encouragements.

'Notice how his limp is gone?' Audun said.

'I think he's just having too much fun,' Thormund said. 'He's genuinely happy, I think. Like a dog with a purpose. Lob him a chunk of meat once a day and that one would follow Sigurd into Hel.'

'I fear that we might have to test that,' Audun said.

'Heads up,' Mouthpiece hissed next to them.

At the front, Sven was signalling for halt. The square stopped and hands tightened around pommels and spears.

Up ahead stood an unmoving wall of Danes and death.

'We seek an audience with Sweyn Forkbeard!' Sigurd shouted out.

No response.

'Forkbeard! Come out!' Sven shouted.

Still no response.

King Jolawer Scot stepped forward. One step, then three, then five – until he was standing well ahead of the square. He spoke softly, but his words carried on the wind. 'King Jolawer Scot, Lord of the Svear, ruler of Uppsala and all of its lands, seeks parley with King Sweyn Forkbeard, Scourge of the Seas and ruler of Denmark.'

Then he simply stood and waited.

Ulfar caught Sven and Sigurd exchanging glances, but the two old warriors snapped back to guard duty remarkably quickly.

There was a brief ripple of motion in the centre of the line and a gap opened up. A man of middle years stepped out. He was dressed simply, but there was a way about him that made the men behind him look smaller, somehow. He carried no weapons and wore little in the way of decoration. His thick brown beard was woven in two long braids.

A woman strode behind him. She was taller than him by half a hand, but she did not need the height to look down on the world. In the dusky light the blonde hair that fell straight down to her shoulders looked almost white.

This time Audun was prepared. As he knelt with the rest of the men he wondered whether that meant he was learning something about the world.

'Speak,' Forkbeard said.

Undaunted by the superior force, King Jolawer Scot weighed up his counterpart. 'There are challenges to driving a force of men through the land of the Svear,' he began. 'And easy to see how a few bands of angry soldiers could peel off the main force and go raiding, and there would be nothing even the strongest of kings could do about it.'

'Oh, he's *good*,' Thormund muttered.

Beside Audun, Ulfar nodded.

In front of them, King Jolawer Scot continued, 'So I do not come here to speak of that. I bring you news of a mutual threat that, if left unchecked, will wash over both our lands like a plague of vermin. I invite you to join forces with me.'

Audun stole a look at Forkbeard, who was looking at Jolawer without even a flicker of interest. 'Why should I want to "join forces" with your sad little group?' he said, almost wearily.

King Jolawer Scot did not rise to the bait. Instead, he raised his arm. Audun didn't need to look to know what was happening about a hundred yards behind them.

Led by Alfgeir Bjorne on the left and Prince Karle on the right, hundreds of men were walking very calmly out of the woods, filling the enclosed space with bodies. The fact that they were very carefully spaced out to appear twice as many mattered less than the surprise.

When King Jolawer lowered his hand, all his men banged their shields twice and screamed 'SVEAR!' at the top of their lungs, as planned. The noise sent a wave of black birds flying out of nearby trees.

There was a note of amusement in Forkbeard's voice. 'Very well,' he said. 'Let's talk.'

As one, the men of Stenvik rose. King Jolawer gestured, and Sven and Sigurd stepped up behind him. 'These are my advisors, and they will stand beside me.'

'Nonsense,' the tall woman spat. 'Sweyn, you're not going alone against three men.'

'Sigrid—' Forkbeard began.

'It's nonsense,' she said. 'And you know it.'

Sigurd leaned in and said something to King Jolawer Scot,

who nodded sagely. 'My advisor suggests that we could go to one side and they would be most happy to wait with your wife,' he said.

'That will do,' Forkbeard said.

The tall woman's face turned sour in the blink of an eye and she stormed off to her left. 'Fine. Do what you want,' she hissed. Sigurd and Sven sauntered after her.

Forkbeard sized up his opposing number and nodded to the right. 'Come on then. Tell me about this "threat" of yours.'

The two men walked off to the side.

'What do you make of this?' Audun said to Ulfar.

The tall Swede watched the kings for a moment. 'There's two ways this could turn out,' he said after a while. 'Either we fight now – or we fight later.'

'Just my luck,' Thormund muttered.

Karle and Alfgeir caught up with them just as King Jolawer Scot returned. Sigurd and Sven were just a step behind.

'Well?' Sven said.

'Forkbeard accepted the truce,' the young man said. He looked like he'd aged about five years since they saw him last. 'I told him of King Olav, the northern chieftains and the risk he posed. To my surprise, he agreed. It didn't even take a lot of convincing.'

'I bet it didn't,' Sven said with a smirk.

'What do you mean?' Jolawer Scot said, glancing at Alfgeir Bjorne, who looked bemused.

'Before he was king and before she'd earned her nickname, Olav and Sigrid were to be wed,' Alfgeir said. 'Then he ran off to go a-Viking.'

'Judging by what we heard,' Sven said, 'Sigrid the Haughty has very little good to say about King Olav Tryggvason.'

King Jolawer Scot raised an eyebrow. 'And none of you thought to tell me this before I talked to the man?'

The mirth vanished from the group and suddenly the terrifying warriors looked vaguely embarrassed.

'Well, we . . . um . . .' Alfgeir searched for words that didn't come.

'Long time ago,' Sigurd muttered to no one in particular.

'Wouldn't have done you any good,' Sven said. 'Might have clouded your judgement.'

Jolawer Scot spoke next. 'Fine. But don't let it happen again. Next time I wish to have *all* of the available information.'

The urgency of the nods and murmurs all round made Ulfar smile. If a man had to choose a king to march with, he might as well pick one who could do that to these men.

That night the two armies camped together, but kept a distance. 'But really, though: who's in charge? Who decides what goes where?' Ulfar asked Thormund as he inched closer to the sad little fire they'd managed to make with the soggy firewood they'd scrounged.

'Just kind of happens, doesn't it?' Thormund said without looking up. 'Get enough lads together who know what they're doing and no one needs to shout much.' His fingers worked constantly, twirling horsehair into rope.

The rhythmic metal scraping next to them stopped. 'Jolawer, then Alfgeir and Sigurd, Prince Karle, Sven and Oskarl,' Audun recited. 'That's who's in charge.' The scraping resumed as another blade hit the whetstone.

'Hm,' Ulfar said, frowning. 'I suppose that means if I wanted to go and have a look at the other camp I'd have to find them, in that order.'

'Yes,' Audun said.

'Excellent,' Ulfar said as he got to his feet. 'I will do that then.'

'Good,' Audun said.

'Good,' Ulfar said.

Thormund looked up as Ulfar left the light of the fire and headed to his tent. 'He's not going to do that, is he?'

'No, he isn't,' Audun agreed.

Moments later Ulfar came out with a square board and a leather bag that rattled when he walked.

'He's just going to walk right into Forkbeard's camp?' Thormund said.

'Yes, he is,' Audun said.

Thormund coiled a long string. 'Hm. I hope he lives. I was starting to like him.'

The two men both went back to their craft, working their hands in silence.

King Forkbeard's camp was laid out simply, the rows of tents and lean-tos separated by broad walking paths. The tents formed a square with minimal distance from the far corners to the centre. Cook-fires had been erected in four different places, and people lingered close to the warmth and the light.

Ulfar sauntered up to the nearest one.

'I don't suppose there's any stew going?' he asked.

'Get your own, Swede,' the cook snarled back. 'This is for Danes only.'

'Ah, yes. Serves me right. No Dane would ever give anything away.'

'Din't say that,' the cook grumbled. 'Just said you can't have any.'

Ulfar paused, as if he was thinking. 'Do you know Tafl?'

A while later a small crowd had gathered.

'You'll have the shirt off my back next,' Ulfar said as the cook moved his king out of trouble. 'My position is clearly lost.'

'Let's say that, shall we? You win this one and I get your shirt.
It'll be great for cleaning out my pots. And if you win, you can have
all the stew you can eat.'

There was a cheer from Forkbeard's men.

'I wouldn't do that,' a woman's voice said.

'Why?' the cook shouted into the crowd. There was some movement and a short blonde woman appeared.

Ulfar's heart raced but he fought to keep his face calm.

'Because I know him,' Inga said. Behind her, Ulfar could just
about make out the shadow of Arnar.

'Oooh! It's all coming down on you now, Swede!' the cook said.
'And how do you know him, girl?'

She looked deeply at Ulfar, searching for something in his face.
When she was satisfied that it wasn't there, she put on a coy smile.

'None of your business, old man,' she said to the cook and the
crowd at large. 'But let's just say he knows how to take care of his
pieces.' Catcalls and whistles drowned out the sound of Ulfar's
next move.

'Pah,' the cook exclaimed, 'he's not as good as he thinks he is.
His position is—' The move was quick, obvious and— '. . . shit.'
Wrong. He'd walked straight into the trap.

Ulfar looked him in the eye. 'By rights I could now take your
entire pot.'

'No! I said all you could eat!' the cook wailed.

'Well, yes,' Ulfar said. 'But you didn't specify a time, and I am
pretty sure I'd get through it eventually. However, I doubt your
men would love you well if you told them that you'd gambled away
their stew, and I am nothing if not a kind soul. I'll take a bowl for
me and one for each of my friends here.'

The cook huffed, and scooped the thick reindeer stew into three
bowls. 'Here you go, Swede,' he growled.

'Thank you,' Ulfar said. 'And for what it's worth, you had me for a while. At least the first five moves.' He dodged a lazy ladle swing without tipping any of the bowls and retreated. 'See you later,' he said and then turned to Arnar and Inga, who had lingered after the crowd dispersed. He handed them a bowl each and sat down.

'So. You're here,' he said.

'So are you,' Inga said. Arnar sat next to her, frowning deeply. 'What happened back in the marshes?'

Ulfar looked at both of them in turn. 'I don't know,' he said, 'but if what he said was true, Loki possessed Goran when he'd been fatally wounded, and then came to me to convince me to lead an army against Jolawer.'

This time they both frowned.

'Do you expect us to believe that?' Arnar rumbled.

'I don't know if I believe it,' Ulfar said, sighing. 'But Audun – my Norse friend – is in the same boat. He's over in Jolawer's camp.'

'Humph,' Arnar said, but he didn't move away.

'How did you come to be here, then?' Ulfar chanced.

'We ran into Forkbeard's men soon enough after leaving you,' Inga said. 'They took us in. Arnar fights, I mend things.' She scraped up the last of the stew, then put her spoon down. 'I really don't know what to think about you. On the one hand I saw you murder a friend. On the other, Lilia loved you truly. I guess we'll find out soon enough what you are. See you around, Ulfar.' With that she got up and left, Arnar following soon behind her.

Ulfar watched them leave. 'That went well,' he muttered. Then he finished the stew and licked the spoon clean. Around him, snow fell gently on the rows of tents. Ulfar didn't notice the tall, hooded figure almost gliding through the camp; he didn't notice how Sweyn Forkbeard's men found urgent reasons to be somewhere else.

Suddenly a soft voice behind him asked, 'Who are you?'

Ulfar spun around, his hand unconsciously reaching for the hilt of his sword.

'Drawing iron in here would be a *bad* idea,' the figure said, with a hint of a smile to the voice. She was a woman, clad head to toe in light blue, with a fur-lined hood, and almost Ulfar's height.

He drew a sharp breath and forced the hand away from the blade.

'You are not one of ours,' she said.

When he finally identified the voice, Ulfar felt the hairs on the back of his hands start to rise. 'No, your Majesty,' he said.

The woman drew back her hood and blonde hair fell over her shoulders. Her pale skin seemed to shimmer in the cold. She smiled at him, and Ulfar fought the urge to retreat.

'Please. Call me Sigrid.'

THE FAR NORTH
DECEMBER, AD 996

Grey skies. The black trunks of snow-covered trees. Jagged mountain ridges in the distance. Valgard scoured the horizon for any movement at all, but there was nothing alive for miles around, save for him and his fellow travellers. The first time he'd seen the fleeing animals, the day they'd set off from Egill Jotun's valley, he had been shocked. Now he would have been more surprised to see any animals at all.

After Loki had told him where to find the runes, Botolf Arnarson had been a good one to try them on – he'd been dying anyway. The results had been, for want of a better word, eye-opening. The others had been stunned into a fearful silence, which had allowed him to keep reading the old runes out loud, and with every pass the words had fit better in his mouth, sounded better coming out. He'd still lost a few to mispronunciations and skipped words; the results of that had not been pleasant.

He considered his travelling companions. Botolf had already started growing and was easily a head and a half taller than him now. Ormslev just seemed to firm up, somehow; he was as close as they'd get to a walking wall. Skeggi's skin had turned white as the snow, then taken on the bluish tinge of a frozen lake. A strong man to start with, he now looked like he could wrestle a bear and win. Skeggi's two young toughs, Ormar and Jori, who had survived the caves, were also growing bigger, broader and taller by the day. And they all did what he told them – no potions, no tricks, just *command*. He didn't understand it yet, but it was working.

Valgard winced as his back reminded him just how much he'd walked. He had considered using the runes on himself, but something made him hold back. He'd heard the echo of a whispered voice in the back of his mind, the voice he'd heard since very early on. The voice that dripped with contempt at the sight of the big, strong raider-boys showing off, laughing at him for being a cripple. The voice that had kept whispering, saying he was *different* from the others. *Better*. 'I'm special,' he said, smiling to himself. The others heard him but didn't speak. They hadn't, in fact, for a while. They spoke when spoken to, but speech didn't seem to be high on their list of needs. 'Let's move,' Valgard said.

They continued walking south, back the way they'd come a long, long time ago, towards Trondheim.

Audun applied the final touches to the last blade.

'Your man has been gone a while now,' Thormund said.

'He'll be fine,' Audun said. 'What could happen to him, anyway?'

Thormund did not reply but glanced off to Audun's right.

Audun looked up. In front of him stood a rather haggard young man who wore his years badly next to a young blonde girl with hard eyes and a mean mouth. There was a distinct similarity to their features. *Cousins*, he thought, *or something like that, anyway.*

'Is Ulfar here?' the young man asked.

'Good evening to you too,' Audun said, and received a mute stare in return. 'No, Ulfar is not here,' he continued.

'Well,' the boy said, and when the girl elbowed him none-too-subtly in the ribs, added, 'Tell him that – that Greta and Ivar wish to see him. To apologise.'

'I will do that,' Audun said.

Without a word, the pair turned and walked away.

When they were out of earshot, Thormund turned to the darkness behind them. 'You can come out now,' he said.

Ulfar walked into the circle of firelight. 'Apologise. Don't believe it for a moment. But consider me told. We'll see what's what in daylight.'

'They're quite a pair, them two,' Thormund said.

'They are,' Ulfar said. 'Sometimes I think she's more dangerous than he is.'

'Women can be very dangerous indeed,' Thormund said.

'They can,' Ulfar said. 'And on that subject . . .'

'Oh – *now* what?' Audun said.

The stars twinkled up above as the lanky man sat down by the fire. 'I think we may have a little bit of a problem,' Ulfar said.

Prince Karle clambered out of his tent just in time to catch the very first rays of weak sunlight creeping over the horizon. He stretched, grimacing all the while, and rolled his shoulders. 'Damn that, damn all of this and damn all of you,' he muttered to no one in particular.

He looked around at the camp gradually waking up around him. Alfgeir Bjorne was already stomping around the tents, growling and threatening. If the big man noticed that Karle wasn't where he said he'd be the night before, he didn't say. 'Bah – he can do the morning rounds.' He pulled his cloak tight around his shoulders to fend off the morning chill. 'Galti!' he snapped.

Within moments, Galti's angular form was close enough for conversation. 'Yes, my Prince?'

'Walk with me. I'm bored. Tell me what the men are saying,' Karle said as he stepped onto a path between the tents.

'Well,' Galti said. 'Ehm. Well. I think – I think the men are content, more or less.'

'Galti,' Karle said, a note of warning in his voice, 'we talked about this. How many people are listening?'

'None, my Lord.'

'And what do you say then?'

'Everything, my Lord.'

'So what are the men saying?'

'They're tired and cold,' Galti offered.

Karle shrugged. 'Better, but that's the deal, I'm afraid,' he said. 'Food?'

'Stew and roots,' Galti said. 'The old Stenvik bastards always seem to have extra. The men love them for it.'

Karle looked to the skies, took a deep breath and eased his clenched fist open. 'I suppose,' he said, 'that that is a good thing.'

'Only if you allow them to do it,' Galti said, a glint in his eye.

'What?' Karle said.

Galti smiled. 'You *could* suggest to Jolawer that all food should be shared equally, by his decree. That way the men of Stenvik cannot argue and cannot use their surplus to buy the men's affections, everyone loves Jolawer and you look good.'

Karle looked at Galti. 'That's . . . a very good idea,' he said. 'What's got into you?'

'I've been watching you lead,' Galti said. 'It's . . . inspiring.'

Karle couldn't help but grin. 'I'm impressed. Now leave. I'll have to find some humility to approach his baby-faced Majesty.'

'As you wish,' Galti said, walking away. Karle watched him pick his way towards the camp. When his assistant was halfway there he stopped, looked back and scratched his head. Karle waved him on, and the angular young man turned again, heading in the direction of Jolawer's tent.

'Weakling,' Karle spat. 'One good idea and he thinks he can speak to me like an equal.' He'd have to watch the boy, see if his new-found confidence and flair for mischief was there to stay. Karle walked on, further away from the camp, dropping the sneer and trying on a bashful face. 'Your Majesty, it occurred to me . . . no. What do *you* think about . . .' He walked further into the forest, looking for game and muttering deference, trying to get used to the taste.

A while after he'd spoken to Galti he saw a big black fox in the forest, but his arrow missed its mark and the fox was gone.

'Oh, you absolute cock,' Sven said, pulling his herb-pouch shut, then grabbing a nearby branch and rising to his feet with some difficulty.

Behind him, Ulfar shuffled nervously. 'I didn't know what to do,' he said. 'She's very . . .'

'Terrifying?' Sven offered. They could just hear the sound of the camp in the distance. Further into the woods the hunters were doing their work and the sounds of animals dying regularly rang through the trees.

'Yes,' Ulfar muttered. 'She's . . .'

'One of the most dangerous people you'll ever meet and no mistake,' Sven said. 'Our boy Jolawer has done well diverting Fork-beard, who has never and will never be stopped. And for all of his power, old Hair-face does what *she* tells him to.'

'He didn't when we met him,' Ulfar said.

'Oh, but that's not the only place a husband and wife negotiate,' Sven said, a twinkle in his eye. 'She'll run him from pillar to post if she feels like it. If he looks like he is in command, it is because she allows him to be.'

Ulfar frowned. 'Why does he?'

'Because she's captured his heart,' Sven said, 'with silk and steel. Now tell me what happened.'

'She came up to me,' Ulfar said. 'She surprised me – I almost pulled a blade on her.'

'Hah!' Sven said. 'You'd be fantastically dead if you had – little Canute would have gutted you, if no one else.'

'Canute?' Ulfar said.

'Her son. They say he's theirs, but I think she birthed him on the world by herself out of spite. They left him at home, watched over by a great wyrm. He's only small now, but he'll be a proper menace when he grows up, you mark my words.'

'Well, she made me feel like I was a pig at a market. She looked me up and down. I had to check if my clothes were still on.'

'Maybe she was just looking for a little fun,' Sven said. He bent down again and started clawing with bony fingers at the dirt by the roots of the pine. 'So were they?' he added.

'What?'

'Your clothes,' Sven said.

'Yes,' Ulfar said tersely. 'We were outside. It was cold, okay? I don't run around like I used to. But she looked at me like she was wondering whether I'd be . . . *useful*. I get the feeling that I might be her midnight snack in a couple of days' time.'

'Hah,' Sven snorted, crouched on the ground. 'That's my Sigrid, all right.'

'How do you know her?' Ulfar said.

'Oh, back in the day,' Sven said, waving a hand at nothing in particular. 'We all knew each other. The young royals wanted to go and claim glory, and for that it made sense to hire the hardest crew around. Which was us,' he added with a hint of pride in his voice.

'You, Sigurd, Skargrim . . .'

'Old Thormund as well, whiny little bitch that he was,' Sven said. 'And there were others, too. Most of them are dead now. Being hard doesn't make you immortal, sadly.'

Ulfar swallowed. 'There's . . . there's something I need to tell you,' he said.

Sven moved towards the next tree and crouched down, again sweeping away snow and rooting around in the damp earth. 'Apart from you almost stumbling into Sigrid's arms? This morning round is turning out to be quite eventful,' he said over his shoulder.

Ulfar followed at a distance. 'We – me and Audun – think King Olav may not be the most dangerous thing in the North.'

Sven's hands slowed down, then stopped. For a moment the old man didn't move. 'What do you mean?' he said quietly.

Ulfar was sweating, despite the cold. This was it. 'We think Valgard may be stirring up some stuff.' Silence. 'And we fear the gods might be helping him. Well, one god.'

'Which one?'

'Loki,' Ulfar whispered.

'Oh fuck,' Sven said. Slowly, his hands started moving again, rooting mechanically through the dirt, pulling up fledgling green shoots.

Ulfar hovered behind him, waiting for more. 'Is that all you have to say?' he eventually stammered.

'What – do you want more swearing?' Sven said.

'No – I, um—'

Sven still didn't look at Ulfar. 'If you're wrong, it doesn't matter. If you're right and that weak boy I took on and saved from certain death many years back – my *son* - has turned into something else, then that'll need to be dealt with. And regardless of whether you're wrong or right, everything suggests that we're going to need more herbs for poultices. So if I were you I'd stop talking and get digging.'

Ulfar's words caught in his mouth.

Sven turned and looked up at him. His voice was cracked around the edges, but surprisingly gentle. 'Now would be as good a time as any,' he said.

Within moments, Ulfar was down on his knees and rooting around under Sven's direction.

Later, when they returned, the camp had been packed up and only the cook-pots remained, surrounded by cold, hungry people awaiting their turn.

'Something's different,' Sven said under his breath.

'What?'

'I suspect we're about to find out.'

They marched to the Stenvik camp, only to be met by a fuming Oskarl. 'They took our food,' the big Eastman grumbled.

'Who did?' Sven said.

'Alfgeir. Said the king had decided all food should be shared equally. But we were sharing plenty,' Oskarl said. 'Maybe we should share something else.' He cracked his knuckles absent-mindedly.

Sven's grin was cold and unpleasant. 'That's not old Alfgeir's decision, and your type of sharing won't be necessary. We will all get what we deserve in the end.' Around them, pots clanged as the armies of Jolawer Scot and King Forkbeard fed for the march.

THE FAR NORTH
DECEMBER, AD 996

Night fell. The whipping wind was a freezing fire on his face, drying out his eyes and cracking his lips. Valgard could taste salt and water, blood and iron: the flavour of frost. Of course they didn't feel it. His army. His men – could he even call them men any more? He glanced at Botolf, striding through the snow like a plough horse. There was something relentless about him, some-thing indomitable: the river in spring and the wind in autumn. He was walking towards Trondheim and when he got there he'd destroy everything.

Valgard smiled. That would do nicely. He turned to Skeggi. 'What is it like, in there?'

'In where?' the big troll rumbled.

'Inside you, I guess,' Valgard said. He had briefly considered having one of the big brutes carry him, but in the end he'd decided there was something fundamentally undignified about that. He was no one's potato sack.

Skeggi wrestled with the question. 'Me?' he said. 'I do not understand.'

'I suppose something has to give way,' Valgard mused. 'What do you remember?'

'Cold,' Skeggi said. 'The cold that lives in the Halls of Hel. A cold embrace, a cold pain, a cold suffering.'

'Mm,' Valgard said. His own dull and predictable aches suddenly felt much more manageable. 'And nothing else?'

'Your voice,' the troll muttered. He sounded even less happy about that than the cold.

'That's right,' Valgard said, 'my voice. And what did I tell you to do?'

'Go to Trondheim. Kill King Olav,' the trolls around him chanted in unison, their voices almost too deep for hearing.

'Well done. Now keep going,' Valgard said. 'I worry that you'll scare away any chance of a decent conversation.' He scanned the wasteland around them. The snow coated everything in the same bluish-white sheen. Trees in the distance looked like dark scratches through cloth. Far away he could see clouds; he knew they would be over the sea. They would be louring over Trondheim. They would be sitting on top of King Olav, who'd allowed others to insult and sneer at him, who'd been all too happy to listen to every single word of slobbering praise and who would, with his wild-eyed fervour, definitely make an *awful* king.

Valgard's eyes twinkled as he looked up. He liked those clouds.

It was Ormslev who found the stag. Well, maybe 'found' was a bit generous. Valgard winced at the snap as the troll, who could not weigh less than half an ox by now, stepped on the snow-covered antlers and broke them. They hadn't seen a single animal in days, so this one had to have been old, Valgard reasoned. Maybe its heart had given out as it was running away from the scent of the walking six leaving it here, sprawled and half-frozen.

Valgard looked down at the animal and tried to think back. When had he last eaten? He couldn't remember. Did he need to eat now?

Not really.

'Move on,' he said. The words almost caught in his throat.

As the blue-skinned giants set off, Jori caught a root with his toe and went toppling over and crashing into Skeggi who snarled and pushed him away. Jori flailed back at him, swung off-balance, missed and connected squarely with Ormslev's face. A meaty forearm swung back and hit Jori in the chest, sending him crashing back towards Botolf.

The words were out of Valgard's mouth before he could think. '*NO!*'

All five trolls stopped on the spot.

'Now stand back,' Valgard growled, buzzing with anger. He walked towards Skeggi and looked up. 'You. Don't do that.' The big troll looked at him with undisguised hatred, but did not move. Valgard turned to Ormslev. He was aware that his back was exposed, but he didn't care. Fury was his shield. 'And you. Don't hit other trolls. Understood?' The pot-bellied troll looked at him dully and shrugged. 'Good. Now let's get moving. I'll tell you who to hit and when. Try to stay on your feet,' he said to Jori.

Before long they'd fallen into rhythm, the brief flare-up forgotten. *They're like children,* Valgard thought. *Massive, scary children.* He thought of Harald, and how he would have fitted right in. *Only these ones do exactly what I tell them to.* There was a pleasant buzz in the core of him, almost like he was drunk on summer wine. So this was what real power tasted like.

The snow didn't bother him so much any more.

THE SOUTH OF SWEDEN
DECEMBER, AD 996

White and grey, cold and wet.

The army marched north, then north-by-northwest. Forests of snow-covered pine gave way to white fields, sinking ever deeper into winter. They marched as far as they could in the dusk, but when the dark crept over them the cry went out and the army made camp in a big field close to the woods.

The men of Stenvik stood by their own camp and watched as Jolawer Scot's men assembled theirs quickly and effectively.

'Look at that!' Sven said.

'Told you,' Sigurd muttered.

'They're getting better,' Oskarl said. He thought for a moment. 'If we can challenge King Olav to a camp-making contest, we should be fine,' he continued.

'Who's that?' Ulfar said. A stick of a man was striding across from Forkbeard's camp, heading towards Jolawer's tent.

Sigurd and Sven shared a glance. 'Some business happening, no doubt,' Sven said. 'Probably nothing to worry us.'

Forkbeard's messenger ducked into Jolawer's tent. A very short while later, Alfgeir Bjorne came out with him. They shook hands and the messenger returned to the other camp.

'Or maybe I'm wrong,' Sven muttered. 'Maybe I'm very wrong indeed.'

Alfgeir turned towards them and walked with a purpose. 'Good evening, men of Stenvik,' he said. 'Sigurd, I need a handful of yours to go help me. They need to be strong and handy with an axe.'

'Of course,' Sigurd said. 'I'll do what I can. Might I ask what we're doing?'

'We're going to start a fire,' Alfgeir said as he walked off.

*

The dark shapes of log stacks were surrounded by flickering flames of white-gold set to dancing by gusts of wind. Built a hundred yards apart, the pyres had been raised in a race between the two camps. Jolawer's men had won, after a fashion, but Forkbeard's stack was neater and better crafted. The result was that the space between the two camps was now illuminated by two burning wooden towers. Forkbeard's men sat on one side, Jolawer's on the other.

Alfgeir Bjorne stepped into the light. 'Men of the North!' he shouted. Slowly the murmur died down and he had the eyes and ears of every man and woman around the two fires. 'We live in dangerous times. This is an age for the brave!' A cheer rang out. 'And before we march to the North, to show King Olav who owns these northern lands, your kings – Forkbeard and Jolawer' – the cheers turned to roars and water-skins full of sour, strong mead were passed around – 'have decided that we should have a contest!'

Sitting far enough back so that the heat from the fires was comfortable, Ulfar glanced at Audun and Thormund, then pointed at Sven and Sigurd, who were deep in conversation.

Alfgeir Bjorne, standing between the two armies, continued, 'The King of the Danes and Scourge of the Seas, Sweyn Forkbeard!'

Half of the assembled fighters roared their approval as Forkbeard stepped out into the circle. Dressed in a simple warrior's garb, he still radiated enough authority to turn thousands of men silent. 'In the world, we are known!' he began, with a voice that had clearly carried across a battlefield or two. 'They fear us for we come in the night with fire and sword. They fear us for we come in the day with powerful sails and death on the edge of an axe.' Behind him, Alfgeir and the tall messenger were commanding a handful of men, who were erecting two logs, hastily cut to resemble the shape of a man. 'So the first test shall be – targets!'

The crowd roared, and started chanting names. Unmoved, Forkbeard pointed to a man on his left. He had a thick red beard to go with the broad, powerful shoulders of a lumberjack, and three hand-axes in his belt. The axeman took his place twenty yards from the wooden targets. Then he looked to the crowd, spread his arms and waved to encourage applause. Forkbeard's men were only too happy to oblige, and the axeman slowly started stepping backwards. Twenty-two – twenty-five – twenty-eight . . .

'Too far,' Thormund muttered. 'Cocky bastard.'

With a roar, the bearded man whipped an axe out of his belt and launched it at the target. The audience fell silent immediately as the axe sailed through the night and hit the target with an audible *thunk*. The point was buried in the top of the figure, where its head would be.

The crowd erupted.

The axeman took two quick steps back. Metal flashed in the firelight and the flying axe sunk into the wood next to its sister, with only a thumb's width between them. The crowd roared its approval, but the axeman did not move. Instead he just stood there, soaking in the sound, rolling his shoulders and limbering up. As the crowd grew quiet, he looked at them, surveying them as a king would his lands. Then he reached for the third axe, hefted it and without warning flung it towards the wooden figure.

Sparks flew as the blade squeezed in between the two axes already there.

Even Jolawer's men could not stay quiet.

'Did you see that?' Mouthpiece hissed. 'Did you fucking see that? One in each eye, and then one in the nose! I've never seen anything like it!'

'Bastard has a good hand on 'im,' Thormund muttered. 'I'm glad they're on our side now.'

'Shh,' Ulfar said. 'Our turn.'

Jolawer Scot had walked into the circle. His shadow danced behind him, stretching into the darkness. In his hand he held a stick with a thickly swaddled end. 'Give cheer to the Dane's hand!' he shouted.

'Give cheer to the king's voice,' Audun muttered. 'Where does he keep all the noise?' Beside him, Ulfar shook his head.

'We could never hope to present anyone of the Svear who could throw an axe like that. In fact, standing here, I'm not sure I'd reach halfway to the target!' Jolawer said, grinning at the laughs from the audience. 'No, we Svear should probably hang our heads in shame!'

Cries of outrage from his own men mingled with the delighted whoops of Forkbeard's soldiers.

'What the fuck is he up to?' Mouthpiece muttered. 'He's giving in!'

Ulfar saw it first. 'No, he isn't,' he said.

Enveloped in the heat of the burning pyres, Jolawer was warming to his role. 'Yes! We should! Prince Karle – stand up!' In the front row, Karle rose to his feet and walked into the middle. His bow was slung so casually over his shoulder that it looked a part of him. A boy of no more than thirteen winters followed him. Jolawer turned to the tall prince, dressed all in white. 'Karle – can you do that? Hit a target that small, only the size of a man's head, from thirty yards? With an axe? *THREE TIMES?*' Half of Forkbeard's men cheered, but the other half had gone quiet.

'No, my King. I cannot,' Karle said, just as loudly.

'Well, then – you are no use to me! You are banished to the shadows!' Confusion set in on Forkbeard's side, and there was a smattering of boos as Jolawer Scot thrust the stick into the boy's arms. Karle turned and walked towards the far end, close to the other pyre. When they passed, the boy stuck the stick into the fire and it flared into light.

'A torch?' Mouthpiece said.

'Yes,' Ulfar said.

Moments later, boy and prince had disappeared into the shadows and all that could be seen was a hazy outline in a ball of firelight.

Fifty yards beyond the first pyre the torch stopped, and the audience could just make out the boy lifting it up high to illuminate Karle.

The movement when he unslung his bow was smooth and silent. The audience could just about make out the twang as he released the bowstring.

They all saw the arrow, flying through the flames.

When it sank into the forehead of the target, Jolawer Scot's men cheered loudly and looked out into the darkness – but the torch was already moving. Another ten, another twenty yards out. They could just about make out Karle's face as he loosened the second arrow, slicing the night air in half.

The cheers turned to roars as it found its target, precisely next to the first one – but then they turned to shouts of dismay as the torch kept moving, further still. 'What's he doing?' Audun said. 'That's an impossible shot.'

Ulfar just shook his head. 'He's enjoying himself. That's what he's doing.'

The torch stopped, and from the darkness came a roar. 'SVEAR!' Prince Karle shouted. Jolawer Scot's men roared and shook their fists in response, only to be met with shouts of incredulity from Forkbeard's men.

'Prince Karle! I will allow you to return to my realm!' Jolawer Scot shouted over the noise. Five arrows were buried in the forehead of the target, on an area no bigger than two thumbs.

Forkbeard's axeman walked out into the performance area and waited. When Karle emerged from the shadows, the bearded man bowed his head. Forkbeard stepped out next to them and held up his hands to quieten the crowd. 'We must concede, Danes, that the Svear have beaten us fairly. They are very good with a target . . . that doesn't move! It's time for the Svear to show us their wrestling champion!'

At this, Forkbeard's men roared again.

In the front row, Jolawer Scot turned to Alfgeir Bjorne, who looked to Sigurd and Sven. After a short conference Jolawer Scot took to the floor.

'They're not going to . . .' Ulfar's voice trailed away.

'What?' Audun said.

'He was a champion back home for a decade, but then he killed a man so he swore never to—'

Jolawer Scot's voice rose in volume. 'We will give you Alfgeir Bjorne!'

'Oh shit,' Ulfar said.

Alfgeir stepped into the centre, between the fires. Already there was something different about him. The years were dropping off the old man and revealing something quite terrifying. In the front row, Sven and Sigurd were grinning like boys sharing a joke. Alfgeir turned to Jolawer Scot's men. 'It's hot down here!' he roared. He peeled off his furs and his shirt and there was an audible, indrawn breath in the audience. The man in the light was built like a prize bull, with a layer of fat covering bunched-up muscle and long, strong arms.

'This is our champion, King Forkbeard,' Jolawer Scot said. 'Alfgeir Bjorne, reigning wrestling champion of Uppsala, Gotland and nearby areas. Who have you got?'

Forkbeard looked over the crowd, but no one moved.

'Will the Jutes rise to the challenge?' he shouted.

'Against *that*?' someone shouted from the crowd, to ripples of laughter.

The king kept calm. 'Will the Fynsmen step up?'

A grey-haired chieftain rose, near the back. 'I have no one who can compete with Alfgeir Bjorne, my king. His name alone weighs more than half my men.'

'Well,' Forkbeard said. 'If that is how it is, then I suspect we'll just have to yield—' Under a rising chorus of boos, the gangly messenger strode up to him in the centre and whispered something in his ear. The king raised his arm and motioned for quiet.

'We have a challenger!' he said.

A rousing cheer went up on the side of the Danes. Over on the side of the Svear, Audun leaned over to Ulfar. 'What's going on?'

'I don't know,' Ulfar said. They both looked at Thormund, whose brow was knotted in concentration. 'I heard some stories,' he muttered, 'but I don't think . . .' His voice trailed off as Forkbeard left the circle.

'Where is the brave soul?' Sven shouted.

The tall, gangly messenger turned towards the Svear and bowed. The noise rolled over him in waves as grown, dangerous men almost cried laughing.

To the side, Alfgeir Bjorne clapped his hands loudly. 'Are you going to face me, *boy*?' he roared.

The messenger answered by shaking out of his shirt. His skin was so pale it almost shone.

'Look at 'im! All skin and bones and no feathers! He's a chicken!' A chorus of clucking followed the voice from Jolawer's camp.

Then the messenger started to move.

'Oh shit,' Ulfar muttered.

'What?' Mouthpiece hissed.

'This is not good. This is not good at all,' Ulfar said, his eyes trained on the two men.

Alfgeir Bjorne crouched down into a perfect wrestler's stance, looking for all the world like he'd be the one better off in a collision with an ox. 'Come on, then!' he roared.

Forkbeard's messenger stepped closer, tentatively.

'Look,' Ulfar said, pointing to Forkbeard's men. In the massed ranks of the Danes, eyes glittered with anticipation.

'They're not afraid,' Audun said. 'None of them.'

At that moment, without warning, Alfgeir launched himself at the skinny messenger, huge arms spread wide like a killing beast swooping down. Nothing could escape that, surely? The fight, if you could call it that, would be over and he'd crush the messenger—

—who was no longer there. Somehow the man had danced out of Alfgeir's grasp and was now behind him.

The big Swede growled, turned around with surprising speed and launched himself at his opponent, and this time, now they knew what to look for, they could actually see the tall man moving, spinning out of the way, grabbing Alfgeir's outstretched hand and *twisting* and suddenly Alfgeir was crashing to the floor, brought down by his own force.

The air went out of all of King Jolawer's men at the same time.

The messenger took three steps back and nodded at his prone opponent. 'Yield?' he said, loud and clear.

'Like the seven tits of Hel I will,' Alfgeir growled, clambering to his feet.

In the front row, Sven turned to Sigurd with real concern in his eyes. Ulfar could make out the words *break his neck* and *a bit tricky*.

This time Alfgeir didn't rush but circled the messenger. 'You're fast, boy,' he rumbled, 'and clever. I like that: it's fun. It's *different*. But I've killed faster and smarter men.'

The messenger just smiled, and reached in. Alfgeir slapped away his hand, but, lightning-fast, the messenger's other hand had latched on to his forearm and suddenly the gangly man had

Alfgeir's arm over his shoulder and was pushing up as the old wrestler lost his balance, then moving under the falling man and pushing, *pushing*, until Alfgeir's own weight carried him over his crouching opponent and up in the air.

When he landed this time he didn't get up.

'I'm having no part of that man, even with any kind of weapon,' Ulfar stated, and around him, Audun, Thormund and Mouthpiece nodded.

Forkbeard stepped into the ring and checked Alfgeir, but the old wrestler managed to raise his hand, then clambered to his feet, wincing. When he'd risen he turned to the Danes. 'I have never in my whole life been beaten like that, especially by a twig of a boy. Hail the champion!' He made his way over to the skinny man and clasped his hand in a warrior's grip.

The Danes screamed in approval, chanting, 'Thorkell! *Thorkell!*'

'Now that means the games are even,' Forkbeard announced. 'Your challenge,' he said, bowing down to Jolawer Scot.

The young king rose and met Forkbeard between the burning pyres. 'The Swedes have bested you at targets.' A cheer from his men. 'But you've defeated us at wrestling.' A louder cheer from the Danes. 'These are all heroic efforts, and I believe they deserve telling – in verse!'

All around Audun and Ulfar, men started clanging anything they could get their hands on together, slowly at first, then faster and faster.

This clearly pleased Forkbeard. He waited until the noise had reached a peak, then held up his hand and immediately every man in the clearing stopped. 'If the game is verse, there can be only one fair pairing. In the soft courts of the South and the West, the fat kings sit on cushions,' he said, his voice rising, 'and have painted lily-boys sing them songs. In the North I will hear of no king who is not a skald! And so I challenge you, Jolawer Scot, boy-king of the Swedes!'

If the young king was concerned by the unexpected challenge, or by the roar of the crowd, he showed no sign. He stepped into the centre of the fires and looked at Forkbeard.

> *Feared and fearsome*
> *Forkbeard, Dane-king*
> *Hides behind the*
> *hem of Sigrid!*

Catcalls and laughter washed over them from King Jolawer's men.

Forkbeard grinned and nodded appreciatively before speaking.

> *Time will tell*
> *the un-tried king*
> *What joys be wrought*
> *by woman's hem.*

Insults rained from the Danes, but Forkbeard silenced them with a raised arm.

> *Lack-beard king*
> *Lost, no wedding*
> *Heirless half-man's*
> *Hand's for bedding!*

'Ouch,' Audun muttered to Ulfar as the crowd went wild, adding hand-gestures and insults.

In the circle, Jolawer laughed along with the others and waited.

As the noise started to die down, he extended his arms to encourage silence. When the whoops and hollers had finally gone, Jolawer cleared his throat. Then, with impeccable timing, he bowed formally to Forkbeard and got a ripple of laughs for his trouble.

> *Flatland ruler*
> *Fiercely yapping*
> *Li—*

'Hear my words, Kings of the South!'

The voice rang out in the darkness, thick and gravelly, cutting Jolawer off. In the light of the fire, thousands of men sprang to their feet and a whole host of edged weapons were ready within moments.

'Weapons DOWN!' Forkbeard roared.

'NOW!' Jolawer Scot added.

'Reveal yourself,' Forkbeard said to the darkness. There was steel in his voice.

A moment passed, and then another. The shadows shifted gently as a man rode into the half-light at the far edge of the fire. Behind him, a row of men rode – all battle-hardened, all equipped for war. Ten of them, armed like men of note.

The rider in front, a big man with broad shoulders and a twice-broken nose, leapt off his horse and kept his hands well clear of the sword in his belt. He walked into the centre, between the fires, towards the two kings.

An arrow whistled past his shin and thwacked into the ground behind him.

'That's close enough, stranger,' Forkbeard said. Behind him, Karle nocked another arrow. 'Who are you, and what are your words?'

The stranger looked around at the assembled men and nodded appreciatively. 'My name is Erik, son of Jarl Hakon the Great, ruler of Trondheim. I bring news from the North, and it is not good.'

'I thought it would never end, this one,' Hjalti muttered as he pulled his jacket closer. Around him, men were grudgingly shovelling paths between houses and shaking off hangovers in the pale morning sun. The air was cold enough to leave a burning feeling in his lungs.

'The locals say it's been a while since it was this bad,' Einar replied, 'and they're used to it,' he added. They were standing outside the door to Hakon Jarl's hall, which they'd just about managed to open. The snow had been wet and hard-packed, up to a grown man's chest. Hjalti had tried curses and threats to get the men off their arses, but in the end it was King Olav who won through to them. He'd simply sat in the high seat and waited until they'd all fallen silent, then asked them to do it – for him and the Saviour. The oddest selection had stood up first – burly warriors, narrow-faced cut-throats, jesters, thieves and hard men – and soon enough they were all on their feet, ready to do their king's bidding.

'We'll be getting visitors soon,' Hjalti said.

'So they say,' Einar said.

'Might be trouble,' Hjalti said.

Einar shrugged.

They stood in silence for a spell, watching the men shovel and push the snow away, creating corridors for walking between houses. What children there were left in Trondheim were already out, hollering at each other, throwing snowballs and pushing each other off the emerging snow-hills.

'Einar! Hey Einar!' one of them yelled, a girl of maybe ten years, watching them from about fifty yards away. 'Show us!'

'Show you what?' Einar yelled back.

In response the girl started making a large snowball.

Moving calmly and without taking his eyes off the little girl Einar reached for a handful of snow, forming it slowly in his hands, packing it firmly.

Hjalti watched as kids all around stopped what they were doing to watch. The girl with the snowball checked Einar to confirm. The youth gave the smallest of nods.

The girl launched the snowball high up in the air.

Einar Tambarskelf's arm whipped round. The small missile in his hands sliced the air with an audible *whoosh*. The big lump of snow burst in midair to wild cheers from the kids. Some of the men even shared amused glances.

'If there's trouble, there's trouble,' Einar said.

A while later, Hjalti's mouth closed.

Grey skies and heavy clouds heralded Storrek Jarl's arrival, and Olav's scouts had alerted him to the time. By the time the jarl had made it to the longhouse, fires had been stoked and food was ready. Hjalti waited by the entrance to the hall.

'Storrek Jarl!' he exclaimed. 'Welcome to—'

'Shut up, squeak,' the chieftain snapped. 'I'm cold and wet, and you're not the king I came to see.'

Hjalti's words caught in his throat. 'I – uh – the king—'

'Af-af-af-af-af,' the chieftain mimicked. 'Shut the fuck up. Are you going to invite me in or will I have to carve my way through?'

Defeated, Hjalti stepped aside just in time before Storrek barged through. 'Storrek Jarl,' he shouted into the hall. 'Arriving before King—'

'Shut *up!*' Storrek yelled over his shoulder. 'I would love to punch you right in the noise-hole. Hel's teeth, but you are annoying.' Behind him, his four long-suffering attendants fanned out and walked in procession towards the dais at the end of the hall.

'King Olav?' Storrek shouted. The king rose from the high seat, but did not reply. The fat chieftain looked him up and down, then waddled to the end of the long table at the foot of the dais and sat, wheezing with effort. King Olav walked down the steps and took a seat opposite him.

'Here it is,' Storrek Jarl said. 'I don't like you.' He searched for a response in King Olav's face, but got none. 'I don't like your god, and I don't like the way you rule.' Still the king did not respond, and behind Storrek, his followers shuffled nervously. 'But,' the fat chieftain said, louder, then, 'but—' he said again, voice more controlled this time, 'I can also count.'

King Olav looked him straight in the eyes and smiled.

'So what do you want?' Storrek Jarl said.

King Olav leaned forward. 'I would like to commend you on your honesty,' he said.

Storrek pulled back, confused.

'Yes, I would,' King Olav said. 'You are precisely the kind of man I could do with more of. And I am sure' – the king leaned forward further, lowering his voice – 'I am sure you will absolutely observe the new rule and respect the word of the Lord when you go back to your home up in the Dales. Even though I have no way of keeping an eye on you,' he added, lips pursed in a conspiratorial smile.

Storrek looked suspiciously at the king. 'You . . . could. Yes,' he said. 'And what do you want from me?'

'From you?' the king said, eyes wide open. 'What could I want from you, Storrek Jarl? You're *here*. Just by honouring me with your presence, you have given me assistance that is almost invaluable. Your name is your gift. The people *trust* you, Storrek. They trust you because you say what needs to be said. And if you trust me, the people will trust me. The Lord will take those he can reach, and he will deal with the others according to their conduct,' King Olav said. Then, 'And when I say invaluable, I tell a lie. I mean, of course, worth at least double the sacks of grain that Hakon Jarl would give you in times of trouble. I gather it wasn't much to begin with,' the king added as an afterthought.

'Tight-fisted bastard,' Storrek muttered.

'And that is not worthy of a man of your . . . influence,' King Olav said. 'Speak to Hjalti on your way out. But please don't punch him in the mouth.' The king smiled. 'If you do he'll be useless on the door.'

Storrek Jarl struggled to his feet, still eyeing King Olav with suspicion. 'And that's it?'

'That's it,' King Olav said. 'We will of course entertain you and your men for as long as you wish.' The king spread out his hands to indicate the great hall. 'Udal is coming, and Gunnthor is already here. I would very much like to hear tales of the area, if you would humour me.'

'I will think about it,' Storrek Jarl said. He turned and shuffled off, motioning angrily for his attendants to keep up.

King Olav watched him leave, reached down to his knee and squeezed it as hard as he could, until he thought his fingers would snap. He drew breath, once, twice, then exhaled slowly.

'Is everything well, my Lord?' Hjalti said, hovering nervously at his shoulder.

'It is,' Olav said through gritted teeth. 'It is.' At the far end of the longhouse, the door slammed on Storrek Jarl's followers. 'Or will be,' the king added.

'Look! There it is!' Heimir shouted.

'Shithole,' Udal Jarl said, spitting for emphasis.

'Look at all those *houses*,' Heimir said. 'How does it even smell in the summer?'

'Trust me, son,' Udal Jarl said, 'you do not want to know. Do you remember what to say?' The wind picked up again, slicing at the back of their ears.

'Yes, *Father*,' Heimir said, screwing up his face in a grimace of mock honesty. 'We are honoured and grateful to meet you, King Olav.'

'Good. Come on then. Let's get a move on. Maybe they've got some half-warm piss in a mug at the king's table.'

Suddenly Udal's horse bucked and twisted to the side and the jarl pulled hard on the reins. 'Whoa! What's the matter with you, eh?' The animal tossed its head and snorted, eyes rolling and nostrils flaring. 'Did the North Wind get to you?' The horse snorted, neighed and shook its head violently. 'Come on, boy. Come on,' the Jarl whispered into the animal's ear. 'You're not going to throw me. Not me. Not after all these years.'

Just as suddenly as it had begun, it was gone again. The wind died down and Udal's horse whinnied in protest at the pull on the reins. 'He must smell King Olav's pansy arse,' one of the men quipped.

Udal Jarl shrugged as he guided the horse down the hill towards Trondheim. 'Probably.'

His son and his men walked behind him, the wind at their back.

*

A while later, Hjalti stepped cautiously towards the dais and the motionless figure of King Olav. 'He's here, my Lord,' he said. 'Udal Jarl.'

'Send him in,' the king said without looking. 'And get the boy to put more peat on the fire. Wind's picking up again. And Hjalti – we will require mead to be brought to the table. Fast as you like, when I call for it.'

'Yes, my Lord,' Hjalti said. He turned sharply and strode towards the longhouse doors.

Olav blinked and looked around at the hall. It couldn't be called great any more by any stretch; the greying timbers would need to be replaced in a couple of summers and the roof needed re-thatching in at least three places. There was a certain smell of decay to the place that was hard to isolate. He thought of Hakon Jarl. 'As with the lair, so with the bear,' he muttered.

At the far end, the doors opened and a large, red-haired man with an unmistakeable air of command strode through. Olav rose and very quietly allowed his hand to drop down by his side, brushing his belt.

'King Olav!' Udal Jarl shouted.

'The same!' Olav hollered in reply. 'May the men of Udal Heath be welcome in my halls!'

'Thank you, my King,' Udal said as he walked up towards the dais. 'We've come a long way to meet you.'

'So I gather,' he said, stepping down from the dais and moving to grasp the chieftain's hand. Udal Jarl was half a head taller than him and at least two hands wider, and even through the wet wool and snow Olav could smell his rotten teeth. The big man looked down on him and smirked, as if the king had been weighed, measured and found wanting.

'It is interesting to see you, finally,' the jarl said. 'Your stories travel fast.'

'So does a fly in summer, but in winter there are none around,' the king said. 'Stories are stories. We are above such things.'

'Hm,' the jarl said. 'Allow me to introduce my son. Heimir!'

A red-haired youth with broad shoulders and a straight back stepped up to the jarl's side, and nodded curtly at the king. 'I am Heimir, son of Udal, son of Thormar of the Heath. It is an honour to set foot in your halls, my King.'

'More so for the visit of proud, strong Northmen like yourselves,' he replied, noting the cloud of confusion briefly passing across the young man's face. 'Sit! Please, sit! Hjalti – mead!' Moments later two young men appeared, set down six mugs on the table and hurried away, disappearing out of sight behind a pillar. The men of Udal spread out behind their jarl and his son. 'Welcome!'

'Thank you,' Udal Jarl said. 'We left as soon as we heard of your landing.'

'No mean feat, coming this far in winter.'

'Well – no. But it is a poor chieftain who doesn't come to see his king,' Udal said. 'A poor chieftain indeed.'

The king smiled and raised a mug. 'To Udal!'

Quick to react, Heimir grabbed a mug and raised it. 'To the North!' Udal and his men followed soon after.

The king lifted the wooden mug up to his lips, drained it and slammed it on the table. 'Hjalti!' Six more mugs appeared quickly. 'To cooked words and raw flattery!' he shouted.

'Hah!' Udal barked. 'To rich kings and poor chieftains!'

Down went the mead.

'Hjalti!' the king roared, one hand under the table to steady himself. Moments later, more mead arrived. 'To cold winters and hot women!'

Udal downed his mug and banged it on the table. 'To Thor's—'

Quick as a flash, King Olav smashed a heavy hunting knife, point first, into Udal's mug and nailed it to the table. Udal recoiled, almost losing his balance.

'No,' the king said, voice firm and eyes steady. 'Not in this house. Not any more.' Behind him, Hjalti, Einar and ten of their chosen men stepped out of the shadows, swords very visible at their hips. 'We can drink, you and I. We can sing songs together. But you will not salute the Old Gods in my house, and your son will not go on with the old ways.'

Udal rose from his bench. 'I see,' he said, 'what my king is made of. So be it.'

King Olav did not rise. 'You are welcome to stay with us as long as you wish,' he said. 'Gunnthor and Storrek are here. We'll eat reindeer, I am told. And' – he glanced at the handle of the knife, then looked Udal straight in the eye – 'we've got more mugs.'

Moments later, when the door slammed on the red-haired chieftain's retinue, Hjalti moved to the king's side. 'You've shamed him in front of his men,' he said. 'He will never forgive you. He will hate you for ever, and seek to destroy you.'

'Excellent,' King Olav said. When he rose he was smiling. 'That is exactly what I want him to do.'

Hjalti and Einar watched King Olav walk up onto the dais and sit down in the high seat, surveying the hall before him. The sound was very faint, but the king was unmistakeably humming a tune.

Sensing that they were not needed, the raider and the young archer made their way towards the exit. 'Do we tell him about the dogs?' Einar said.

'He's in a good mood. It can wait,' Hjalti said, tugging absent-mindedly on his beard. 'It can probably wait.'

'Do it!'

'Get a move on, fishwife!'

'You fight like your mother!'

The cries bounced off the walls of the great hall. Excited by the visitors, the men had quickly formed a wrestling ring and now bets were flying and coins were changing hands. Gunnthor's men – two of them, neither a day younger than their chieftain – had politely declined to participate, but the followers of Udal and Storrek grappled enthusiastically with all comers.

King Olav surveyed the room.

'They seem happy to bark at each other,' Hjalti said at his shoulder.

'They are,' the king replied, 'but there are too many of them, they've got too little to do and the space is too small.'

Hjalti hesitated. 'Do you – do you want me to clear some out? Move them, maybe, to other houses?'

He looked at Hjalti then, studying him like a collector would a rare specimen, and sighed. 'No, Hjalti. I can name every man in this hall. They have marched with me across half of Norway and halfway to the winter sky. Every last one of them would step in front of a spear for me, and most of them have, at one time or another. They have done so because I have given them a part of myself. I have given them a reason to live. I have kept them close. I've got them now. So what happens if I push them away into the snow and the cold in a strange place?'

'You . . . lose them?'

'Quicker than you'd think. I saw a lot of captains make that mistake out west.'

'So we keep them in, then?'

'Keep them in. Where are our friends?'

'Udal is over there—' Hjalti pointed to where the big red-bearded chieftain sat, yelling encouragement at the wrestlers. 'Gunnthor is there—' With one of his followers at his shoulder, the old jarl had found a nice corner where he appeared to be regaling some of the locals with a story. 'And Storrek is there.' Sitting midway between the two, Storrek was nursing a mug and talking to a grey-haired man.

'I see.'

'Um . . . there is one more thing I need to tell you,' Hjalti said, clenching his fists.

'What's that?' King Olav said, his eyes trained on Storrek and the grey-haired man.

'Today, just after Udal came in, there was a . . . well, something happened with three of the dogs.' The story tumbled out of him. 'I've never seen anything like it. The wind changed and it was like they smelled something. They fell on each other, snarling and biting – no provocation, nothing. I know those dogs, too. They got on just fine yesterday, and the day before that.'

'Anyone near them? Anyone hurt?'

'No – and the moment they started, no one wanted to go anywhere close.'

'And the dogs?'

'Well, here's the thing: they ripped each other apart! The big one, the black Dane, was the last one standing, but when the others were dead he started biting and tearing at his own flesh until he bled to death. We couldn't believe it.'

'Hm.' The king's gaze strayed to the rafters. 'That's unusual. Have you—?' Shouts from the far end cut him off and his head snapped back to search for the source of the noise.

'What the—?' Hjalti exclaimed.

'Sigthor!' King Olav shouted, but to no avail. At the far end of the hall a great block of a man with a bushy beard and long, thick blond hair had risen. The man he'd smashed to the floor with his mug was writhing in agony beneath Sigthor's feet. The big man clambered up onto the table.

'HE HAS RISEN!' he bellowed.

'Come on then!' one of Storrek's men shouted back from the wrestling ring. His shirt was off and clumsily carved runes decorated his muscled torso.

Sigthor roared and jumped off the table. Mysteriously, even in the packed hall, space seemed to appear around him. 'HE COMES!' he said. 'HE COMES FOR YOU!'

'Well, he should get on with it,' the wrestler shouted back to gales of laughter from the men.

Olav's legs had started moving before he had even quite decided what was happening. 'Go and get the others,' he growled at Hjalti before grabbing his mailed gauntlets off the table and pushing his way through the crowd.

'Come on then!' the wrestler shouted. He was out of sight now that King Olav was down on the ground. 'Come on, you big fu—' The crowd recoiled as one at the wet crunch, then shouts of outrage rang out in the hall.

'Weapon!'

'Rule-breaker!'

'Watch out!'

The crowd parted and suddenly Olav found himself face to face with Sigthor, who was coated in the blood of the wrestler. The man's corpse lay on the ground, discarded like a broken toy. The head was split open, the face a bloody mess.

Sigthor, clutching a wedge of firewood, looked down at Olav. 'He's coming,' he said, softly this time, and a chill ran up the king's spine.

'Who's coming?' he said, pulling on his mail gloves, but Sigthor just smiled. 'WHO IS COMING?' the king roared, and out of the corner of his eye he saw some of his oldest soldiers take one look at his mailed fists and take another half-step back.

'They'll see,' the big man said, 'they'll see! They'll pay for judging him – but he will need my help. He'll need all our help.'

Olav felt the ranks close behind him. With a grunt of effort, Sigthor swung at the king, who ducked and twisted, then threw a hard punch that forced a wet cough out of the raider.

A primal roar ripped through the hall and Sigthor turned, but he was too slow; the king had found his balance again and this time when he swung, he connected squarely with his opponent's jaw. He felt the chains on his gloves dig into flesh; the skin on his knuckles split as the bones in Sigthor's face shattered and the raider crumpled before him.

Gritting his teeth to avoid shaking the hurt out of his hand, he turned to the assembled men. 'Clean this up,' he said, forcing calm into his voice. He found Hjalti's eye and walked towards him. 'Slit his throat and feed him to whatever dogs we have left,' he said, loud enough for every man in the circle to hear. When he was closer, close enough not to be overheard, he added, 'And bring me ice and bandages for my hand. I'll be in the back room.'

On the way back he walked past the three chieftains, standing together a safe distance from the wrestling ring. He looked them up and down, speaking before they had the chance. 'Storrek, your man's life will be paid in full. To all of you – join me in the back room, will you? The men will be quiet out here for a while.'

As he turned away, he could feel their eyes on his back.

'And then?' Einar's eyes were wide open despite the early hour. He'd been out since dawn and had brought down an elk and two deer. The rest of the hunting party had gone off to eat, but Hjalti had helped them drag the carcases the last bit of the way and now they stood together up against the wall of the pantry, watching a thick-armed butcher carve up the meat.

'He just sat there, hand on the ice block, listening to them,' Hjalti said. 'He dropped in a word now and then, to lift their stories, make them feel good about themselves,' he added. 'His hand must have been killing him. It was swollen purple and black, and he had ring marks all over his fingers.'

Einar made the sign of the cross. 'I'm just glad he's on our side,' he said.

Hjalti laughed. 'Hah! Yes, we're lucky there. Really, *really* lucky.' The smell of blood was getting too strong to ignore.

'I'm off,' Einar said. 'If the dogs stay away, then so should we. Are we still going riding with the king?'

'You speak the truth,' Hjalti said. 'And yes, we are. We're leaving right now. Don't make a face. You'll get to ride next to the king. It'll be a good trip.' He watched the tall youth roll his eyes, leave and turn towards the longhouse before hurrying out himself and checking to both sides before heading in the other direction.

Heimir Udalsson cracked his knuckles. 'This hut is tiny,' he said. 'They've put us in a fucking dead man's box.' He cracked his knuckles again.

'Stop that,' his father growled. The boy glared at him, but stopped and all but disappeared under his furs. 'So. Tell me one more time.'

The grey-haired man by the doorway took a half-step into the house. 'My chieftain—'

'Gunnthor,' Udal said.

'. . . Gunnthor, yes, he says he was told by Storrek that they were ready to move. Gunnthor wanted you to know this because while he trusts Storrek Jarl—'

'He fucking shouldn't,' Udal snapped.

'—ahem, fully, he thinks we would all benefit if you were on our side, with your men. King Olav is cocky; he doesn't post that many in the way of guards. With eight to ten men it's easy, but it would be harder with four to five.'

'And this advantage you say you have?'

'He doesn't expect us,' the grey-haired man said. 'And we can make sure he's alone.'

'How can you do that?'

The old advisor smiled. 'We have our ways.'

'Bloody Southerners,' Udal muttered. 'Wouldn't know a straight answer if it stuck you in the eye.'

The grey-haired man smiled again. 'Does that mean you're ready?'

Udal spat and shrugged. 'I'll think about it. Until midday.'

'That will do,' the grey-haired man said as he turned towards the door. He cast another glance at the assembled men. 'That will do. If you're in, come to the back entrance at midday, ready to do the work. We'll be inside.'

When the door closed on the grey-haired man, Heimir's nose reappeared above the furs. 'Can I come?'

'Shut up,' Udal snapped. 'No one's said we're going.'

His three kinsmen shared a glance.

'But we are, though?' Heimir said.

Udal did not reply.

Around and behind him his men started preparing their weapons.

THE FAR NORTH

DECEMBER, AD 996

The voice whispered to Valgard, insinuated its way into his mind like smoke from a secret fire. The cold in his feet faded from memory and he was soaring, hunting.

Call him

Call him to you, reach out to him with your mind

Like that. Yes

He will do your bidding

He will obey as long as you can hold your thoughts

Yellow eyes. Hot breath. Fangs.

Wolf.

TRONDHEIM, NORTH NORWAY
DECEMBER, AD 996

'There's no one here,' Heimir muttered. 'They must all be out hunting or something.'

Udal Jarl looked around for the sixth time since they'd stepped out of their hut. The shovelled paths were empty and Trondheim felt lifeless. Above, the sun was a dull orb of light behind a thick layer of milky-white cloud.

'Don't fucking chatter,' he hissed. 'We've got work to do. Remember, it was like this when we got here too, and the bastard was just sitting in his longhouse, waiting for us.' They picked a path that took them around the backs of a long row of houses and suddenly the great hall loomed over them. 'There,' Udal said. 'Back door.' A modest door was set into the wall, almost tucked in beside a beam half again as thick as a man. Udal looked at his men. 'Here we go.'

The door swung open without a sound and the five men stepped into the great hall.

'Look!' Heimir whispered. On the dais, King Olav's chair was overturned, and someone had tipped over three long tables and more chairs at the far wall. A scream broke the silence, and sounds of clashing blades carried from the back room.

'Quick!' Udal said, running towards the noise, his men following at a sprint, blades drawn. 'He's mine, the fucker!' He leapt up onto the platform, strode to the back room door, gave it a good solid kick and stepped in.

He didn't see the spears hurtling towards his men from the shadows.

He didn't see the warriors rising from behind the overturned tables in the great hall and advancing from the sides.

He did see Storrek Jarl standing calmly at the back of King Olav's back room, holding two swords. The fat man looked him square in the eye, smacked the blades together twice and shrieked, 'Help me!' in an exaggerated voice.

'Father . . .' Heimir staggered into the room as screams echoed throughout the hall, 'they're behind us – they were waiting – it's . . .' Heimir's voice grew faint, and he coughed up blood as he fell to the floor.

Udal stared at his dying son, then at Storrek. 'You—'

The hand-axe took Udal in the back of the head, split his skull and ended his life. Gunnthor stepped out from the shadow behind the door. 'It was his time,' he said, kneeling down and pulling hard to dislodge the axe.

'It was indeed,' Storrek said. Outside the hall, the sound of slaughter was dying down. 'And the best thing is that the cocky little bastard king will think he paid for this – for my *loyalty* – with a couple of sacks of grain.'

'Which suits us just fine,' Gunnthor said. 'And as we agreed, we split Udal's lands down the middle. Now that the king thinks we're obedient we'll get all the time we need to handle him by ourselves.'

'It's good to be working with an old hand,' Storrek said, grinning. 'You're making this look easy.'

They left King Olav's back room together.

OUTSIDE TRONDHEIM, NORTH NORWAY
DECEMBER, AD 996

The crisp snow crunched under the hooves of eight horses. King Olav rode up front with Hjalti to his right and Einar to his left. Five men, hand-picked by the king, rode behind them.

'Is that the last one?' the king asked Hjalti.

'Last one, yes,' Hjalti replied. 'We've delivered all the sacks we had. A good day's work.'

'Good,' Einar said. 'It'll be good to get to some food and some warmth.' Hjalti scowled at him, but Einar shrugged. 'What? I can stay out here all day and all night if the king commands, but now my feet are wet and my arse is sore and there is no harm in wishing to be indoors for a spell.'

Hjalti snorted and they rode on without speaking, the rhythmic crunch of frozen snow rocking them into a cold half-sleep until suddenly King Olav's mare reared its head and whinnied in alarm, her nostrils flaring.

'Easy, girl. Easy,' the king whispered, but to no avail; the mare started stamping and dancing to the side, all the while twisting to get out of the snow, out of the reins, out of her skin. Within moments the other horses had caught whatever it was that King Olav's horse had sensed.

'*WOLF!*' Einar's voice rang out loud and clear over the protesting horses and King Olav looked up from struggling with the reins and sure enough, there it was, a hundred yards up ahead: grey, with bluish-white flecks in its fur. Narrowing, yellow eyes seemed to home in on the king.

Time slowed down for King Olav as the horse, frantic with fear, bucked under him. He adjusted his weight, but the horse kept tossing and kicking, all the while pulling at the reins. When drops of blood from the animal's mouth landed in the snow he did the only thing he could do: he stood in the saddle, bunched up the reins and threw them to Hjalti, then swung his leg over and jumped off, landing in the knee-deep snow in front of the men and the panicking horses.

The wolf saw him and kicked off, pushing itself through the white powder. *It is everything*, the king thought: *the wolf is the world, bearing down on me with teeth and eyes and darkness in its jaws.*

Though he was struggling to control the rampaging horses, Hjalti still couldn't stop staring at the king, who just . . . *stood there*, in the path of the onrushing wolf.

'Einar!' He turned to the youth, who was struggling to keep himself in the saddle while getting his bow ready.

Ten yards.

'I can't!' Einar shouted back.

The horses reared wildly as the scent of the wolf hit them full-blast.

Five yards.

The wolf *leaped* and the king swung his sword, but the weight of the animal bowled him over, sending his sword spinning to the ground. The wolf, furious, went straight for the king's throat, and only King Olav's mailed glove saved him as slavering jaws clamped down on the armoured hand. The beast growled as it pulled and worried at the metal. The king screamed as he fumbled for his sword. The wild-eyed animal let go of the metal glove and lunged for the king's face—

—and suddenly the head was pulled to the side, hard, like someone had yanked on a dog's leash, and blood was gushing over Olav's eyes from the hole that the arrow had punched in its throat. The noise of scrambling men reached him.

'The king!'

'Speak, your Majesty! *Speak!*'

A push, and he was free of the animal. 'I'm fine,' he growled. 'I'm fine.'

Einar Tambarskelf stood beside the skittish horses, breathing heavily and holding his bow, another arrow already nocked. 'That's the biggest bastard wolf I've ever seen,' he panted.

Olav was reaching for his sword when one of the riders shouted, 'Beware!' and he whirled around and watched in astonishment as the wolf clambered to its feet, growling.

This time, the king did not miss.

Hot, dark blood sprayed the snow and the wolf's head fell away from its body.

'Look!' Hjalti said, pointing to the exposed neck wound.

The men came closer – cautiously, still – to see what he was pointing at.

A strange bluish tinge ran through the flesh of the wolf.

'It's dead. Move on,' King Olav snapped.

The men mounted up only too quickly and were soon back on track. Trondheim's houses were about the size of a thumb when they saw the boy.

'The king! The king returns!' he shouted, turning and sprinting towards the town.

'Home at last,' Hjalti said. 'It'll be good to get back to the fire and the pots, eh?'

'What do you mean?' Einar said. 'Shouldn't you be praising the snow? Out riding in nature? Taking the word of the White Christ to the people?'

'Oh, shut up,' Hjalti said.

'Both of you,' Olav snapped, 'hush up. Something's wrong.'

A group of men was assembling rapidly in the open space before Hakon Jarl's great hall. Gunnthor Jarl was there, looking concerned, and flanked by his two grey-haired men, as was Storrek Jarl. Their numbers swelled as the king's party drew closer – even Hakon Jarl ventured outside.

As he got close enough, Olav pulled on the reins. 'What's going on?' he said.

'We've had great troubles in your absence, your Majesty,' Gunnthor said.

'Where's Udal?'

Gunnthor wrung his hands. 'Ah – see, the—'

'The bastard was going to kill you,' Storrek Jarl snapped. 'Him and his rat-faced shit-for-brains son were going to wait in your back room and cut your throat.'

'Is this true?' King Olav scanned the faces before him. They were familiar, but not known. Suddenly he missed Finn's quiet, stolid presence. He'd hoped Udal would misjudge, but not like this. He'd wanted to be there himself, to see it and make a show of it.

'Some of your men overheard them and came to me,' Gunnthor said. A handful of Hjalti's warriors nodded. 'We went to Storrek, who was more than ready to help.'

'Never liked the fucker,' Storrek growled. 'No honour in an ambush.' Beside him, Gunnthor looked grave.

King Olav dismounted swiftly and stormed into the great hall without a word. Einar looked at Hjalti, who shook his head. No one else volunteered to follow the king.

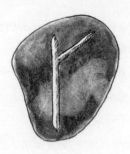

Valgard coughed and stumbled, sending pain shooting up his spine as he pushed the animal out of his mind. The hunger had been explosive, consuming and terrifying, borne on a tidal wave of smells and sounds, and the raw power of it had exhilarated and terrified in equal measure. 'Fucking hell,' Valgard muttered through the sour spit, 'that was . . .' He looked at the trolls, but none of them were registering any sympathy. 'Yes, well,' he continued, coughing again to clear his throat. Somewhere in the back of his mind he could feel the beast powering through the snow, seeking out its target, keeping the scent of King Olav in its nostrils. It felt good to think of the so-called king as the hunted rather than the hunter. He scooped up a handful of snow, put it in his mouth to rid himself of the taste of bile and walked on. He could feel the cold flowing into him, replenishing what the wolf had taken. It was happening quickly, too. His body felt better every day. There were many things to be happy about these days.

He didn't allow himself to think about the voice he'd heard, or the cave where he'd heard it last.

Twenty miles north of Trondheim, Valgard found himself once again considering his options as he trudged in front of his silent companions. Behind them lay the Northern Wastes, but they held nothing but reindeer and Finn-witches.

To the east was the land of the Svear – a possibility, sure, but the time felt wrong, somehow.

No, there was only one way to go: Trondheim.

The experiment with the wolf had been partly successful – mostly because it was such a strong animal; it had broken free of his command. But he'd get stronger. He'd get *better*.

Valgard smiled.

He'd get a lot better.

Fifteen miles north of Trondheim, Valgard tasted the air. He could feel his tongue flicking at the cold, darting in between points of frost and bringing back sensations – smell, touch, presence. He could sense the bodies of the creatures behind him, standing still, looking ahead. They did not question his leadership; they followed, stolid and slow, like a glacier wall. He could feel his own power rising. Like the glacier, he'd crush everything in his path. He would be the walking frost. He would draw the veil of cold over the land so it could rise again.

The only warm thing in the world was the bag resting against his chest, underneath his layered clothes and furs. The runes within felt as heavy as the world. He couldn't remember much of Loki and the cave, but he remembered what happened afterwards well enough: Botolf, dying on the steps; the weight of Egill Jotun's throne and the crash as it toppled over; the ornate box that just sat there, innocent and quiet. And when he'd opened it, time had slowed to a trickle around him, flowing around his legs like a lazy river. The squares of calfskin had spoken to him – the ancient runes had leapt off the pages and into his head, whispering the unfamiliar sounds as he opened his mouth. Unbidden, the image of Botolf's flesh came into his mind as he mispronounced the first words. The way it had warped and spun and *turned* on itself had almost made him throw up, but something Loki had said made him stick with it.

They never respected you because they never feared you.

A slow smile broke out on Valgard's face as his nose and his tongue found what he was looking for.

Well. We'll see what they think now.

His mouth moved, and old words snuck back into the world on a whisper.

TRONDHEIM HARBOUR, NORTH NORWAY DECEMBER, AD 996

'Here?' the raider grunted at Hjalti.

'Doesn't matter. Just throw it in already,' Hjalti snapped. 'It's freezing out here, if you hadn't noticed.' Stars twinkled overhead.

'Fuck off, goat-boy – you're not carrying anything,' the raider said. 'Heave!'

Beside him, eleven men moved in concert and six bundled corpses flew off the pier, hit the water with a deep splash and sank almost immediately. The men on the docks stood quietly and watched as Udal's men faded out of view.

'Njordur keep them,' someone muttered.

Hjalti turned away from the men. 'Shut it,' he snarled. 'Whoever said that – *shut it*. I didn't see who spoke, but if he hears you, you're next.'

'Calm d—'

'Finish that sentence' – Hjalti turned around, looked at the raiders and put a hand on his sword-hilt – 'and I will personally end your life, right here.'

The raiders exchanged looks and then backed away, silently. Hjalti watched them leave. When the last man had disappeared he exhaled and turned to look at the water.

The waves glistened, raven-black, reflecting the stars overhead. There were no signs of bodies anywhere.

'Njordur takes what Njordur wants,' Hjalti muttered.

He walked off the docks and turned north. When he saw the great hall he turned east, towards the outskirts of Trondheim. He had just a handful of moments to think, to imagine questions and plan answers, and then he was there.

The house looked nothing out of the ordinary – just a regular northern warrior's home – but it still filled him with unease.

'Honour demands,' he muttered. Four steps took him to the door. His knock felt feeble.

Moments later, light spilled out and one of Gunnthor's grey-haired men stood in the entrance. He looked Hjalti up and down, then ushered him in.

Hjalti felt the walls closing in on him almost immediately. The house was lit by two tallow candles set in metal that bounced the light around, but it stayed away from the corners. He could just make out the shape of Storrek sitting by the wall, looking serious. Next to him were two of his men, who in the half-light looked nothing like bullied and whipped followers. Everyone was quiet; everyone was looking at him.

His eyes met Gunnthor's.

'Cousin! Welcome to our little gathering.'

Feeling the drops of sweat slide down his back under the furs, Hjalti inched into the house and closed the door behind him.

Gunnthor had folded his arms and was leaning back in his seat, smiling. 'Repeat what you told me. *He can be caught alone when . . .*'

'. . . he prays,' Hjalti said. 'Every night at midnight.'

'We'll nail him then,' Storrek growled from the corner. 'Do you think six of us will be enough?'

'Seven, with Hjalti,' Gunnthor said, still smiling.

Hjalti became uncomfortably aware of the grey-haired men behind him, outside his field of vision. 'Yes,' he said, 'seven, with me.'

'Very good. Where is the moon?' Gunnthor asked.

'High above,' Hjalti said, 'but we should be able to catch him if we leave very soon.'

'Then that's what we do. Come on!' Gunnthor rose with a speed that belied his age. 'We settle this now.'

'Oh for fuck's sake,' Storrek grumbled as he levered himself up out of the chair. 'Give us some notice, will you, Grandpa?'

Gunnthor's grey-haired men ushered him out and the cold hit Hjalti square in the face. 'Hairy arse of Thor, but it's cold tonight,' Storrek growled behind him.

'We'll get a fantastic summer after this,' Gunnthor said. 'You know what they say: it's always worse before it gets better.'

'Unless you die,' Storrek added.

'Unless you die,' Gunnthor agreed. They walked along, seven of them, soon settling into an easy stride that looked at least partially guilt-free. Up above, stars twinkled.

A lonely raven croaked at them from atop the beams of the longhouse, soon answered by another. They could hear the clamour from within.

'Sounds like it's back to usual in there,' Storrek said. 'They didn't spend much time grieving for the fallen.'

'They know Udal didn't give a lamb's turd about them, so they offer him the respect he deserves,' Gunnthor said. 'Besides, it works to our advantage. No one will hear him scream. Where's his sad little god's hut?'

Hjalti pointed to the lee side of the house. 'Over there.'

That first day, King Olav had annexed what had used to be noble-men's lodgings set a few yards from the back of the great hall, turning it into a god-house for his One God.

'Must get lonely in there,' one of the grey-haired men said.

'He likes it that way,' Hjalti said.

'He's a fool,' Storrek said. 'Let's do this.'

Gunnthor pointed Hjalti to the rough wooden door and he reached for it and pushed. Soft candlelight spilled out onto the snow.

King Olav's voice came from within. 'Who's there?'

Hjalti stepped into the chapel, followed by Gunnthor, Storrek and their men. This was the first time he'd set foot in the king's holiest space and for a moment he struggled to think.

Every surface in the small, converted house had been stripped bare. A man-sized cross had been suspended between two beams, and the way it hung like a human body made him shiver. It caught the light off four flickering candles set in buffed shields that cast an eerie glow on the men crowded by the door.

At the far end of the house, a small table held what was easily the biggest book Hjalti had ever seen.

King Olav knelt before the book, head down, facing away. 'You know I do not wish to be disturbed,' he said.

'I know, my King,' Hjalti said, and cursed himself inwardly. Old habits died hard. 'It's just that—'

'We're going to negotiate,' Gunnthor said.

There was a moment's silence before the king spoke. His voice was cold. 'We have already negotiated,' he said. 'Leave me to my prayers.'

'Turn around, you little shit,' Storrek growled. The king didn't reply and he repeated, 'I said, turn around and face us.'

'What – like a warrior?' the king said. He sighed and rose, still facing away, and closed the book almost tenderly. 'What do you expect, Storrek? Fear in my eyes?' He turned around, made the sign of the cross and looked all seven of them up and down. He was unarmed.

Storrek didn't flinch. 'Listen, you puffed-up Southern arse-badger! We don't want you here, we don't want your stupid god and we don't want your new rule.'

King Olav looked at Gunnthor, then Hjalti. 'Why are you with them?' he asked.

'Gunnthor is my cousin on the father's side,' Hjalti said.

'Blood is blood,' Gunnthor said.

'Enough chat,' Storrek said before the king could speak. The big man reached for the sword by his side. 'Let's—'

A high-pitched scream from outside drowned the rest of his sentence.

A deep, guttural roar followed.

'What the—?' Hjalti's words caught in his mouth as something thudded into the wall, shaking the big cross. Like the others, his eyes flashed towards the movement, and when he looked back it was too late. Hunched down, elbows out and shoulder first, King Olav swung a punch at Storrek, crashed through the group of men and launched himself out of the door.

'*GET HIM!*' Gunnthor roared.

One of Storrek's lumpy followers was closest, and Hjalti watched him barrel through the door after the king, only to be swept out of sight as something big and darker than the night crashed into him.

'What's going on out there?' Storrek snarled, pushing towards the open door. Shouts carried in from the darkness to meet him.

'We're under attack,' Gunnthor snarled, holding back the fat chieftain and staring at the door. 'Think for a second, you oaf.'

King Olav's voice rang out, strong from years of use at sea. 'TO ME,' he shouted. 'DRAW STEEL! MEN OF THE NORTH, TO ME!'

'Shit,' Storrek muttered.

Gunnthor whirled around, eyes blazing. 'No, we're still in this. If we rush out now – right now – if we rush out, rally the men and fight whatever's out there beside him he cannot have us murdered in front of his own. He'd have to kill Hjalti too, and his men would never trust him again. Go! We'll face what's out there together.' As he spoke he moved to the door, pushed through it – and came face to face with a brown bear, reared up onto its back legs. The corpse of Storrek's man lay discarded to one side, nothing but a sack of meat and broken bones.

Something cracked behind Hjalti and he was pushed to the side as Storrek passed him, muttering curses under his breath. 'GET BACK,' he roared at the bear, taking up position next to Gunnthor and brandishing the butt of the six-foot cross. 'GET BACK, YOU BASTARD!'

The bear roared back and swatted at the wood, but it missed and Storrek used the opening, put all his heft behind it and rammed the thick wood in the bear's chest. Roaring in pain, the animal fell back down onto all fours and ran away through the snow.

'Out! Everyone out!' Gunnthor commanded. The men fanned out behind him with blades drawn. The king was nowhere to be seen.

'There's blood in the air,' Hjalti said.

'Oh, you fucking *think*?' Storrek growled at him. 'There was a fucking *bear* right in front of us!' Nostrils flaring, the big chieftain looked ready to attack the next closest thing, which was Hjalti.

'Fight the enemy,' Gunnthor snapped. 'We need to move. They're around the corner.' Storrek turned again, but spared Hjalti a killing glare. The seven moved away from King Olav's prayer-house, staying close to the wall of the longhouse. Sounds of battle bounced off the walls around them.

'Look at this,' one of Gunnthor's men said. 'Tracks.'

'That would be the bear,' Storrek growled.

They rounded the corner of the longhouse and stopped. 'Not just the bear,' Gunnthor said quietly.

The square in front of the great hall was crowded with men and beasts, all fighting for their lives. A handful of men with spears had formed a line facing an enraged elk, who was laying into them with no regard for the metal points digging into its flesh. Two forest cats the size of well-fed dogs tore at the throat of a body in the snow, claws digging into dead flesh, but within moments the beasts were up again and bounding towards their next target. Fighters streamed out of the longhouse, but they were held back by a group of men struggling to strike at a swarm of huge rats running at and over them and heading into the hall.

At the far end of the space outside the longhouse, King Olav and another four men had cornered the bear and were laying into it. As Gunnthor's men watched, one of them stepped too close. The bear's paw crushed his skull in the blink of an eye.

'This is where we get it back,' Gunnthor hissed. He drew a deep breath, let out a battle-cry, immediately echoed by the men behind him, and charged into the fray.

King Olav delivered mercy to the bear, but not until the beast had taken four men with him. Hastily dressed fighters had rushed into the square after he'd called, wielding anything they could find; when the frenzy was over they counted eight dead, five badly wounded and three men covered in cuts, bites and already festering scratches from the rats.

The old chieftains stood over the body of a big forest cat,

struggling to catch their breath. Blood leaked from a nasty gash on Gunnthor's leg. 'In my whole life I've never seen anything like this,' he hissed. Storrek didn't answer but noisily cleared his throat several times, then spat.

Animal roars echoed out in the dark. 'To me!' the king shouted, charging out of the square towards the noise, and well over a hundred warriors followed.

'See that?' Gunnthor said.

'We need some way to get him away from the men,' Storrek said.

'We won't do that here,' Hjalti said. 'We need to be in the middle of it.' With that he ran after the king, joining the warriors heading towards the main road into town, following the sounds of lowing, hissing and roaring.

Gunnthor glanced at Storrek. 'Little fucker has a point. MOVE!'

The old chieftains followed Hjalti into a nightmare.

Fangs, claws and pointed horns were everywhere, enemies in many shapes, united only by the fear-crazed look in their eyes. Wounded men were screaming and the rich, thick smell of blood permeated the night. Hjalti swung his sword and connected with the shoulder of a wolf. He raised his foot to push off the animal and pulled the blade free, only just avoiding the snapping jaws. An elk came charging through the crowd, head down, spearing anything in its path and tossing it into the air.

King Olav was in the thick of it, pushing and cutting, striking and blocking, screaming at his warriors to stand firm. Fat Storrek, reborn in battle, was throwing his weight around with fierce joy on his face. Life and death was decided, moment by moment by never-ending moment.

Hjalti pushed away everything that made him human and gave himself to the battle.

*

Olav exhaled and watched the white cloud in front of his face. The fighting men had fallen silent around him as the fear drained out of them and now the stench of the dead animals was everywhere – in the air, in their clothes, in the snow. The butchers had been at the carcasses, but they were all inedible, all blue-tinged like the wolf.

Now hundreds of faces stared at him as he turned to Gunnthor and the traitors, feeling for his sword as he did. He thought of something to say, but nothing came to his mind. Suddenly Olav felt every one of his thirty-eight years. 'You fought well,' he said.

'Thank you, my King,' Gunnthor said.

'And you, Hjalti,' he said. He turned to the gathered men, a good three hundred or so. 'Hail Hjalti! Tonight I saw a side of him that I didn't know existed. He was brave – almost foolishly so, one might say!' A multitude of voices cheered, and for a moment everything was all right with the world. He noticed the glint in Gunnthor's eye a moment too late.

'But why were they running, my Lord?' the old man said. 'And what were they running from?'

Storrek saw the opening immediately. 'Are we even safe here?' he shouted.

The idea spread through the cold, exhausted men like poison in the blood and Olav could almost see the control of the situation slip out of his hands. He took a moment, a deep breath – there was only one option.

'Of course we're safe!' he shouted with all the command he could muster. 'But we have a responsibility to the people of Trondheim and to each other, so I will take all the volunteers I can get and go and have a look.' Out of the corner of his eye he saw Gunnthor smirking, and anger flared within. There was maybe still a way to turn this to his advantage. 'I will request only the presence of brave

Hjalti Elk-Slayer – we could probably handle whatever spooked the animals, just the two of us!'

Another cheer from the men, and Olav looked at Gunnthor and Storrek as fighters swarmed over Hjalti, eager for something to do. He cleared his throat and stepped towards the two chieftains. He noted with some pleasure that Storrek had to fight not to draw steel.

'If there's something out there,' he said, 'It will get what it deserves.' He held their stare for another couple of heartbeats. 'My enemies usually do,' he added before he walked towards the longhouse door.

When King Olav stepped out again, armed and armoured, eighty men on horse waited for him, Hjalti at their front. Olav quickly scanned their faces and found he knew the names of three men in four. That would have to do.

'Let's go hunting!' he shouted as he mounted his horse, to cheers from the men. Fear turned to joyous anger very quickly, he thought. It was remarkable how quickly their mood changed with the promise of violence.

And then the column was ready to go. Hjalti rode at his right shoulder. The man looked like he was trying to make himself take up the least space possible. Good, Olav thought. It showed the bastard still had some survival instinct. Behind him rode the volunteers, three abreast, all heading out of Trondheim and up towards the North.

They could see the broken branches and trampled snow where the stampede had come through: red, brown and yellow lines ground into the white where the fear had driven the animals. King Olav's horse tossed its head; behind him he could hear a smattering of riders commanding their mounts to be still.

King Olav turned to Hjalti. 'The horses don't like the smell of it, do they, Hjalti? Death? It's all a bit much for them when it comes that close.'

'Yes, my King,' Hjalti muttered, staring at the back of his horse's head.

Satisfied, Olav turned and looked north. The moon was up, colouring the sky a dull grey. All shadows deepened in moonlight. They rode on up the stampede trail with the stink of fear in their nostrils. It came and went, dulled by the cold and caught in the trees, but there was no mistaking the sour smell of blood and guts from up ahead.

Olav raised his arm and signalled for the halt. 'Hjalti ... ?' he said, gesturing ahead.

Head bowed, the lanky man rode forward. The snow dunes curved up, then away. Just past a high point he looked down to his left and stopped, then swung off his horse and knelt. His head turned slowly towards Olav. 'You need to come see this.'

The king urged his horse onwards, gently, keeping an eye on Hjalti's blade all the while, but it stayed sheathed. 'What is it?'

'Look,' Hjalti said. Almost as if reading the king's mind, he took three steps backwards.

The elk lay on its side, its entrails strung out behind it for a good thirty yards, alongside erratic hoof-prints and a line where its broken back leg had dragged in the snow.

Without a word, Hjalti gestured to the animal's stomach, or what was left of it.

'What did this?' Olav asked, when he'd found the ability to speak. More than half of the skin on the underside of the elk was gone, exposing the empty inner cavity. 'Bear?'

'There are no claw-marks.'

'Blade?'

'Look at the edge.'

King Olav leaned closer, trying to breathe through his mouth and to keep his eye on Hjalti's position. 'It's been—'

'—ripped, yes.'

The king rose. 'Cover it up with snow, quickly – mask the smell.' When Hjalti frowned, he explained, 'For the horses.'

Not waiting for an answer, he saddled up and rode past the dead beast, further into the forest, trying hard not to think about its fate. The tracks ran parallel to the trail of destruction, and soon other corpses started appearing: a trampled fox, sheep with badly mangled heads – some without heads altogether – and a bear with a shattered front leg.

Slowly, the hardened fighters behind him had gone quiet, and now the only sound to be heard was the crunching snow under hooves and the occasional snort of disquiet from the horses, quickly followed by soothing whispers. The scent of pine needles mixed with the blood in the snow.

'Our Father, who art in heaven,' King Olav muttered to himself. 'Hallowed be Thy name. Look down on Thy servant, and shield him from whatever it was that did this.' The ground had been sloping gently upwards for a while and the corpses that littered the ground were now hardly recognisable.

'They must have run down through here,' Hjalti said, 'trampling each other.' King Olav didn't answer and he went on, 'They've stripped the bark off the trees.' The king still didn't reply. 'I couldn't do anything, my King. They threatened to kill—'

The wind changed, and King Olav's horse went mad, and moments later, the animals behind it started squealing and bucking, followed by the angry shouts of the riders. Hjalti was thrown clear of his horse; he watched it barrel down the path at speed, back towards Trondheim.

'WE'RE UNDER ATTACK!' King Olav screamed.

'Not yet,' a calm, familiar voice said from the top of the hill.

With the reins twisted so tightly around his hand that he was sure he could feel the bones snapping, King Olav kept hold of his horse – but only just. The figure, back-lit by the moon, stood tall on the ridge, fifty yards away, clear of the trees.

The king didn't dare look behind him but he could hear the horses bolting easily enough, along with the outraged shouts of the men. Something niggled at him. Something about the voice . . .

SOUTHERN NORWAY
DECEMBER, AD 996

Helga from Ovregard leaned over and stroked Streak's neck.
'What's the matter, girl?' The horse tossed its head and snorted.
'Are you just being an old grouch? Or . . . ?' She tugged on the reins
and Streak stopped all too readily. Helga dismounted smoothly and
tasted the air. It had started snowing when they sailed across the
channel, but it wasn't cold enough to stick. Not yet. A white veil
would appear overnight, vanish in the day and return when the
temperature dropped. It would stay in about a week's time, she
gathered, and from what the bones had told her it would stay for
a long time.

'A long time,' she muttered, pushing the quiet aside for a
moment.

There was a scent on the air, something . . . *wrong*. The forest
could hide her from prying eyes, but it could also shelter all kinds
of other things. Helga felt for her carving knife, though if there
was anything about it would be about as useless as a harsh glare.
Still, she remembered the times when it had saved her life and
found some strength in that. Whatever was out here might have
her, but it would not take her easily.

Streak snorted and tossed her head again. 'Yes, I know,' Helga
muttered. 'I can smell it too.' And the thing was up ahead, so there

was nothing for it. 'Let's go, girl,' she said, inching forward. She'd met many men who would say she was being weak and womanly, that she needed someone to protect her. They had many things in common, those men. They were all brave, and strong, and very dead.

Helga of Ovregard would take her time.

The reins felt rough in her hands, but Streak trudged along. Sometimes Helga thought she could hear the mare's thoughts, and they were in a voice not entirely dissimilar from her own. Thoughts went unbidden to Audun's hands, folded in his lap. Then they went somewhere else entirely, and she had to shake her head to dislodge them. 'Oi,' she muttered, half annoyed with herself for losing focus but not entirely able to shake the wolfish grin. It was getting colder and she couldn't be blamed for warming herself on something, even if it was just memories of what could have been.

A chill settled in the base of her spine and shook her gently from the centre and out. It was a raw cold, flavoured with the scent of pine trees and bark and earth covered in rotting mulch. She felt the familiar tingle, the metallic taste on the back of her tongue that spoke of sparks and shifts in the world.

When she saw the tree the breath caught in her throat and escaped with a low hiss. She looped Streak's reins around a branch, muttered a half-hearted command and walked towards the thing, half-entranced.

The trunk had been stripped of bark and *twisted*, pulled down, branches warped and twined around it in unnatural curves that made the eyes hurt. From a distance it looked charred but when she drew closer she saw that the surface of the tree was smooth, like raven-stone. Helga's head pounded with the wrenching *wrongness* of it and she staggered away, staring down at her feet to avoid looking at the black thing that stood out in its curves among ramrod-straight pines – but the ground felt wrong as well. The bile rose in her throat as she realised what she was looking at and she forced her head up to confirm it.

A circle around the black tree, maybe ten yards wide, was dead. Wizened roots from other trees poked up through the under-growth, and the ground looked like some kind of ash. Her eye was drawn to the black trunk then, following it up through curves and bends that felt so alien and horrible. The familiarity of them hit her like a rock and she started muttering, 'No. No, no, *no*.' She'd seen them; of course she'd seen them – but they had just been too *big*, too *wrong*. Impossible. Her hands started knotting and fidgeting of their own accord, making the signs and un-making them, trying to make it go away like a child with a bad dream.

Streak neighed loudly, and Helga snapped out of her trance. Anger flooded her and she clenched her fists so hard she could feel the nails digging into her palms. The pain was enough to get her moving towards her horse. Unlooping the reins in one move-ment, she turned her back on the black thing in the forest, then led Streak away.

With every step away, the wrench in her chest loosened and the anger subsided until suddenly the tears flowed. 'Oh come on, woman!' she growled, gritting her teeth and trying her best to swallow some spit. 'Bawling like a baby? Stop it!' The reins sud-denly went slack and Streak's head was by her side. The smell of warm horse washed over her and ever so gently, the massive head came in for a soft nudge. A smile broke out on Helga's face and she reached up to stroke the horse's jaw. 'Don't you go soft on me too, you old nag,' she said, 'because if you buckle too, we'll just be two old girls in the middle of nowhere. And if this is true, we've got work to do.'

Even when they'd ridden for a good while she could still feel it pulsing behind her, a dark lover's heart: a tree twisted into runes that spelled out 'winter' and 'eternal' and 'war'.

Ragnarok.

Helga wasn't afraid of the night. She'd seen too much, and on more than one occasion the shadows had saved her life. However, there was something about the campfire that gave her a feeling of unease. In times like these, anyone who lit a fire that big clearly did not have a care in the world. No effort had been made to cover it up – it could be seen from hundreds of yards away, the light bouncing off tree trunks and throwing shadows around. She was still quite a way off, too far off to be illuminated, and Streak, well attuned to her moods and by all accounts a very smart horse, knew to be as quiet as possible.

A faint smell of roasting meat drifted her way and made her stomach rumble. Placing every step with care, she inched forward. If what the rune had told was true, she would need information, and she'd get that from travellers. As an afterthought, Helga stopped and rooted around in the mulch. Moments later she found what she needed. A few flicks of the rune-knife carved what she wanted and the wood chip disappeared into folds in her dress, along with the knife.

Something shifted, off to her side, and as Helga froze, Streak halted beside her. Another rustle, then a squawk – and a startled woodpigeon flapped up to a branch as a shadowy, four-legged creature slinked away. Helga exhaled slowly and sniffed the air. Burned twigs, pine resin . . . earth . . . none of the wrongness of the big rune. That was a good sign. She'd got this far north, which meant whatever the gods were up to had moved slower than she'd feared. This could only—

The blade touched her throat gently, and only after that did she feel the warmth of the man behind her.

'Nice and slow,' he said. 'Move and I cut your throat.'

Beside her, Streak whinnied in surprise as another man stepped up to her side and started muttering soothing sounds.

Fat lot of good you did, Helga thought bitterly.

'How many of you are there?' the man behind her asked calmly, without raising his voice. She noted that his arm did not waver.

'Just me,' Helga said, fighting to keep her voice level. 'Travelling north. Saw the fire. The nights get cold.'

'Down here? *Pfft*.' There was genuine mirth in the voice. 'You lot need to eat more seal fat.' There was a gentle tug on the reins and Streak was led away towards the fire. Helga could only just make out a pair of legs beside the horse, but the man clearly knew what he was doing. 'Move,' the man behind her said, pushing gently at her back.

With the body of the man behind her and his strong arm in front, she curtailed all impulses and allowed herself to glide forward. She'd need to see what this was before she could make a decision. When she got closer, she started catching reflections of the fire in small, sparkling diamonds: sentries in the shadows, almost inseparable from the forms of the trees, still as the grave, and all of them watching her.

The smell of the burning wood was more intense now, and the light spread around her field of vision. She turned her head to find Streak and caught a glimpse of her, led to a tree and tied up there. Her captor stayed with the horse, brushing her down. A good sign.

The nudge in her back was firm. 'Forward,' the man said.

The camp, if you could call it that, was a loose collection of men. It had a relaxed air of competence, and Helga recognised the spirit of a fighting company. These men had seen a lot, and seen it together. She saw young men sitting alongside more weather-beaten soldiers, but all of them were the same: hardened.

A youth stepped in front of them. Wiry, and tall for his age, which could not be much more than twelve summers, he moved with barely suppressed energy. A nasty, thick scar followed his jaw-line from his ear to his Adam's apple, and glittering black eyes sparkled in the firelight. 'What's this, Ygval?' he said to the man behind her.

On instinct, Helga looked straight at him. '*I* am Helga Finnsdottir of Ovregard,' she said, 'and I'm a woman. If you work on your manners, maybe you'll get to meet one.' She could hear a quickly suppressed laugh behind her, and feel the attention of the closest men.

This would either save her life, or go very, *very* wrong indeed.

The boy looked her up and down. 'Nice try, grandmother, but I like them only up to twice my age.' This brought a chorus of guffaws and catcalls from the men.

'What's that – eighteen summers?' Helga asked.

More men drifted towards the exchange. Good, Helga thought. That would bring—

'Ognvald!' The gruff, deep voice was like a kick in the spine.

The boy winked at Helga and took two steps back. Helga followed the glances of the men, looking to the shadow of an old pine, where something moved. A large man rose, slowly, and stepped into the light. At least half a head taller than the next man, he stretched languidly and rolled his shoulders. 'What's the noise for?'

'Ygval's found a stray cat,' the boy said.

The man emerged from the shadows and Helga felt her heart sink. Black hair braided in a thick plait and a bushy beard twined in warrior's grips framed a hard face. His eyes squinted into the light. There was no give in this man, Helga thought – no angle, no finesse, just brute power and will.

He turned and looked over his shoulder. 'Visitors,' he said.

'Oh for fuck's sake. The *one* time you useless beard-braiding goat-fuckers don't gut someone on sight is the *one* time I'm trying to get some sleep,' a woman's voice said from the darkness. 'Kill her and be done with it.'

The big man frowned at this. 'No,' he said eventually. 'She's out here, on her own. I want to hear what she has to say first.'

Helga looked around her at the circle that had formed: the camp was now interested. She drew a deep breath, turned and looked straight at the big man.

'I am travelling northwards,' she said. The boy had sidled up next to him, and there could be no mistaking father and son. Two thick scars adorned the big man's throat, but they looked more like markings than battle wounds. Half-remembered stories of some very bad men rose to the surface of her mind, then sank again. This was not going as well as she'd hoped. Helga's heart hammered in her chest, but she would not show it: not now, not to them. She reached for old memories of worse situations and found very few, but still – she'd survived those too.

'Why do you travel alone?' the big man said. 'There's foul things about. Most of them in this camp.' This brought wolfish grins from the men around the fire.

'I have to get to the North,' she said. Suddenly nothing seemed real. She felt a drop of sweat slide down her spine.

'You with the king?' There was a hard edge to the big man's voice.

'No,' Helga snapped. 'And there's worse things than King Olav Tryggvason.'

The mood in the camp changed then.

'Right then. I'll kill her myself if you don't stop your fucking rumbling.' A woman emerged from behind the big man, not much more than half his height. Her short cropped hair made her look like a bottle of lightning. She turned her eyes on Helga. 'Right, *sister*. I'll give you' – she counted thoughtfully on her fingers – 'three words before I spill your guts and drag you into the woods for the ravens so I' – she turned and glared at the big man, who suddenly looked less than comfortable – 'can get some *sleep*.'

She looked back at Helga and showed her teeth in what was probably supposed to be a smile. 'If I don't get my sleep I tend to lose my temper.' She gestured to the men. 'They've seen it happen. That's why they've all taken a couple of steps back. Now. Your last three words. Go.'

'Loki walks,' Helga blurted out. The sting was so sharp that it reached her before the sound of the slap did. An uncomfortable warmth spread from her cheek, and the left side of her face throbbed. She reached up and touched the sore spot gingerly. Three drops of blood came away on her fingers.

The woman before her stepped back. 'You want to watch your mouth,' she snarled. There was no trace of mirth in the circle of men now. Helga felt more than saw them tense and slip into their fighters' minds, but the woman before her kept her hands free of the daggers in her belt. For now.

'The North,' Helga continued, tugging nervously at the folds of her dress, forcing herself to look at the woman. 'Loki is on the move, stirring up the beasts of the underworld, seeking to raise armies and get as many people killed as possible. Nowhere is safe.'

The woman turned to the big man. 'See? You should have gutted her. She's wrong in the head.'

'If she is, then what were those men searching for, up Egill's way?' the big man rumbled.

'I don't know, and I don't care.' The woman turned to Helga again and sneered, 'They're dead now. Maybe I just don't like her. That's been reason enough a couple of times.' Her hand went to the hilt of a dagger.

Helga threw her arms up in the air. 'Fine! Condemn all of the North to death, why don't you? It looks like it would save you time, you b—'

Loud shouts of warning drowned her out.

'THE FIRE—!'

'BLADES – NOW!'

The fire was burning faster now, and brighter, hot enough to pull at the skin. The men next to it dived out of the way and underneath the flames, in the hollow space that was just heat and smoke, something stirred.

'Back up,' the big man bellowed. 'Ognvald, fetch my axe.'

All around Helga, blades were being drawn – hardened spears, axes and swords – the men moving as a unit, forming lines and staying well away from the fire.

The flames danced faster and faster, spinning around each other, sucking the golden air into shapes as the logs underneath crackled and snapped, groaning as they burned.

'Scouts: watch our backs,' the big man commanded, and immediately men peeled off the edge of the lines facing the fire and disappeared into the darkness.

'Don't you fucking move,' the woman growled at Helga.

The flames bucked and tossed now, exploding upwards in showers of embers. The trees around the fire were bathed in white light and the faces of the men were suddenly clearly visible. Somewhere in the shadows, Streak screamed in fear.

The thing rose from the flames, half again the height of a man and thick like a tree trunk. It had the shape of two legs, but instead of arms, long, thick rope-tendrils of flame swung about. It had no head, but there was an uncanny feel to its trunk, as if it was looking right at them.

A young man at their side screamed and charged, but a thin

line of fire lashed out and effortlessly caught his spear, snipping it in two. And still the flames grew. Helga saw the faces of the men, sweat-covered and fearless, but uncertain, no idea how to deal with this new enemy. Underneath its feet the ground was drying out, hissing with steam where water evaporated, charring and fusing. The thing stumbled out of the fire, towards their little group, and young Ognvald screamed in frustration, grabbed swords off two men and charged towards the fire demon.

'STOP!' his father bellowed, but the youth had his head down and was pushing against the oppressive heat.

Now.

Now was the time.

Helga reached and grabbed the woman's shoulder. 'Give me a knife.' A bony hand shot up, faster than she'd thought possible, and latched onto her wrist, but Helga had worked a farm for twenty years and she held on. The flames reflected in the short woman's wild eyes and in a blink her blade appeared at Helga's throat.

Still Helga didn't flinch. 'Give. Me. A. Knife.'

To her surprise, something of a glint of genuine amusement twinkled in the woman's eye. 'Here you go,' she said, twirling the blade around and offering it, hilt-first, with a sensible step back as soon as Helga's grip loosened.

Grabbing the knife, Helga steadily turned around and caught Ygval's eye. The man was in his mid-thirties, handsome in a wolf's way, with a neat, grey-streaked beard and thick brown hair. She drew a deep breath and put everything she had into two words.

'Trust me,' she said.

Ygval looked at the short woman, then at the blade. Even in the rising heat, he looked bemused. 'All right,' he said.

'Show me your shoulder,' Helga said. At their side the fire roared as someone screamed in pain; out of the corner of her eye she could see Ognvald, staggering backwards, slapping at flames dancing on his arms and legs.

Ygval did as he was told, pulling down his shift to reveal lean, hard muscle.

'I am going to cut you,' she said, looking him straight in the eye.

He stared straight back and grinned at her. 'Won't be the first time,' he said.

She smiled back. At least she'd had a little luck in the picking. She checked his hips. Sword. Good. Nice hips, too. Reaching down into her folds she very quickly substituted the woman's knife for her own rune-carving blade. *This lot would most likely have taken my head off on instinct if I'd pulled a concealed blade*, she thought as she made four sharp incisions into the fighter's flesh.

He looked down at his shoulder, at the blood that welled up through the thin cuts. 'Nice rune,' he said. 'What does it—?'

His eyes opened as wide as they went, and he shuddered.

'Take your sword and stab it in the heart.'

Ygval nodded, almost in a trance, and turned towards the raging, walking fire. The circle had expanded as wide as it could. Around the fire, anything that could burn was now alight. The fighter drew his blade and walked, slowly but surely, into the blazing circle.

Helga watched the big man, his son and the woman staring at Ygval. Everyone around the fire held their breath.

A tendril of fire lashed out and caught him right across the chest; there was a hissing sound and clouds of steam rose around Ygval's head. Without a word, not even a cry of pain, the fighter went up to the fire-thing and stabbed his sword into the centre of it.

The fire hissed and spilled, the flames dancing away from the red-hot blade, but they couldn't escape. Ygval moved to the left and slashed at the fire creature's legs, then stabbed the creature once again before hacking at the tendrils. Everywhere he touched the monster, the fires softened and the temperature dropped another notch. Stunned silence turned to shouts of encouragement, then screams of triumph as the fire grew smaller and smaller, until with a final stroke the creature simply turned in on itself and vanished—

—and darkness flooded the forest circle.

'Eyes,' the big man growled, 'get a new fucking fire started right now, but make it small. Someone see to Ygval.' The smell of roasted flesh, sickly and shamefully delicious, was chased away by the rush of wind whooshing back to fill the space left by the fire.

Something sparked down by the ground and soon enough a small fire rose to replace the original campfire.

All through the men's activity Helga could feel the heat of the small woman's stare. It was like being watched by a vicious guard dog. Her face drifted in and out of darkness, sometimes hidden by the shadow of the big man, who was striding around the camp, establishing that everything was set up to his liking.

Helga looked at the short woman then. Her face was scarred and hard, the face of someone who had spent precious little time indoors by a cosy fire. Her body was lean, almost boyish. Her cropped hair stuck out at odd angles – in fact, all of her looked spiky; there was not a soft curve anywhere on her. All through the examination the woman's stare didn't waver, and she gave nothing away.

'Bring her over,' the big man rumbled, and the woman grabbed Helga and dragged her without ceremony to where the big man and his son were standing next to Ygval.

'Who the fuck are you, and what did you do?' the big man asked.

'Protection,' Helga said. 'It's very crude, and won't last long.'

'You a witch?' the boy said.

Helga looked at him, thought about his question for a moment and then said, 'Yes, if it makes you feel better. I know, and I've seen. That was a fire-troll – it was small and weak, but they'll just get bigger and stronger, and because Loki walks they will be looking for ways into our world to join him.'

'And can you protect us against the forces of Loki?' the big man rumbled.

'Yes,' Helga said.

'Well then. We'd better get up North and see if we can stop the fucker from walking too much,' he said.

There was no cheer, no rousing speech. If the big man's followers had even noticed that they'd been summoned to war, they didn't appear to care much.

A massive hand was in front of Helga. 'I am Skadvald,' the big man said.

She shook it, waiting for the crunch of bones, but the man was surprisingly aware of his strength.

'And this is my boy, Ognvald.'

'Well met,' the youth said.

'Well met,' Helga echoed.

'And this—' Skadvald started.

'—is Thora,' the short woman interrupted. 'And I have no time at all for runes and magic. So the moment I find out that you're not what you appear to be, or if I see you messing with any of my boys' heads' – and she fixed Helga with a cold look – 'I kill you. With a knife. In the face. Understood?'

'Understood,' Helga said.

'You're going to make yourself useful, and if you make trouble between the men . . .'

'That won't happen,' Helga said, and something about the way she said it seemed to be enough for Thora; she turned away and walked off into the camp, followed by Skadvald and Ognvald.

Suddenly Helga was standing all alone in the middle of the men, watching the camp get back to rotations, fire, rest and food.

She looked at the three men laid out on the ground. One of them would not live through the night. The other two would be in an awful lot of pain for a long time, and they would never get rid of the scars.

The rune that summoned the troll had been very crude; it had been tricky to throw it into the fire, but she'd managed. It was a shame that the men had had to suffer, but there had been no other choice. Loki's plans had to be stopped.

Helga checked to make sure that no one was watching, allowed herself a small smile and went over to tend to Streak.

The black winter night stretched overhead, dotted with white. Valgard luxuriated in his senses, savouring the height of the sky above him and the sensation of the cold, cold ground. He could hear them coming from far away; they were at the foot of the hill, stumbling through the woods with weapons clattering and armour clinking.

Two steps brought him to the top of the ridge and it didn't take him long to spot them down there, shifting shadows in amongst the trees. Their scent drifted ahead of them: sweat and fear.

Good.

King Olav led from the front, pushing through the snow as if it were a personal affront to him and his reign, looking to find the source of the stampeding animals. It had been terrifyingly easy to find their minds and give them a reason to run, and the effect had been pleasing.

Valgard pushed a thought out into the air.

—see me—

Like someone remembering a dream, the king's head rose and he scanned the top of the ridge. In the moonlight his face looked gaunt and drawn.

'WE'RE UNDER ATTACK!' he cried.

'Not yet,' Valgard said, surprised at the calm authority in his own voice.

'. . . Valgard—?'

'Yes,' Valgard said. 'It is me.'

King Olav cracked a tired smile. 'Old friend – we thought we'd lost you!'

'You did,' Valgard replied. 'And your kingdom, too.' Off to King Olav's side he could see the lickspittle – Hjalti, that was his name – wading through the snow. Behind them Valgard sensed movement: soldiers. Looked like the king had decided to bring a hundred of his friends with him.

The Lord provides. He smiled.

'What do you mean?' The king sounded confused.

'This is my country now,' Valgard said calmly.

For a moment the king looked flustered and confused, as if he were struggling with a memory. Valgard tried reaching out to his mind . . . and tasted torchlight, iron and the touch of Loki like a drop of honey on his tongue.

The king was still staring at him. 'We must get you to Trond-heim, Valgard! There's something out here – something dangerous.'

'I know,' Valgard said, and finally he saw comprehension dawn on the king. He could almost feel the way the years of fighting took him over; how easily the mask of the warrior slipped over his head.

'BLADES!' the king screamed, and was rewarded with a concert of steel leaving sheathes in the darkness.

Valgard did not move. He just smiled. 'Those won't do you any good,' he said conversationally.

'We'll have to see about that,' King Olav growled and strode towards him, quickly closing the gap to forty yards.

Valgard motioned with his hand and they came out of the night to stand beside him: five of them, hewn of frost, all at least six and a half foot tall. They looked inhuman. There was a stillness about them that reminded him of trees and mountains, and winter predators waiting for the soft meat to come closer.

King Olav waded on, snow up to the middle of his shins, and Valgard watched him coming towards them and felt a curious absence of fear.

Behind the king Hjalti spoke up, his voice quavering. '. . . *Botolf?*'

The king glanced up at the tallest of the blue-tinged creatures. There was only a faint suggestion of recognition there, but not enough. He drew his sword and closed in.

Valgard couldn't help smiling – it was all so amusing. He looked the king in the eye and took a half-step back, behind his men, and that was enough to tip King Olav over the edge.

Fury took the king, who charged, screaming, and his sword dug into Ormslev's shoulder.

—*go*—

—*break them*—

Valgard pushed the thought out and watched Ormslev deliver a furious back-handed slap to the king's ribcage, driving the air out of the man and sending him flying, spinning like a child's thrown rag doll. Whatever was left of Valgard the Healer winced as the ruler of the Norsemen smashed backwards into the nearest tree, then collapsed face-first in the snow. Botolf and Skeggi were moving too, with Jori and Ormar close behind. A brave warrior stepped in front of them, a big man, swinging an axe in a menacing fashion. Botolf knocked the weapon out of his hands and seized the man by the shoulders, and without breaking stride Skeggi grabbed the man's knees, sweeping him off his feet. As the big man screamed in pain, Skeggi and Botolf *pulled*, and the inhuman noise was followed by the sound of snapping and ripping.

Valgard walked in their wake, observing with detached interest the hot blood colouring the snow, spurting from the broken axe-man. King Olav's men were beginning to look less interested in fighting than fleeing, shuffling backwards, struggling to find ground to hold. To his far left a young warrior dropped his axe and turned to run for it.

Stop him—

Valgard had no sooner thought it than Jori bolted like a hunting dog after the man, catching him in twelve steps. A moment later he turned and walked back towards him, leaving the twisted, lifeless corpse where he had dropped it.

At least that settled it for the soldiers. They retreated a couple of steps into the forest to get the advantage of trees for cover, then bunched tighter together and formed up, albeit quivering, into something resembling a shield-wall facing Valgard and his five trolls.

Valgard searched for the cold, hard minds of his trolls, finding them more easily now, like silvery fish in a lake.

Kill them—

—kill them all—

Botolf moved first, snapping off a branch as thick as his arm as he passed the first trees. Skeggi followed, then Ormslev, Ormar and Jori. Valgard felt an odd surge of almost paternal pride as he watched them: they appeared more confident, more assured now, less stiff and lumbering, more fluid. Less bear, more wolf.

The second of King Olav's men died messily, Botolf's tree branch wedged in his face. The third fell, clutching his smashed kneecaps and screaming, until Ormslev stepped on his throat.

Something in the back of Valgard's head hummed, a flaw in the pattern, a grain of sand in his mind's eye. There was a ripple, a shimmer in the darkness – and then a flame.

Shield your eyes, fool, the voice hissed at him, hoarse with anger.

Valgard quickly averted his eyes, seeking the broken bodies of the king's warriors, then glancing sideways at the light.

'Odin,' he spat.

The runes in the bag glowed white-hot against his skin and words bubbled into his mind, and just as the heat was becoming unbearable, cold relief flooded from his fingers as ancient rhymes spun from his lips. He could feel the bodies of the trolls ahead of him and the power of the frost flowing from his fingers and into their spines, spreading throughout them with every breath. Reinvigorated, Botolf and Ormslev pushed against the physical force of the heat.

You can beat him—

—he's an old man—

—you deserve this—

The voice hissed in his ear, insistent, urging him on almost like a lover, until Valgard, swept away on a wave of dark desire, ceased to be in the world and became just consciousness, free of physical constraint . . . and finally, the beast rose from the lake in his mind.

It was beautiful, and terrible: powerful square jaws and a low brow, with thick bronze scales leading away from a gaping maw filled with sharp, curved teeth. Emerald-green eyes were set deep in a flat skull sitting on top of cords and cords of muscle that pulled the rest of his body, flowing and dancing, adder-like, ripping through the hole in reality. In the distance somewhere he could feel Odin's consciousness, holding fast, but weakening in the face of Valgard's belief.

He *deserved* this.

He had finally reached the point where a lifetime on the edge of the world, a lifetime of hurt, derision and scorn, had given him the power to push back – and he was going to push back *hard*. He could feel the point of the grey-haired man's walking stick tearing into the flesh of the trolls, into *his* flesh, but he was fear and cold and death and he didn't care.

Then, suddenly, he felt reality's pull again and he flailed against it, thrashing like a caught fish, but he could do nothing. Half-born, Valgard was pulled back into the world.

Odin's voice was loud and commanding. He was speaking to someone: 'Join me, King Olav! Command the men to attack! We can overwhelm them!'

The king.

Valgard blinked, and tried to make sense of the world again. Improbably, King Olav had somehow made it to Odin's side and stood there, ghostly pale, clearly favouring his right side. His brave fighters cowered behind Odin's fire-shield.

'Who are you?' the king shouted.

'I have many names,' Odin shouted back, 'but we can talk about that later.'

King Olav's face turned bright red and words tumbled out of him. 'THOU SHALT NOT WORSHIP FALSE GODS!' he screamed. 'BEGONE!'

The world drew its breath, and held it.

Watch out—

—the voice hissed at him.

A blink of the eye, then—

Valgard turned away just in time as the wave of force washed over him, knocking him back a step. Dazed, he reached for the words – but they weren't there. He couldn't speak. His head swam.

Odin turned towards the king, sadness in his eye. 'Time was, in battle I could be sure of a man's belief,' he said, almost quietly. 'But if you will not allow yourself or your men to believe in me, Olav Tryggvason, there is nothing I can do for you. '

And in the moments between the blinks of the world, Odin

the Almighty stuck the torch in the ground and walked off the battlefield.

Consciousness flooded back into Valgard's mind like cold water on a hot day. He shook his head to dislodge the last of the All-Father's spell and searched for the minds of the trolls.

They were there, groggy but recovering.

Destroy—

The thought was in his mind, but another one crept in.

—most of them—

Destroy most of them.

Botolf reached for the long torch and knocked it over. The others were already moving towards the cowering soldiers.

Valgard saw two shadows in the distance, running downhill like their life depended on it, but then the screaming started and he knew what he had to do.

All King Olav could hear was his breath and the thumping of blood, always the blood, as his feet decided what was best for him and sent him hurtling away from the slaughter, down the hill, caring not a second for his broken ribs. He waded through the snow, tripped and rolled, screamed in pain, rose and ran again.

A hundred yards over to the left, Hjalti ran alongside him. The younger man was faster, and when the king got to the bottom of the hill Hjalti had already rounded up two horses. They could hear the tortured screams of the men they'd left behind, along with the roar of those . . . *things* . . .

'Here, my King: we'll ride back to Trondheim, tell the men, get some fires start—' Black blood followed the words as King Olav's skinning knife dug into Hjalti's stomach and up, up towards his heart, until the hand holding it was almost inside him.

The last thing Hjalti saw was King Olav's face, glaring at him.

'Don't act like you didn't expect it,' he snarled. 'You led them to my church. You brought this upon us. Our Saviour may forgive you, but I won't.'

He pulled the knife out with a wet slurping sound and Hjalti collapsed, coughing up blood and clutching his stomach. 'Please . . .' he wheezed.

King Olav took the reins of the nearest horse, looked at the man at his feet and felt nothing but contempt. He opened his mouth to speak, but a wrenching scream drifted from the top of the hill. The horse threw its head and snorted.

'You're eager to go,' the king muttered. 'I understand.'

He clambered up onto the horse's back and rode off towards Trondheim, putting the hill and the corpses of his men far behind him.

Valgard could still smell the stench, even in the cold. He looked down with detached curiosity at a form that had been human a while ago; now it just looked like it had been dropped from a great height. The trolls had struck King Olav's terrified men down where they stood, knocking some out and breaking others: a quick, brutal attack. They'd fought to the last man and would no doubt be going to Valhalla eventually – but not just yet.

He had a use for them.

By his feet was a warrior, only half-conscious, staring up at him. The man's face was bloodied and his left leg was bent at an odd angle. 'Please . . .' he muttered, eyes wide with fear.

'What – do you want mercy?' Valgard sneered. 'I'll tell you what I'll do: I will deal with you according to your conduct, and by your own standard I will judge you. How does that sound?' A vicious kick turned the man's words to whimpers.

The old words stung Valgard's lips.

Rise, brave warrior
Born of darkness
Fear and blood
Your sworn companions
Walk in winter
War's compatriot
Raise your blade
For Loki's promise

The man's body twisted and warped in the snow as the darkness flowed into him. Muscles coiled and twisted and knotted, ripping apart and reforming. The warrior's mouth flew open and his face turned red in a silent scream. Valgard saw him, saw through his clothes and his flesh and his meat into the very core of him, and envisioned the frost creeping up through the man's feet into his shins, past his knees, the big muscles in his legs, thickening them, turning them a shade of blue as the flesh somehow died and came to life again. He was being reborn into something stronger. Something bigger. Something *better*.

The change was complete.

The warrior lay in the snow like a squeezed rag, but there was already a different look to him. He was thicker and broader across the chest, but stiffer, less human. He was more like someone's idea of a warrior. His skin was tinged with blue.

Jori approached and looked down at the soldier. 'Take him?'

'Yes,' Valgard said, and the gangly troll hoisted the man over his shoulder without difficulty and carried him over to a group of slumped fighters. Next to them sat Ormar, looking bored.

Valgard counted. That made twenty-four.

On to the next one.

TRONDHEIM, NORTH NORWAY
DECEMBER, AD 996

Snow hung off the eaves of the great hall in cascades of soft white curves. Inside, the fire roared and the old songs echoed off the walls, sung in full chorus by those who could and shouted by those who couldn't. In the right-hand seat, Gunnthor leaned over to Storrek. 'Listen to them. Makes me feel almost thirty years younger, this,' the grey-haired man said.

'What, only seventy?' Storrek shot back, grinning. His features had been softened by untold jugs of mead – he'd stopped counting after six. 'You're doing the right thing, old man,' he said. 'You're making them feel at home without all that God-crap.'

'Keep it down,' Gunnthor growled. 'You never know who's listening.

'Right, right,' Storrek said, sobering up a little. 'Keep it down.'

Across the hall, Einar Tambarskelf watched the two men converse across King Olav's unoccupied seat, but the stench in the hall was becoming too much for him, and he pushed his way towards the door.

Outside, the clouds cleared, revealing the black sky covered with twinkling dots. The night air was crisp and clear and the smell of blood had blown away. Red stains still marked the ground in front of the longhouse, but the nightmare was over.

'Einar.'

The whisper was borne on the wind, softly, like a thought.

'Einar!'

Einar Tambarskelf turned to find the source. Something in the shadows by the corner was moving . . . His dagger was in his hand and poised to throw when King Olav emerged, hands outstretched, palms facing forward.

'I am putting my faith in the Lord,' he said in a soft voice that only just carried on the wind. 'I am hoping that you are not one of the conspirators.'

'. . . *what?*'

'Gunnthor, Storrek and Hjalti, all in on it – some of their men must have driven the animals in towards us, because the hunt was a set-up. They were going to kill me. I only just escaped, but I am wounded and in no shape to fight.'

Einar's face contorted in fury. 'Bastards,' he hissed. 'I'll take their eyes out,' he continued, feeling for a bow that wasn't there.

'You will not,' King Olav said. 'There are too many of them. Instead, gather sixty of our best men. When the traitors realise I'm still alive none of us will be safe. We'll sail from here tonight, go back to Stenvik and return in force in the spring – we'll leave them with too many mouths to feed; they're bound to whittle each other's numbers down. Meet me by the harbour. We'll take *Njordur's Mercy.*'

Einar took some time to ponder his king's words, but finally he spun on his heel and marched inside.

King Olav resisted the urge to cough and stepped back into the shadow, holding his ribs. He couldn't tell Einar what he'd *really* seen – he wasn't even sure himself. The throbbing ache in his side was the only real thing about it.

The moon had inched half a house-length across the sky and gone into hiding behind a thick bank of clouds when they appeared at the harbour: about sixty of them, all of them soft-spoken and quiet in the manner of men who know when they need to be.

The king met them on the pier by the *Njordur's Mercy*. In moments tasks were assigned, and six of them went into the town to fetch rations. King Olav had selected twenty men to prepare sails and get the ship ready when he noticed the blossoming light of a torch between nearby houses on the approach to the harbour. When the guard turned the corner and saw the quiet activity, the first thing he did was to shout a challenge. The second thing he did was to claw, coughing, at the arrow wedged in his throat. Einar drew again and the second arrow struck the guard in the chest. His torch fell and fizzled out in the snow.

Very soon after, the six reappeared carrying two stuffed sacks each, and with that, the *Njordur's Mercy* was ready to sail. The rowers pulled and the big ship lurched forward, but with each stroke she moved more smoothly until she was gliding across the water.

King Olav glanced back at Trondheim once before moving towards the bow of the ship and staring into the dark up ahead.

'Look!' One of the men hissed and pointed to the sky.

Up above, the last of the cloud drifted away to reveal a blood-red moon over Trondheim, as raw as a fresh wound. King Olav noted with some satisfaction that everyone he saw formed the sign of the cross.

Valgard crested the hill and looked down on Trondheim.

The scent of the king's fear-sweat still hung on the wind, shoved in his face by the wind coming from the sea, making Valgard lick his lips. The rich, salty taste of it thrilled him. There was something particularly delicious about King Olav's fall, about him realising that he was in fact very, very mortal. And now he, Valgard, was about to walk back into Trondheim.

This was going to be *fun*.

'Skeggi, Botolf, Ormslev,' he snapped, and like trained animals the three trolls stepped forward. Compared to the others, they looked massive: Botolf was reaching seven foot now, and Valgard wasn't sure he and Skeggi could shift Ormslev if they tried. They'd do. They'd do just fine. 'Take what you need and go to the far corners of the town. Move as quietly and quickly as you can. Don't break more of them than you have to. We will need them.'

When he finished talking, the trolls stepped back.

'Ormar and Jori, you come with me. And you,' he said pointing to the figure on the left. '*Especially* you.' Around him there was movement as bodies shifted in the dark.

There'll be a lot of tracks in the snow, Valgard thought, *but then again, soon that won't really be a problem.*

THE SOUTH OF SWEDEN
LATE DECEMBER, AD 996

The man who called himself Erik and claimed to be the son of Hakon Jarl, chieftain of Trondheim, cleared his throat. He was a good half-head taller than Forkbeard and had the bearing of a man who'd spent his life in hard places. A lean, tough frame and broad shoulders, straight back and sharp features were complemented by black hair with streaks of grey pulled into a thick riding braid. Behind him was the faint hiss of snowflakes on open flames.

'King Olav has left the North!' he shouted. 'He is coming south-wards, and he is coming fast!' Chatter spread out like waves in a pond from the man at the edge of the light, but it was interrupted by Forkbeard, who had grabbed the nearest man's shield and axe and was now banging them loudly together as he stared at the assembled warriors.

Slowly the men's mouths stopped moving.

Forkbeard smiled and waited until the gathering was absolutely silent. When he spoke, he spoke quietly but clearly. 'My friend from the east' – he nodded to Jolawer – 'will be glad of the interruption, because he was clearly losing.'

Shouts erupted on both sides, and Ulfar struggled to contain his grin. 'That's how to win a crowd,' he whispered to Audun, but Forkbeard hadn't finished.

'However, all things must come to an end. Return to your camps. We march tomorrow morning.' Reluctantly, the rows of assembled men broke up and sauntered off to their tents. Forkbeard, Jolawer and a small selection of their chosen men remained.

'Do we stay?' Mouthpiece whispered.

Ulfar was about to reply when Sven answered the question. 'Ulfar. Audun. Over here. Others – get lost,' he said.

'There you go,' Thormund said, hurrying to get to his feet. 'No good comes of named men talking.' The old horse thief disappeared into the dark, Mouthpiece following on his heels.

Emerging from the dark, a line of men formed behind Forkbeard and Jolawer to match Erik's chieftains. Oskarl stood there, calm and solid, next to Audun and Ulfar, his height matched by Alfgeir Bjorne, while Sigurd, Karle and Sven were joined by Thorkell the Tall. Sigrid had stepped up next to Forkbeard.

'Well met,' Forkbeard said.

'Well met,' Erik said.

'When did King Olav move?' Jolawer said.

'News travels slow in winter,' Erik said. 'Perhaps ten days ago.'

Jolawer shot a sharp glance at Alfgeir; Forkbeard didn't move, but his shoulders tensed. The kings were lost for words, caught unawares at the gaming table.

A sharp voice cut the silence. 'How many men?' Sigrid said.

'Sixty,' Erik said.

'That's one ship,' Sigrid shot back. 'He brought forty ships to Trondheim. Do you think we'll believe you?'

'Why did he leave?' Forkbeard added. 'And who's in charge up there?'

'There have been no travellers from the North for a while,' Erik said, and Ulfar felt his insides twist. This was bad: very bad indeed.

Erik continued, 'These men' – he gestured to the silent group behind him – 'are from the mountains, some from the deep valleys inland. They agreed to ride with me and put their names towards raising an army to take back Trondheim.'

'But you don't *know* what's up there,' Sigurd said.

'No,' Erik said. 'We don't.'

Forkbeard looked over at Jolawer, then Sigurd. Finally he looked at Sigrid. 'If Trondheim's less important to King Olav,' he said, 'it is less important to me.' He turned again to the young King of Sweden. 'Jolawer?'

'We're going to need some information,' the young man said. 'We'll meet at first light tomorrow.'

'Agreed,' Forkbeard said.

Audun looked at Ulfar and whispered under his breath, 'Could this be—?'

'Not now,' Ulfar said quietly. Forkbeard, Jolawer and Erik were already heading off with their retinues, but Sven and Sigurd had lagged behind, deep in quick, quiet conversation with Oskarl.

The two friends found themselves standing alone in the trampled snow and flickering firelight, the marks of a thousand men littering the field.

Audun sighed. 'It's never easy, is it?'

Ulfar smiled. 'Easy?' He glanced at the stocky blacksmith. 'Where's the fun in that?'

Daybreak brought with it more snow still.

'This weather feels like we should be a damn sight further north and later in the year,' Thormund muttered as he packed up his tent.

'You're just not fat enough,' Audun said, patting the bony old horse thief on the back.

'These are lean times,' he replied, 'lean times for man and beast. Although your mother didn't seem to mind so much.'

Audun tensed, but Ulfar, crouched over the disassembled tent, interrupted, 'Now, now, Thormund: age is getting to you! You're confusing things again. I've never met our Norse friend's mother, but I'm pretty sure that unlike your girlfriends she didn't have hooves.'

Beside them, Mouthpiece chortled, an odd, wet sound, but no less honest for it.

'Whelp,' Thormund said.

'Codger,' Ulfar replied.

'Get up!' Oskarl said, striding across the campsite. 'Up and ready! Now!' His calls were largely unneeded by now, though: the men from Stenvik had been well-drilled and Sigurd's warriors were good to go soon after the first man woke.

Elsewhere in the camp, Ivar turned to his sister. 'I wish that fat Eastman would shut up,' he muttered.

'He will,' Greta muttered. The siblings sat hunched together under a pile of old blankets. 'He'll catch an axe one day – hopefully with his face.' Next to her, Ivar chortled. 'What?' she said.

'Oh, nothing,' he said, grinning at her. 'Because you're definitely angry at the Eastman.'

Greta punched him in the arm. 'Shut up,' she snapped.

'Ow! Go and punch Ulfar if you're still this mad,' he said.

'Neither of you will do anything.' Karle's voice came from above and behind and the siblings scrambled to turn around, knocked their heads together and flailed as the blankets fell off them, revealing an assortment of rags stuffed down into trousers and up sleeves.

'We're sorry, Prince Karle,' Greta said on her knees, trying in vain to sort out her clothing.

'Yes,' Ivar added, 'we're sorry. We won't—'

Karle looked down on them as they shuffled around on their

knees self-consciously. 'No, you won't. But you will keep an eye on Ulfar and that thick-necked friend of his. Understood?'

'Yes! Yes, understood,' Greta blurted out. 'Keep an eye. Not too close. No punching.'

'Good,' Karle said. 'Report back to me.' He crouched down and looked them in the eye. 'And me *only*,' he added.

The white-clad prince rose and left.

When he was out of earshot, Ivar turned to his sister again. 'This is all your fault! If you hadn't insisted on following the army just so you could see that stupid, skinny, moon-faced idiot one more time—'

Greta punched him again, but Ivar didn't stop; he went on crossly, 'We could be at home now! In front of a nice warm fire – with hot broth!'

'We'll still get there,' Greta said, 'and what's more, we'll get there with the goodwill of Prince Karle, which means we'll do plenty of trade in Uppsala.'

'How?' Ivar whined. 'You have no idea! It's cold and miserable and if I have to eat more slop I'll die. Come on then – tell me your plan!'

Greta didn't answer; she just kept her eyes trained on the shapes rising in Sven and Sigurd's camp.

Black tree trunks and white snow turned the world grey, cold and wet to the touch. Forkbeard and Jolawer's armies trudged across the never-ending fields and valleys, through the forests of towering pines and past lakes coloured steel-grey by the thickening clouds overhead.

'Is it just me,' Mouthpiece said, 'or are we going back exactly the way we came? To the Danes?'

'I liked him better when his face was broken,' Thormund muttered behind him.

'Feels like I've not seen the sun for a hundred days,' Audun said.

'Cold,' Ulfar said, 'and getting colder. Oh, look,' he added, not even bothering to hide the disgust, 'there he is. Our saviour.'

A bright white man-shape was clearly visible, coming out of a copse about two hundred yards to their left, a bow slung over his shoulder. Behind Karle were four men, struggling under the weight of a full-grown elk.

'I don't care what he did,' Mouthpiece said. 'I'm having stew tonight.'

'Careful,' Thormund growled behind him, 'Or you'll be having only the bits you don't need teeth for.'

Mouthpiece spat. 'That's the way of it, old man,' he said. 'I'm hungry.'

'We all are,' Audun said. 'Doesn't make Karle any less rotten.'

'That's one way to say it,' Thormund muttered.

They walked on in silence, listening to the shouts of the hunters as they delivered their prize to the cooks and disappeared again into the distance. As the day passed, they left one forest in the distance, only to find themselves entering another.

'This is an old wood,' Audun remarked, stroking the bark of a pine tree as he passed.

'Just like Thormund's—'

'Shut up, whelp. I can thwack just as well with an old stick,' the old man interrupted, to chuckles from the men around them.

'Not a lot of life here,' Ulfar noted.

'Just like in Thormund's trousers!' Mouthpiece started, ducking a swiftly thrown snowball.

A pale dusting of snow had reached the forest floor, but above them a canopy of white and green filtered and dampened the light.

'Careful where you tread, boys,' Thormund said. 'Don't smack into any trees and don't trip on roots. A bit of bad luck and that's your neck snapped.'

They picked their way uneasily through the woods, breathing a collective sigh of relief when they saw clear sky once again. In front of them, low hills and snow-covered fields stretched as far as they could see.

Audun leaned in towards Ulfar. 'What are we going to do? They're headed south. We're going in the wrong direction.'

Ulfar took his time before answering. At last he said, 'We'll have to make our own way.'

Audun looked at him. 'Tonight?'

Ulfar nodded.

A while later, with light fading, the forest just a thumb's-width-wide line in the distance and the field before them stretching on for ever, the hunters came back for the third time.

'What's this?' Audun said, peering at them.

'Hmm?' Ulfar said, not quite bothering to move his head any more.

'Someone's missing.'

Karle's hunting crew was reduced to him and two others, one of whom was walking with a limp, and this time they were empty-handed. Ulfar glanced up the line and could vaguely make out Sigurd, Jolawer and Forkbeard in conversation.

Soon after, Alfgeir Bjorne's voice boomed over the heads of the men, 'Stop! We're sleeping here. Tents!'

Lumbering like oxen, the men trudged into their assigned groups and spread out around the field. Soon enough, weary voices were barking commands and teams of axe-men walked off towards a nearby cluster of trees to fetch firewood.

As the light faded completely, Karle's team arrived, and Audun watched from a distance as the tall, white-clad hunter dismissed his men and stormed towards the leaders' tents.

'He looks miserable,' said Ulfar, beside him. 'That's good for a little warmth.'

Beside him, Audun chuckled. 'I'll drop a hammer on his toe for you one day.'

'Don't do that,' Thormund said. 'Boy'd catch fire from pure joy.'

Smiling to themselves, Ulfar and his men continued building tents.

The armies of the two kings fought the darkness by building a host of small campfires. Food was prepared and distributed, and slowly quiet descended. After the day's march, no one was in much of a mood to do anything but sleep.

Ulfar, Audun, Thormund and Mouthpiece had just settled when Sven came over to the small fire they'd built.

'Hello, old man,' Thormund said. 'What happened?'

'Karle said they were attacked by a rabid wolf,' Sven said. 'I pointed out that wolves live about thirty days' hard ride north of here, but he didn't budge. Wolf, he said. Ripped out a throat and got the leg of another before they got a clean shot. Took six arrows to slow him down and another three to kill him.'

No one had anything to say to that, until Mouthpiece broke the silence. 'And Karle didn't take him as a pet?'

This got a laugh, but Sven's eyes had lost their customary sparkle. 'There's something wrong with the world,' he muttered. 'I know my bones are old, but I can feel it.'

Ulfar and Audun traded glances, but kept their peace. Sven didn't stay long, and once he'd gone, Thormund crawled under his furs and Mouthpiece followed soon after.

Audun and Ulfar sat in silence and watched the skies. When

wispy grey clouds drifted across the moon Ulfar got up, went to his tent and picked up his walking bundle. He was joined by Audun, who silently pointed towards the hill and the treeline in the distance. After taking their tents apart they moved, like ghosts, between the dark triangular shapes on the ground.

Ulfar's hand shot up and they both instantly crouched down, making themselves as small as possible in the darkness. A large man was moving towards them.

Oskarl.

Without a word, the big Eastman stopped, sniffed the air – and then burped loudly, ducked down and crawled into his tent. Within moments a sharp, nasal snore cut through the darkness from his direction. Audun tugged at Ulfar's shirt and motioned him forward. Ulfar rose and picked his way through very slowly, very carefully. Guards had been posted, but they were all half asleep and the two men slipped through their grasp easily.

After the sea of tent-hides the snow dunes were uncomfortably bright in the moonlight. Ulfar led, striding through the powder, Audun following on his heels.

They had not got more than fifteen paces away from the camp when a torch flared up ahead of them, a slice of sunlight in the darkness. A pile of snow shifted and a figure rose, slowly and clumsily. 'Stop!' it shouted.

Night-vision thrown by the flames, Ulfar squinted, trying to make out the features. '. . . Ivar?' he said, as quietly as he could.

'Yes!' Ivar shouted, triumph in his voice.

'For fuck's sake, shut up,' Ulfar hissed. 'We're leaving – we're going north. We'll be out of your life for ever.' About two hundred yards to their left another pile of snow changed to a human shape that stumbled towards them.

'No, you're not,' Karle's voice said behind them. Ulfar and Audun turned. The prince stood at the edge of the camp, smiling, with five spearmen at his back and his bow slung over his shoulder. 'We can't have people just running off when things get a little difficult. What kind of army would that be?' The spearmen started wading through the snow towards them, brandishing ropes.

'Do we go?' Audun muttered under his breath.

'No,' Ulfar whispered, 'that's what he wants. We'd be dead in five steps. We'll try our luck with the kings.'

'You must have *really* put some sparkle into your promises,' Audun said, looking at Greta, who was standing by Ivar's side. They looked an odd mixture of smugly triumphant and miserably cold.

'I can't even remember,' Ulfar said as the spearmen bound his hands. 'But I hope this makes us even.' He cast a glance backwards and caught a glimpse of Greta's face. 'And then again, maybe not.'

Karle led the way, walking quickly through the snow, as the two of them were half dragged and half pushed to the outside edge of the camp. Ivar and Greta had tried to follow, but Karle told them to stay. Ulfar was sure he'd heard Greta hiss at the prince.

'This is not good,' Audun muttered.

Ulfar looked ahead, over Karle's shoulder. 'You're right.'

Moments later a stocky guard blocked their path. 'What do you want?' he said.

'Forkbeard,' Karle said. 'Something he needs to know.'

The guard looked suspiciously at them, but Karle did not budge. Turning, he stalked off to a large tent in the middle of the clearing and moments later, Forkbeard emerged.

'What do you want?' he said, sighing.

'Found these two trying to run off,' Karle said.

'Hm,' Forkbeard said, eyebrows lifting a fraction as he looked Ulfar and Audun over. 'Stenvik men, aren't you?'

'Yes,' Audun said. 'Audun Arngrimsson and Ulfar Thormodsson.'

Forkbeard seemed to be turning something over in his mind. 'Fetch Jolawer Scot,' he said. 'Make sure you give him their names: Audun and Ulfar.'

As the guard ran off towards the camp of the Swedes, Ulfar glanced at the man who held their fate in his hands. He looked bored.

When Jolawer arrived, he was accompanied by Alfgeir Bjorne.

'Ah. Jolawer,' Forkbeard said.

'Oh shit,' Ulfar muttered, dread sinking into his bones. Audun glanced at him. He too knew that this was not a good situation to be in.

Jolawer Scot looked at Ulfar, and for the first time he thought he saw shades of the old king in the young man's face. 'Yes,' he replied, looking at Forkbeard.

'These men are under your command, and they were trying to run away.'

'I see,' Jolawer said.

Ulfar glanced over at Karle, who could hardly contain his glee. He'd placed them right in the middle of the game board and Forkbeard had made exactly the move he'd hoped for. Now, in this biting night cold, under the stars, Jolawer Scot was being forced to make a decision on their future.

'They may very well be working for King Olav,' the young king said, 'and as such, they cannot be trusted. Kill them.' Alfgeir Bjorne spluttered beside him, but Jolawer stopped him with a raised hand. 'If they walk away from this, news will spread and it will cost us a lot of men.'

'It'll cost you a lot more if you kill them, son,' Sven said from the darkness, almost conversationally. 'We've taken quite a shine to your boys, you see.' Forkbeard, Jolawer and Alfgeir turned around. Behind them, Sven and Sigurd stood at the head of a group of

Stenvik men at least fifty strong. Standing silent and still in the darkness, they radiated the kind of menace you could only get by living by the blade and refusing to die for a long, long time.

'So if it's all the same to you,' Sven continued, 'we'll pick up our two straying sheep and be gone. You'll round up five times our number on the way south, especially if King Olav is the bait.'

'We thank you for your hospitality,' Sigurd said, 'and value your friendship highly, but we need to leave your service.'

The silence that settled spoke hard words. Guards around Forkbeard moved hands to weapons, but he stilled them with a raised hand. 'Where are you going?' he said, an edge to his voice.

'North,' Sigurd said.

'Why?' Jolawer said. 'King Olav is coming south now.'

'We know,' Sven said. 'We're going to visit a . . . friend.'

The Stenvik faction broke camp before sun-up. There was no noise, no talking and soon, no tents. As the world turned from black to grey to white, Sigurd ploughed forward at the front of the line while Sven drifted up and down, checking on friends, explaining their decision and eventually coming to Audun and Ulfar. Oskarl strode up ahead, near Sigurd, like a mastiff with his master. Thormund and Mouthpiece had stayed behind, arguing sensibly that they had a better chance of survival in a bigger group. Ulfar couldn't help but think that they might have made the wrong choice. After Forkbeard and Jolawer's endless column, walking with only a hundred men felt like a relief.

Sven appeared next to them. 'Fine mess you've put us in, boys,' he said, smiling.

'Didn't have to push too hard,' Audun said.

'True, true. I still don't know everything, but both me and the old bear' – Sven gestured up towards the front – 'have been feeling it for a while. There's something wrong up north, something *different*, and if your tales of Valgard start coming together with reports of King Olav moving at speed without most of his men, and the world breaking, there's only one thing we can do.'

'Which is?' Ulfar said.

Sven's face hardened. 'Go and fix it.'

They didn't say much after that, just focused on putting one foot in front of the other. Sigurd was a surprisingly canny trek-master, making sure they stopped early, camped well and sending out a rotation of men to forage and, on lucky occasions, hunt. While most of the Stenvik men remained stone-forged and silent, those who went out agreed that the wildlife that they'd known all of their lives was acting differently somehow: more skittish.

Though they varied greatly in size, age and bearing, Sigurd and his men all had two things in common: they'd all survived for a very long time, and they were no strangers to hardship. They moved steadily northwards, overtaking the army campsites quickly. When they passed the field where Forkbeard and Jolawer had faced off, moving between the two nearly snowed-over and half-burned stacks of firewood in the middle, Ulfar paused and turned to Audun.

'What if that Erik character is lying?'

'I had thought about this,' Audun said, looking around. The ghost of that night still lingered in his vision – Karle shooting from the dark, Alfgeir wrestling, the flames rising ever higher – but now the field was dead; no life, just snow: grey above, white below. 'I think he's telling the truth, though.'

'Why?' Ulfar said.

'I just do,' Audun said.

'Hard to argue with that,' Ulfar said as he turned to catch up with the group. 'Are you sure?'

'Yes.'

'And what else do you know?'

'Whatever happens, there'll be spring,' Audun said.

'I hope so,' Ulfar said as he fell in with the footsteps. 'I really hope so.'

As they walked, the land changed. The fields took on a different shape, stopped being big squares and became curving slivers, pushed and squeezed by the encroaching lines of thick pine trees. Sigurd skirted the edges of the forest for as long as he could but soon there was no way to avoid it. The dark treeline stretched either side of them as far as the eye could see, and it was impossible to tell which way would be quicker.

'We'll stop here,' the old chieftain said. He didn't need to shout – when he was ready to talk, the men listened. 'Use the last light to get us something for the fire. We'll go in tomorrow at dawn.'

The men dropped their gear and some went about setting up camp, sweeping up snowdrifts to build casings around their tents while others grabbed bows and spears and formed up in two small hunting parties. They headed off in opposite directions.

'What do we do?' Ulfar said.

'Tents, I suppose,' Audun said, 'and then firewood?'

'Sounds like a plan,' Ulfar said. 'Got anything to get it with?'

Audun turned and walked off, returning almost immediately with two hand-axes.

'That was quick,' Ulfar said.

'I've worked every bloody edge in this camp,' Audun said, smirking. 'I know who's got what – and I'll sharpen them both again tonight. They won't mind.'

'Fine,' Ulfar said. 'Let's get the tent up and then go.'

With the tents quickly erected behind them, they checked the paths of the hunting parties and picked a route between them, straight into the forest. An odd quiet settled on them, a heavy curtain of silence as the trees swallowed up the noise along with the light. The ground felt spongy with pine needles under their feet, and there was only a light dusting of white, though the branches above carried thick layers of snow that softened the already fading light; it gave the impression of walking into someone's house.

Audun pointed at a tree trunk up ahead. 'That one,' he said. 'Might as well.' His voice sounded harsh in the silence. Almost as if to spite the forest he strode up to the tree, buried his axe in the trunk and took three quick steps to the side. The heavy load of snow crashed to the ground exactly where he had been standing.

Grinning, Ulfar walked over to the other side of the tree and soon their blades were rising and falling in rhythm. A short while later Audun raised his hand. 'Stop,' he said. Ulfar pulled the axe back and stepped away as the blacksmith aimed three quick, savage blows at the wedge on his side, then stepped back.

They could both hear it. They could almost *feel* it.

The wood creaked and the tree trunk shifted slowly as its weight found no support to lean on. The creaks became groans as the trunk toppled over, snapping branches overhead and crashing to the ground, sending a big cloud of snow to the sky.

'That wasn't so bad,' Ulfar said. 'Now we just need to—'

Audun raised his hand again, staring over the tall man's shoulder. 'Stop,' he said again, quietly this time. 'Turn around.'

As he turned, the first thing he saw was the snow, gently drifting to the ground. Then, in the distance—

'Look at the size of him,' he whispered. The stag's crown reached fully an arm's width to either side. 'Imagine if we could bring that back—'

'How?' Audun whispered back.

Ulfar sniffed the air. 'If you stay here and I circle . . .'

'You're going to take that beast down with a *hand-axe*?' Audun said, eyebrows raised.

'. . . *hm*,' Ulfar said. 'Maybe?'

Audun glanced down at the debris from the fallen tree. 'There may be a way – but we're going to have to be incredibly lucky.'

Ulfar followed his gaze and grinned.

The stag was a good three hundred yards away. For the longest time it stood absolutely still, as if frozen to the spot there among the trees. Ulfar watched it carefully as he moved through the loose snow, slow as the winter itself, circling the big animal.

When he'd finally made the torturously long circuit and found his place, he swallowed, drew a deep breath and charged towards the stag, shrieking at the top of his voice and flailing his arms, making himself as wide as he could.

The animal jerked into motion, big muscles powering it through the snow. Although the fight between them would not have been even remotely close, Ulfar had the element of surprise, and now he sprinted for all he was worth after the stag, herding it towards—

At the very last moment Audun stepped out from behind a thick tree trunk, wielding a broken branch at least as long as a man and thick as a thigh-bone. He planted it in the ground at an angle, then bent down, making himself as small a target as possible. Blood gushed over him as the stake tore into the leaping stag's chest, driven in by the animal's own speed, and within moments it had snapped under the weight as the beast's knees buckled. The animal lowed in pain and scrabbled to get up, but Ulfar was already leaping on its back and hacking at the neck while hanging for dear life onto the horns.

The struggle didn't last long. Dark-red blood went reddish-pink in the snow, and the animal stopped moving.

'See?' Ulfar said. 'Told you. Hand-axe.'

Audun smiled faintly. Ignoring the rich smell of warm blood was easier now, but he could still feel the fire within.

Kneeling, Ulfar finished the blood-letting and moved on to the guts. 'Are you going to help, or what?'

Audun knelt and grabbed a handful of snow. 'Give me your axe,' he said, and when Ulfar had done as he was told, Audun grabbed the blade and packed the snow on it, warming it in his hands, then brushing off the thickening blood. He wiped the edge of the axe on his shirt, then pulled out his own axe and the scraping sound of metal-on-metal filled their quiet bubble as Audun sharpened their blades.

The axe he handed to Ulfar had a wicked-looking gleam to its edge.

'Thank you,' Ulfar said solemnly. '*Now* are you going to help?'

Audun very calmly grabbed a handful of snow and flung it at Ulfar's head, forcing him to duck out of the way. 'If you want you can continue to use something dull to skin it, like your face.'

Grinning, Ulfar turned and sliced open the stag's belly.

The look on Sven's face alone was worth the ache of carrying the massive animal back to camp on their backs. The old rogue just stood there, mouth working silently.

'Oh, come on, old man!' Ulfar shouted as the men gathered around them. 'Have you never seen a stag killed with a hand-axe?'

'Hail the hunters!' someone cried out.

'HAIL!' the response rang and strong hands took the weight off Audun and Ulfar's shoulders and a number of enthusiastic bearded warriors carried the stag in a cheerful procession towards the campfire. Within moments, runners had been despatched to fetch more wood and knives flashed above the gutted animal, carving flesh into chunks to roast on the fire.

As Audun and Ulfar watched the sea-wolves tear into their prey, Sven found his voice. 'How did you do this?'

'We felled a tree,' Audun said. 'We were going to bring it to the fire, but when the snow fell the animal was there.'

'And he didn't run when the tree crashed?'

'He was about three hundred yards away,' Ulfar said. 'He stood still – he didn't seem to care about us.'

'Hm,' Sven said, pursing his lips as the smell of flame-charred deer drifted towards him. 'Well done. Now go and get some before those hairy bastards eat all of it.'

As Ulfar and Audun grinned and moved towards the fire, Sven watched them go, then looked down and squeezed his temples. 'No,' he muttered to the ground, 'no, it's probably fine.' He looked back up at the crowd clustered around the stag, jostling and joking with the two young men in the fading light.

'It's probably fine,' he repeated.

TRONDHEIM, NORTH NORWAY
LATE DECEMBER, AD 996

The guard very quietly cursed King Olav and his insistence that someone had to be outside in the middle of the night and the freezing cold, huddled under a wall-mounted torch that gave out no heat whatsoever, and that tonight, that someone had to be him. 'It's not right, is it?' he said to the dog at his feet. Another of the king's decisions: they had to have watchdogs, apparently so they could smell the enemy in the dark. He didn't mind that, though; the hound was good for company. A big brute of a thing, it reached almost to the middle of his thigh standing up. They'd taught it a little too well to growl at strangers, so a thick cord was wrapped around his wrist and hooked to a wide collar around the beast's throat where it lay at his feet, resigned to its fate and probably dreaming of a fire and a bone to gnaw on.

Rubbing his gloved hands together for warmth, the guard leaned up against the corner of the longhouse and tried to inure himself to the persistent, biting cold.

'Well met!'

His head snapped up, as did the dog's. The voice came from the darkness, beyond the line of huts. He peered into the night, cursing the flickering flame above his head. There! A shape, highlighted against the snow. A man – no, two, one following the other.

'Well met,' the guard said, stepping forward and reaching to his hip for the axe. The winter wind biting at his cloak was sharp with the smell of sea. 'Show your face, stranger.'

'I'm no stranger,' the man said slowly. His voice sounded hoarse but familiar. 'Do you not' – he stopped to draw breath – 'know me?' The man stepped into the light.

'Hjalti! What happened?' The king's right-hand man looked like he'd been dragged through death backwards.

'I need to see the jarls,' Hjalti said. He cleared his throat. '*We* need to see them.'

Behind him the other man stepped into the light as well. He was taller and thinner than Halti and stood silently behind him. His hair was slicked back and he was dressed in simple but well-made traveller's garb, but he looked . . . odd, somehow. Like something that didn't belong here.

'They're inside,' the guard stammered. 'Do you want me to—?'

'Please,' the tall man said. He smiled, which did not make things one bit better.

The guard turned to leave, but the dog at his feet didn't move an inch. 'Come on,' he said, yanking on the dog's lead. 'What's wrong with you?' The beast rose half an inch off the ground and shifted, head down, tail between its legs, staring at Hjalti and the man until they rounded the corner. The moment they were out of sight the guard had a single moment to let go of the lead as the dog bolted, bounding over the snow dunes and disappearing into the night.

Hjalti and the man rounded the corner.

'Oh. Where's the dog?' the man said.

The guard could feel his chest constricting as the tall man smiled at him. 'It . . . ran away,' he managed.

'Interesting,' the man said as Hjalti marched on beside him, grim-faced.

The big double doors to Hakon's great hall swung open smoothly.

'They're in there,' the guard said.

Hjalti nodded stiffly. 'Good.'

'I'd better, um—' The voice inside his head screamed at the guard to *run run now run away* but neither of the men acknowledged him. Someone shouted something from inside the hall.

He managed to retreat two steps before the heavy oak doors swung shut with improbable speed, slamming hard enough to shake the snow off the roof.

The guard threw himself backwards, only barely saving his ankles from being crushed. He could hear the sliding *thunk* of the bar falling into place on the inside.

For a moment he just lay there, heart thudding in his chest, then he clambered to his feet, dusted the snow off his backside and shuffled towards the corner of the longhouse. He took up his position under the torch, but it felt strange without the dog. 'Here! Here, boy!' he called, but the night remained silent. He looked around for the dog. Where was the damn thing?

The light from the torch flickered, and something moved in the shadows.

Valgard and Hjalti stepped into the longhouse. The heat from all those big, sweaty bodies packed shoulder to shoulder hit them in the face first. Then the noise.

'Shut the fucking door!' someone yelled, voice slurred.

As if on command, the big door slammed behind them, to drunken cheers. Someone shouted Hjalti's name and the word spread before them like a ripple in a pond.

A chill travelled up and down Valgard's spine as he recalled what it had felt like to finally emerge into the world, the way his skin had stretched and *felt* . . . The sour taste of retreat followed, and the rangy healer's jaw set. This time there was no Odin to stop him.

'Hjalti!' cried a big fat man sitting on the dais, in the far left seat. Valgard smiled to see the seat in the middle was empty. 'Make way, you bastards!' he called. 'Hjalti – come here!' A channel opened in the throng as people pushed to get out of their way. Halfway down the hall, Valgard got a good look at the other man on the dais.

'Interesting,' he said, but Hjalti didn't respond; he just stared straight ahead as he stumbled onwards, like a child in the throes of sleep. Around them the noise in the hall slowly died down, to be replaced with truculent stares as they reached a square space before the dais, maybe four yards by six, that had cleared of people. The hall was hushed now.

They'll all be hanging on Hjalti's every word, Valgard thought.
Good.

The other man on the dais was a greybeard. His features were open and friendly, on the surface at least, but his eyes said something else entirely.

'Hjalti! Speak, cousin. Where is the king?'

'King Olav has fled Trondheim,' Valgard said.

The fat man's lip curled with barely suppressed rage. 'No one fucking asked you,' he spat. 'Hjalti, speak up! What happened?'

'There was a fight. King Olav lost,' Valgard said.

The greybeard's outstretched hand stopped the fat man from leaping off the dais, but only just. He turned to Hjalti, looking stern and commanding. 'Hjalti! Talk to us – tell us what happened in the woods. And if you don't shut your friend up, Storrek will.'

'I don't think he will be able to,' Valgard said conversationally, enjoying watching the men on the dais as they tried to piece together the meaning in his words and comprehend the sheer scale of his rudeness. They failed.

'See,' Valgard said, rolling his shoulders, 'I think I'll have this thing of yours – *the North*. It's a bit cold, but that's fine. I'll even let you leave on a boat of your own choice.'

Something smacked into the outside wall with a wet crunching sound.

The greybeard ignored the noise and shot him a withering look as silence settled again in the hall. 'I don't know who the fuck you think you are,' he growled, 'but you need to be taught some manners.' He withdrew his hand and Storrek stepped down from the dais.

He walked towards Valgard, all fat-covered muscle and death, and Valgard couldn't help but smirk.

'What's so funny?' the man snarled.

'Storrek, is it?' Valgard said.

'You fucking bet it is,' Storrek snarled, stepping to within an inch of the tall, thin man. 'And you're not saying much more of anything for a while.'

'Mm,' Valgard said, 'I see what you mean. A man like yourself could break a man like me into pieces' – Storrek grinned broadly – 'well, in a fair fight.'

Valgard stopped speaking, but his mouth kept moving.

The smile on Storrek's face stiffened and contorted as the fat man spun on his heel and started moving back up the dais like a dog being yanked on a lead.

'What are you doing?' the greybeard said, half-rising out of his seat. 'Fucking hurt him! Break his—'

The words were knocked out of him: an invisible force flung him back into the seat and pinned him down on the right-hand chair as Storrek crashed into the wooden throne on the left. The two chieftains' eyes blazed with fury, but no word escaped their clenched jaws.

Valgard looked at them then, drew their gazes in and willed them to see him for what he was – and what he could do.

Like a seamstress pulling a thread through skin, Storrek raised his right arm and brought it smoothly to his left hip. One seat over, the greybeard did the same.

The knives slid out of their sheaths without a sound as Valgard walked towards the steps. One – two – and *up*.

King Olav's throne was more comfortable than it looked.

He wanted to laugh as he watched the assembled sea-wolves and land-bears of the North, all staring at him like a herd of milk-cows.

He allowed the thought to slide out of his head . . .

. . . and the sound of the knives hacking into flesh to either side of him grew in strength, half wet slop and half banging against a deadened drum, as the chieftains started stabbing themselves, and soon the smell of gushing blood mixed with the stench of voided bowels until their hearts stopped beating and they left this world.

He released them then, all of them. Hjalti collapsed to the floor, coughing up the blood that had been held inside him, and Storrek deflated as he sank into his seat then started an inglorious slide off his heavy arse to the floor.

The greybeard, straight-backed to the end, took for ever to topple, but eventually his balance shifted and he too crashed to the floor of the dais.

The sound of his head smashing into the wood snapped the war-riors out of their stupor: there was a great tumult as war-cries went up all over the room and hundreds of warriors decided to charge. Valgard could see the murder in their eyes, smell their desire to tear him apart. Of course. He had offended them – he had defied them. Worst of all, he had *frightened* them.

And now they wanted their revenge.

The doors to Hakon Jarl's great hall were made from the biggest, strongest oaks they had been able to find within a day of Trondheim. Each one was easily the width of a man, and they had been crafted together with thick ropes and three-times-quenched steel.

When they splintered and broke, they killed six men.

Botolf and Ormslev pushed through the gap just as Ormar and Jori burst in through the back-room door.

As the blood of the two chieftains pooled around the throne and seeped through the wooden planks of the dais, Valgard leaned back and savoured the panic, the last-gasp calls to Odin and Thor – to *anyone*.

Too late, he thought as his trolls walked among the best of King Olav's army. They broke some and bent others too far, but these were tough bastards. He'd get most of them serviceable, and that'd be a fine number.

The light of the fires was reflected in the widening pool of blood by his feet and he allowed himself a quiet moment of appreciation. Things really were going his way now.

Sighing contentedly, he rose, touching the rune bag. He could feel the tendrils of strength within. There was a scent on the air.

'Fear,' Valgard said. 'So that's what it smells like.'

STENVIK BAY, WEST NORWAY
LATE DECEMBER, AD 996

Black water lapped at the prow of *Njordur's Mercy*. The steep black cliffs rose on their left, touching the thick grey clouds and glowering at the ship with unmovable menace.

King Olav pulled his furs close. Six days' fast sailing had taken its toll on the men, but they rowed on, hunkered down under every layer of warm clothing they could find, no doubt cursing him when they thought he wasn't listening. He did not doubt that the screams they'd heard from the shore as they left still haunted them.

Behind him, Einar shifted to get a better look. 'That's Stenvik, there,' the young man said.

'I know,' King Olav said. 'I know.' He had prayed on the water, talking to the skies and begging for . . . What? Forgiveness? That night in Trondheim still weighed on him. It seemed unreal, somehow – the forest, the one-eyed man, the feel of his sword biting into thick, blue flesh . . . and the cries that carried from the shore and hung on the air far longer than they should have.

The gentle hiss of the prow slicing through the waves wiped his thoughts away. The North just wasn't the right place for him – he'd never have gone there, not this late in the year, if it hadn't been for Valgard.

King Olav looked over his shoulder again, and cursed himself for it. He'd felt *watched* the whole trip, as if the sickly healer had been sitting by his side, smirking at his mistakes. He hadn't even fought his own battles, the weakling; he'd had those brutes do it for him. His ribs ached at the memory of it. The pain in his side had torn his sleep apart; he couldn't find any comfortable way to lie down, and breathing was difficult. It had been a challenge not to growl at the sailors, but he'd learned a long time ago that kings sat on thrones, and thrones belonged on land. A ship's captain had to be a good bit more patient. So Olav kept his anger to himself and waited, counting every moment that brought the *Njordur's Mercy* closer to shore.

'That's strange,' Einar said.

The young archer by his side had been one of the few bright sparks on the journey, and Olav had quickly begun to feel like he could trust the man. There was something about his quiet reliability that reassured, unlike Hjalti. A chill ran down his spine as he relived the dagger buried to the hilt in the man's chest, but he shook it off.

'What?' he replied, more brusquely than he'd intended.

'Their torches are lit,' Einar said.

The sun was hiding somewhere in the clouds, past the mid-point, but not by much – though the light was weak, it was quite enough to see by.

The king squinted and could just about make out the dots of light along the coast. 'You're right,' he said. 'Maybe old Finn has become afraid of the dark. Maybe the South has made him soft,' he added with the closest he could get to a grin. It was hard to smile in the cold. He licked the salt spray off his lips and waited.

Einar kept staring. 'The old town,' he said at last.

'What about it?'

Einar turned to look at him. 'It's gone.'

'Hold the oars,' King Olav barked. They'd reefed the sails a while ago; they needed control more than speed right now. Einar stood beside him, arrow nocked, and half of his crew stood behind him, armed and ready for a fight.

'Are we not out of range, Einar?' he asked quietly.

'For most people,' the young archer replied, not quite hiding a smirk.

Olav could find nothing to smile about. The old town had been levelled: every single structure had been burned to ash; those few beams that had initially resisted showed the white wounds of the axe.

'Where is everyone?' he muttered.

'Movement up on the wall,' Einar said under his breath. 'Pikes – quite a lot of them, too.'

King Olav made his decision. 'Oars!' he shouted, and as one, the men pushed and pulled and the ship sped forward towards the pier. 'Eyes open,' the king barked, and then added, 'Prepare for anything.'

But *Njordur's Mercy* docked smoothly at Stenvik Pier and nothing happened. The thirty armed men were up in a flash, scanning the horizon for enemies and ready to fight – but none rose out of the soggy grey mess that had once been the Old Town. No screaming horde descended on them, no rain of arrows – nothing. The rowers disembarked quickly, strengthening their ranks, but still no one came.

Einar looked at the king.

'Form up,' King Olav said, and behind him, the men moved into position and inched towards the walls of Stenvik.

'Four more steps and we're in range,' Einar said quietly at the king's right-hand side.

'Halt!' King Olav shouted. From here, even he could see the row upon row of silent armoured men on the wall. His ribs ached, his stomach was roiling from the sudden stillness of dry land and he could feel a fever coming on.

He turned and looked at his men. 'Stand your ground. My Lord will protect me,' he said quietly. Then he walked towards the town, arms outstretched, though there was still no response from the wall. When he was sure no one could see his face, he gritted his teeth to squeeze out the pain and drew as big a breath as he could manage. His voice rang out, loud and strong: 'I call for Finn Trueheart!'

This caused some movement on the wall and at five points, men stood up from a crouch, displaying bows at the ready, with arrows nocked.

'Is this how you greet your king?' King Olav shouted.

'Stand down! Open the gates! Open the gates or I'll rip your shitting heads off!' a big booming voice roared from within, and a small bubble of nervous laughter escaped King Olav's lips at the chaos erupting on the wall. The archers disappeared as if they'd been cut down. The silent pikemen dropped their weapons and jumped into action and within moments the grating of chain on stone broke the cold silence, the thick wooden gate started to move and a familiar figure emerged on the wall.

'My king!' Finn shouted.

'Hello, Finn,' King Olav shouted back.

Belatedly, Finn remembered to bend his knee. He was barely visible above the parapet as he gestured to the slowly opening southern gate. 'Welcome to Stenvik!'

The longhouse was much as King Olav remembered it, but the fire and the broth warming him outside and in made it finer than any king's palace. He finished his story, and allowed himself another spoonful.

'Those *bastards*,' Finn growled. 'Conspiring to kill you all this time? And Hjalti – I cannot believe it. I mean, I can, obviously. If only I'd been there—'

'If you'd been there by my side they would have gone for you too,' King Olav said pragmatically, then asked, 'So, what happened to the Old Town?'

'I burned it,' Finn said. 'They . . .' He stopped and swallowed, and then went on, 'They just wouldn't die, the fuckers – Sigurd and Sven, I mean.'

'I saw them. I saw their bodies,' the king said.

'I know – I saw them too. But after Valgard and I buried them and you left, the old guard started disappearing – the raiders of the Westerdrake. And then . . .' The big man's face darkened. 'We chased them through the woods, up the hills and into the Old

Town, and my men died, one by one. Some were trapped in the forest by spiked branches. A number of them fell as they climbed, and more than one was stabbed in the shadows of those shitty old huts. So I burned them.'

Too many questions needed answering. 'How did they—?' the king began, but a cough ripped through him, followed by a stabbing pain in his ribs. He gripped the edge of the table and gritted his teeth.

'You're hurt,' Finn said. 'You – fetch the healers,' he ordered, and the warrior he'd pointed at disappeared into the darkness.

'Had to defend myself,' King Olav said. He felt the snowball rolling down the hill, taking him with it. 'Had to—' Cold sweat broke out on his forehead and he tried again. '—escape . . .'

'We'll sort you out,' Finn said, reaching over and pouring half of his broth into the king's bowl. 'Drink.'

'I don't—'

'*Drink.*'

King Olav looked hazily at the big man's face, but there was no malice to go with the edge of command, just a wide-open, worried face. The king allowed himself a weak smile. 'As you say, chieftain,' he said, enjoying the time it took Finn to understand the joke.

'I – I didn't, um – you need your strength,' the big man said sheepishly.

'I know,' the king said. The broth was delicious, meaty and full of nourishing fat. At the far end of the hall the door flew open and two serious-looking men carrying leather pouches entered at speed.

The king looked down at the spot where he'd sat when he first got to Stenvik – was it really just a few months ago? He remembered the shape of the man kneeling before him, the glint in the eye as the bastard had looked up and thanked God for saving him.

'Valgard . . .' he muttered.

Concern clouded Finn's face. 'Yes – I didn't see him. Where is he?' But King Olav was done talking. Reeling, he slumped backwards into the arms of the healers who'd come up behind him.

Thunder crashed overhead and far beneath King Olav's feet white-tipped waves smashed into the base of the cliff. The wind howled all around him, tugging at him, tantalising with the joy of the fall and the darkness to follow. He looked down and the waves were no longer water but armies: roaring, heaving waves of men, shields locked and charging to meet in deadly conflict. The wind carried their screams as he stepped off the cliff and drifted down, borne by an invisible hand to take his place in the vanguard. The clouds disappeared, revealing a red sun burning in the sky – he felt its heat snapping at him, pinching his skin and covering him almost instantly in a slick sheen of sweat as he stood on the battle-field, holding his sword and staring at the faces of hundreds – no, *thousands* – of blue-skinned monsters. If he squinted, he could just make out Valgard's slim shape behind them, surrounded by waves of blue-green light.

The sensation when his army faded out of view was like having his stomach pulled out through his feet. His heart ached, but then the cross started thumping at his chest and King Olav could feel himself growing – *growing* – stretching to the heavens to meet his maker, getting bigger and stronger and heavier.

The first blue-skin looked up at his form and charged, fangs out and frothing at the mouth.

King Olav lopped his head off in one stroke.

As the current of power ran through him, from his fingertips up through his shoulders and into his head, his heart and the very core of him, the king smiled. 'You shall be weighed and measured before the Lord,' he said quietly into the face of the roaring army. 'And you shall be found wanting.'

Laying about him to both sides he strode into battle, twisting in his sleep.

The old warrior stood awkwardly by the end of the table in the longhouse, waiting for Finn to look up. Finally, he cleared his throat. 'We put the king's men in the stables last night. Roof's tight, and we made sure there was plenty of wood – they were cold, wet and hungry.'

'Good,' Finn said.

'Young one – named Einar – said he'd be in charge of distributing blankets and furs. He asked for healers. . . . er, Finn?'

The big man was no longer paying any attention to the soldier. Instead, he was looking at the crooked figure striding across the floor of the longhouse. Finn rose slowly from the seat to the right of the throne. 'Fine,' he said absentmindedly. 'Leave us.'

'What?' the warrior said.

'Leave us, I said,' the big man snapped, and as the warrior hurried away, out of sight, Finn kept staring at the man he had called king.

King Olav was almost bent over double, favouring his left side. His face was drawn, his skin sallow and his hair hung limply, but there was still that spark in the eyes, a mad glint that demanded – *commanded* – attention.

'Finn,' the king said without ceremony as soon as he was close enough.

'Yes, my lord,' Finn replied.

'You have too many men here,' the king said.

'Yes, we do. But there's little we can do about it,' Finn replied.

'If we let a handful go home to their farms we'll lose half of our army. Everyone else will go as well.'

'But if we make them stay here they'll either start fighting amongst themselves, rise up against us or grow thin, sick and dead.'

'Yes,' Finn said cautiously.

'I want a report on everyone and everything you have in this town: all the craftsmen and the materials.' The king made his way gingerly up to the dais and sat down in the high seat.

When he turned, the breath caught in Finn's throat.

King Olav smiled. 'You're going to build me a ship.'

The raw wind pushed the snow up into Finn's face as he left the longhouse. The faint morning light brought no warmth and Finn felt chilled to the bone. *Ship?* What the king had described . . . The warrior sighed. He'd said yes, of course – but it wasn't going to happen. There was no way a thing like that could be built.

Finn's strides lengthened as he got angrier. Why did this happen to him? What was the reason? He clenched his fist and gritted his teeth. It had been bloody hard, keeping Stenvik from collapsing. The enemy had known it inside out and had used every hidden weak spot to their best advantage – it had been like shoring up a leaky boat in a storm. They'd wounded Gunnar badly on his fourth day in charge, so Finn had taken over. And he was absolutely sure that it was Sigurd and Sven, even though he'd buried them with his own hands. How could you fight men who were already dead?

Head down, Finn barrelled straight into a bony old man and sent him crashing to the ground. 'Watch where you're going,' he growled.

'My sincere apologies,' the man said, lying on his back. He was short and skinny – knobbly as an old wind-beaten branch – with white hair that hung in thick, salt-crusted tendrils covering almost half of his face. He propped himself up on his elbow, wincing like someone who had just lost a hard fight.

Finn felt a tingle of embarrassment. Was that was he'd been reduced to, knocking over old white-hairs? He extended a hand and pulled the old man to his feet. 'No, I'm sorry,' he said. 'I wasn't looking.'

'Something on your mind?' the old man said.

'You could say that,' Finn replied, more bitterly than he wanted to.

'Hm.' The old man scratched his head. 'So what's going on?'

'Oh, nothing. I just have to find the materials in the middle of winter to build a . . . a ship.'

The man seemed amused. 'Plenty of ships down by the harbour,' he said.

'Why are you smiling?' Finn snapped.

'Oh, no reason,' the man said. 'Just find it funny. You must be a fortunate man.' Finn glared at the man, but didn't answer, and oblivious to his companion's rancour, the white-hair continued,. 'You need a ship built, and you walk into a shipwright.'

Now it was Finn's turn to laugh incredulously. 'You're a *shipwright*?'

'Sure am,' the man said. 'Just came in on the boat with the king. I should have introduced myself.'

The old man smiled, and Finn felt oddly at ease in his presence. 'My name is Fjolnir. Why don't we get started?'

THE DALES, WEST SWEDEN
LATE DECEMBER, AD 996

The hunting parties returned later that night with even more meat, although none of them could match Audun and Ulfar. With bellies full, the men traded well-worn stories of old victories, applauding new embellishments with raucous laughter. In the shadows, Ulfar's head dropped to his chest before he started and woke.

'Right,' he said. 'I think it's time for me to sleep.'

'Me too, I gather,' Audun said.

'Hail the hunters!' Sven shouted.

'HAIL!' the cry went out.

Ulfar smiled a wan smile. The tree, the stag and the walk back had taken it all out of him and he could feel his hips seizing up, along with his lower back. For just a moment he allowed himself to be grateful for the knowledge that the aches would be gone in the morning.

The two hunters, bone-tired, stumbled into their tents and were asleep almost as soon as they hit the ground.

The sun was up there somewhere, Ulfar thought, but it did not feel like it wanted to be. The trees were bigger than he remembered, the massive trunks smooth and the colour of a crow's feather. Must be something to do with the distance they'd travelled. The people of the western valleys always banged on about their big trees, how just one tree would do as a house, a boat and a year's firewood for a family and so on. Yes, that had to be it: they must have gone past the big lakes and up into the heavy forests of the west that stood on the edges of the land of the Norsemen. It would get worse before it got better, too. If the stories were true there were days and days of woodland to go before they'd hit the valleys: days of travel until they'd be able to see further than their outstretched arm.

So all he needed to do was place one foot in front of the other. Left, right, left, right, left, right . . .

Ulfar looked down at his feet and his stomach twisted. Thin strands of fog were swirling unnaturally around his shins, floating on top of the snow and covering it in a grey sheen. Around him the trees stretched to the skies, impossibly smooth, impossibly round. The snow felt wrong under his feet, too: like someone's *idea* of winter in a forest, rather than the thing itself.

'Show yourself,' Ulfar said.

The dogs were first to arrive: Geraz, broad-shouldered and pale, followed by Frec, a giant black mastiff with head held low and fangs bared. Above, two ravens settled on nearby branches and *quorked* conversationally at him. A moment later the man was *there*, just as if he'd stepped through an invisible doorway. He was tall, grey-haired, propped up by a thick staff and in all other ways exactly like Ulfar remembered from the walk so many days ago.

'It's you.'

'Of course it's me,' the old farmer replied. 'Fjolnir. You remember, don't you?' Audun remembered all too well. He could see the hut, he could feel the shame as he hid under the bed, and when he left . . .

The old man studied him with a twinkle in his eye. 'Do you still have it?'

'Yes,' Audun said, his voice barely more than a whisper.

'Good. You'll need it.'

'It makes me ill,' Audun said, 'if I use it I'll die.' He remembered exactly where he'd put the belt; it was coiled up in his bag. But no – though he didn't remember putting the belt on, now it felt heavy around his waist.

The old man smiled at that, wistfully. 'We all die,' he said. 'That's how we get in this mess in the first place. But you will need to use it. Keep that in mind. And besides, my gifts are good. I gave you the stag, didn't I?'

'What do you mean?' Ulfar snapped. 'I caught that with Audun!'

'The stag that stood so still that it could have been frozen?' the tall man said. 'The animal that ran away from you, straight at the only other man within miles? Come now, Ulfar. You're sharper than that, aren't you?'

Ulfar felt a surge of annoyance. 'Shut up,' he said, but the words felt limp coming out of his mouth. 'You're—' He went to speak again, but nothing followed.

'Call me what you want,' the grey-haired man said. 'You've already taken one of my gifts.'

'What?'

'The Mead of Skalds,' he replied calmly. 'And you have drunk it, so you have wisdom and understanding beyond any human. It will take you a while to learn that you do, though.'

Ulfar stared at the old soldier. 'You—'

'—are wasting time,' he said, waving away the words. 'You need to go straight north without delay.'

'To Trondheim?'

'No,' the old farmer said. 'Trondheim's gone.'

Audun frowned. '*Gone?*'

'Dead. Overrun. Beyond our scope. Let the kings of men' – he laced the word with contempt – 'deal with that one. No, you're going to Gallows Peak.'

'Why?' Audun said.

'Because that's where he is going,' the farmer said.

'Who's he?' Ulfar said.

'You know.' A dismissive hand-wave.

'And what makes you think I'll do as you say?' Ulfar snapped.

'You hate me,' the grey-haired soldier said, 'but you hate him more.' When Ulfar didn't argue, the man smiled and reached down to scratch Geraz behind his ear. 'So you will talk to your men and you will march up to the mountains. It is the best thing you can do now.'

'Or else?'

The farmer shrugged. 'Valgard fights his way to the Rainbow Bridge and baits the gods into fighting him. He knows that the Fates say the gods will fight on mortal soil when the gates of Hel open wide, so he's figured out that the reverse is also true: he reckons all he needs to do for the end of the world to come about is for him to pick a fight *here*. Naglfari sails, Fenrir breaks his chain, the Wyrm of Midgard rises and the waves along with him, Jotuns walk the earth and it all ends in pain, death and destruction. Then a handful of humans and gods arise from the ashes, but with a new ruler: *him*.'

Audun watched as the old man formed the sentence, chewing on it like a piece of rotten meat.

'In a word,' he said, 'Ragnarok.'

'Wake up—!' Sven's voice cut through the cold morning air. 'Get moving! I want to get home so I can scratch myself twice in the same place!'

'You do that all the time!' someone shouted from a nearby tent.

'That's why we never shake your hand!' someone else shouted from across the site.

'No, that's just because you recognise the smell of your mothers,' Sven shot back.

Around him men were crawling out of their low tents, shaking snow off hides and hair. Before long, Sigurd's group of leather-faced greybeards was ready to walk. Audun and Ulfar packed their tents, neither in the mood to speak.

Snow fell on marching men and wind swept it away. The forest swallowed them on the south side and four days later spat them out on the north. The time passed slowly, in silence.

On the morning of the fifth day, Ulfar approached Sven. The old man had cut himself a walking stick that was his own height and then some and he leaned into it as he walked, pulling his feet out of calf-deep footsteps in the snow and pushing on, one step at a time.

'Where are we?' Ulfar said.

Sven made a noncommittal noise. 'Somewhere in the west of Svealand, I think.'

'How long will it take us to get to Trondheim?'

'At this pace?' Sven said, looking back over the row of greybeards marching doggedly through the snow, most clutching walking sticks of their own. 'We'll be there tomorrow.'

Ulfar hesitated. The old rogue's usual good spirits seemed to have vanished. 'Will it be easier going if we . . . if we turn towards Gallows Peak? There'll be fewer bloody trees there,' he added hastily.

Sven shot him a sideways glance. 'Gallows Peak,' he said. 'You want to go into the mountains? Now?'

'Only to – uh – get easier walking,' Ulfar said, reddening as the words came out.

'We're in the middle of nowhere because of you, the mad bastard with the hammers and the old bear's gut feeling,' Sven said, snow crunching underfoot. 'Unless you want to finish the rest of your journey and face whatever you're going to be facing on your own you *might* want to consider telling me everything, *always* – starting with right now.'

Ulfar swallowed and searched for courage. 'A few days ago, after we caught the stag, someone came to me in the night,' he said.

'Oh fuck a motherless goat. Of course he did,' Sven said. 'Thought his hand might be in this. Go on.'

Ten days' walk to the south, Jolawer Scot marched at the head of his army, Alfgeir Bjorne beside him, and Karle skulking close behind. Some distance away, not close enough to hear but close enough to see, Thormund and Mouthpiece trundled along side by side.

'Thormund,' Mouthpiece said, and watched until the old man on his right turned his head ever so slightly to indicate he was listening. 'Where is he leading us?'

'Towards the coast, I imagine,' Thormund said.

Mouthpiece walked on in silence for a while. A hundred yards or so to their left marched Sweyn Forkbeard's column. Jolawer's army looked small by comparison, but for the moment that didn't matter; they were on the same side. For now.

The snow fell silently, soft and white, all around them: not yet heavy but insistent and unstoppable. Their shoulders were soggy with it and lamb's wool caps glistened with a mix of new-fallen flakes and freshly melted drops.

'It snows a lot,' Mouthpiece tried.

'It's winter,' Thormund snapped.

'All right,' Mouthpiece said. 'It's not *my* fault.'

But Thormund simply huffed, sank his scrawny neck further into his furs and marched on, ignoring him.

'Thormund,' Mouthpiece said.

'*What?*' he snarled.

Mouthpiece shot him a glance. 'Did a mink bite your arse this morning? You're spikier than Sigrid's underskirt.'

Thormund snorted. 'I just don't like where this is headed. Should've stayed with Sigurd and Sven.'

'Why?'

'Because he's taking us to the *sea*, you idiot. Fucking hate the sea.' Thormund kicked at the snow and Mouthpiece took an involuntary half-step away to his right. 'Boats. Always boats, near the sea.'

'Move it,' the man behind him grunted.

Mouthpiece hunched his shoulders and bent his head, but as he put one foot in front of the other and tried his best to stop his mind and his mouth, he couldn't help but think of lambs in slaughtering season.

When the sun started its fall towards the horizon, Forkbeard signalled for the halt. Tents were raised quickly and the camp set up as the sky above them turned from the dirty white of sheep's wool to sword-grey, speckled with fat snowflakes.

'I cannot think of anything finer than a horse right now,' Thormund said, rubbing at the outside of his leather shoes. 'My feet feel like they're my father's, and he's been dead for twenty years. I'd give anything for a horse to ride.'

'Even if you were Forkbeard?' Mouthpiece said.

'All his treasures and his lands aren't making his arse any less cold and wet, are they?' Thormund said.

Mouthpiece made a face at him. 'So you're saying you'd give a kingdom for a horse?'

'Yes,' Thormund said.

'That's ridiculous,' Mouthpiece said. 'I—'

'Shut up,' Thormund said.

'What? I—' Mouthpiece began.

'I said *be quiet*,' the old horse thief hissed, urgency in his voice. 'Listen,' he whispered. Around them the low murmur of tired men ebbed and flowed, the occasional burst of laughter or shouted insult rising then sinking back down into muttered conversation.

Mouthpiece glanced at Thormund, whose face was carved in stone, a picture of concentration. 'What—?'

A bony hand shot up to silence him.

'It's gone now,' the old man whispered after a moment, but his hand was still raised. His eyes suddenly sparkled. '*There*,' he said. 'Listen!'

Mouthpiece strained to sift out the sounds of the camp: there *was* something else, just on the edge of hearing . . . When he realised what it was, he sighed. 'It's a cow,' he said. 'Or, you know, one or two cows.'

Thormund turned to look at him. 'I know it's a cow,' he said slowly. 'I am, in fact, fully aware that it is a cow.'

'Then why are you so scared?' Mouthpiece blurted out.

The horse thief smiled then, and suddenly he looked less like a helpless old man and more like Sigurd and Sven. 'Because I'm alive,' he said, 'and because I like you, despite your face and your *constant* yapping, I'll tell you something: if you hear a cow in pain and it's calving season, that's a *good* thing. But if you hear that same noise in the middle of winter, far away from any farms, in the snow—?'

Mouthpiece fumbled for the truth, but didn't find it. 'I don't understand,' he said plaintively.

His eyes and ears trained on something in the shadows, Thormund pulled the knife from his belt, cleaned it, ran a finger along it to test its edge and, satisfied, stuck it back in its sheath. 'Neither do I,' he said, scanning the camp, 'but something's about to happen, and when it does, I want to be in the right place.' Then he produced another three knives of different sizes from various places, including his sleeve, cleaned them and slid them back into their hiding places.

Mouthpiece clutched the battered club he'd been given. The wood felt comfortably worn in his hands and he cursed himself for feeling scared. He was travelling with possibly the biggest army the North had ever seen and he was allowing a jumpy old horse thief to unsettle him. *No*, Mouthpiece thought, *I'm safe here, safe as I can be*. The realisation made him relax some, enough to get comfortable under his furs and get to work pushing the cold away. There would be another day tomorrow and maybe whatever was bothering Thormund would leave with the rising sun.

As he felt dull, cold sleep crawl over him, Mouthpiece's thoughts were of life by the blade and how it wasn't at all like he'd imagined.

'RISE! RISE, YOU BASTARDS!' Alfgeir Bjorne's voice was followed by thundering, stomping footsteps. 'WE'RE UNDER ATTACK!'

Mouthpiece woke up with a start, his heart in his mouth and his stomach in his feet. He crawled out from under his shelter and into the night and immediately had to throw himself to the side to save his face from a collision with the knees of a group of running men. 'Thormund!' he shouted, but there was no answer; glancing across, he saw that the old horse thief's tent was already empty. Mouthpiece pushed himself onto his feet.

The camp was a sea of flickering shadows under the torches moving swiftly, all heading towards the southern edge of their newly formed tent town. Shouts bounced from one side to the other as the chieftains exhorted their men to get on their feet and get to arms on pain of death and worse. In the distance Alfgeir was bellowing commands. Prince Karle's white cloak flitted into, then out of a pool of light in the distance.

Mouthpiece looked around for someone to ask what was happening, but no one volunteered any information – and then his head finally woke up and he understood what he was hearing.

Underneath and behind the panic, the shouting and the clanking of thousands of men getting up and ready to fight in a hurry was a river of sounds; Mouthpiece, still dazed by the abrupt awakening, staggered towards it, trying to figure out exactly what he was hearing.

There were animals there, somewhere – but there was more, too.

'THEY'RE COMING!' someone screamed up ahead. The closer he got to the south end the steadier the light was. In front of Mouthpiece, Jolawer's warriors were hastily establishing shield-walls, facing south. Mouthpiece noted that they'd tied torches to the longest pikes and stuck them in the ground, enveloping them in a pool of light that created a big half-circle in front of them.

The sounds were coming from the darkness beyond, but Mouthpiece still couldn't quite place it; it sounded like trees breaking, like the sea at night like one continuous wave of dull, dark misery.

There was no warning, no official declaration, no command given to stand firm. One moment the flickering flame-lit circle was empty and then, they were there: a herd of white-eyed cows staggering at them out of the darkness. Swords rose and fell, but it all took too long; the big beasts didn't go down quickly enough and the shield-wall, after holding for a heartbeat, collapsed under the sheer weight of the animals blundering forward. Time slowed down for Mouthpiece; he saw the breach in the shield-wall ahead of him and felt the push as men staggered backwards, pushed by

the onslaught. He took two steps back – and was almost shouldered
to the ground.

'Get *back!*' Alfgeir Bjorne roared as he charged past, yanked up
a pike with a torch on it and thrust it at a dying cow. Steam rose
up from its flanks as the flames melted snow and consumed flesh,
but the animal didn't flinch. Mouthpiece heard Alfgeir's muttered
curses mixed in with the screams of men suddenly plunged into
darkness.

'More light!' the old warrior screamed. 'More fire! And get *back!*'
But it was too late: ahead of them men were trying in vain to
stem the tide of mindless animals lowing their disquiet at the
world. 'More fire! *Quickly!*' he kept repeating as disembodied noises
drifted on the air, the unnerving pain-sounds of the cattle weaving
and twining with the dull thud of blades hacking into flesh and
the sharp screams of fighters being trampled, breaking under the
weight of the animals.

And now there were other sounds in the night as well: dogs
barking, bleating sheep and human voices: a discordant, broken
chorus of them.

'*He has risen.*'

The words, repeated over and over in dull voices, made Mouthpiece's skin crawl. He turned to run – and saw a wave of torches,
sweeping over towards them from the other camp.

Forkbeard.

The words were out of his mouth before he could close it. 'FORK-
BEARD'S COMING! GET BACK!'

A heartbeat later Alfgeir Bjorne's voice boomed, battlefield-loud:
'STEP BACK – NOW! SHIELD-WALL!'

Mouthpiece watched as if in a dream as the line of torches coming
towards them broke into three sections and flowed smoothly away
from each other like water down a hill. The middle slowed down as

the other two groups curved around the dots of light surrounding Alfgeir Bjorne.

A bony hand closed on Mouthpiece's shoulder and yanked him away from the flickering flames. Before he could turn, Thormund hissed into his ear. 'Shut up, boy, and stick with me.'

'But—' Mouthpiece began.

'*No*. This is about to get messy,' Thormund said, pulling the younger man deeper into the dark, away from Alfgeir and the heart of the battle.

'Let me go! I'm not going to run and hide from—' A hard elbow to the chest silenced him and he sank to the ground, coughing and struggling for breath. Stars danced in his eyes. He buried his hands in the snow and pushed until he'd managed to stagger to his feet. It took him a few moments to regain his night sight, but by the time he could make anything out in the darkness again, Thormund had disappeared.

The torches moved in clusters, the distance between them closing up, and a vision of his father's farm came completely unbidden to Mouthpiece. He remembered the hired hand they'd got one summer, a short, stocky man with a scythe who'd swept through the grass like water, leaving no blade uncut.

The soldiers of the Danish king fell on the attackers head-on like a pack of wolves, bodies surging past Alfgeir's men, and suddenly the surge of half-lit hell-beasts was held at the line. Mouthpiece stared as the other two companies fell on the flanks of the remaining attackers, and the flickering torches threw shadows of men, horses and even a stag dancing in the night as they all pushed mindlessly towards the same goal.

Forkbeard's men set about them with a will, hewing down man and beast where they stood.

Mouthpiece, frozen to the spot, couldn't see it in the dark, but very soon the whole camp could feel it: the quality of the sounds had changed. The mindless murmur was dying down, step by step, throat by cut throat.

The three lines of torches met in the middle, and it was done.

'Give us some light!' Alfgeir Bjorne shouted, but the edge was gone from his voice. Torches flared up around him, revealing the dead and dying.

'Drag the bastards away,' the big warrior commanded, and slowly, moving as if they were waking up from a particularly bad dream, work teams started forming. Mouthpiece blinked at the light and the bodies being dragged away into the dark, the sudden *change* in the atmosphere.

'There's nothing here for me to do,' he muttered. '*Nothing*. I missed it. He made me miss it.' With a host of thoughts he could not properly voice swirling in his head, Mouthpiece turned and headed for his tent, picking his way past smashed shelters and hobbling soldiers. When he got back to his own lean-to on the north side of the camp he saw Thormund was already in his shelter, sleeping.

When he was safely under his own furs, Mouthpiece looked at the old man across from him. 'Coward,' he muttered as sleep took him.

It was the smell that woke him up: that pervasive, sickly smell of spoiled meat. The sky was no longer black but the light hadn't quite pushed the dark away. As he blinked and tried to get his eyes used to the half-light, voices drifted in on the breeze: short commands, quiet but insistent. The events of the night before crept into Mouthpiece's consciousness along with the snatched words: blood gushing from a warrior's snapped leg; axes cleaving a bullock's neck, with precious little blood flowing out; the shield-wall breaking; Forkbeard's torches in the dark, sweeping in.

He rose, glanced over at Thormund and grimaced. The old man lay on his side, still as a statue, sharp angles not softened by the blanket of sleep. Disgusted, Mouthpiece walked off. The old man should have let him fight instead of knocking him down and running away. It was all Thormund's fault that he hadn't been able to get stuck in.

Coward.

Caught up in his thoughts, Mouthpiece didn't see the damage until he was almost standing in it. The south end of the camp was one gaping wound.

In the dark it had felt like they were being attacked by thousands of enemies, but in the cold and creeping morning light the truth was revealed: trampled tents and packed snow stained with reddish stripes led the eye to a pile of carcases. Mouthpiece, trying to estimate, guessed that the herd might have been about fifty strong. Scattered randomly amongst them were a handful of sickly-looking dogs and a couple of unhealthy sheep. Gaping wounds stared back at him from anywhere he looked, challenging him to look at the uncomfortably blue-tinged flesh within. Mouthpiece could see the crowns of two separate stags and the horns of a bull moose as well.

Something felt odd, though. There weren't nearly as many animals as he'd thought. Then he looked to the side and bile rose in his throat.

The corpses were laid out in ordered rows. He counted fifteen men before he stopped, and that wasn't even half of them. He felt disgusted, but curiosity pulled him in. Numb with horror, he staggered towards the corpses, one thought echoing over and over in his head: *could have been me.* Over and over. *Could have been me.* Even though their eyes were closed, every face was judging him.

'They're gone,' Alfgeir Bjorne said behind him.

'Yes,' Mouthpiece mumbled, heart thumping in his chest.

'They are no longer cold or hungry and none of them misses home. Fair trade for a bit of fear and a bit of pain, wouldn't you say?'

Mouthpiece turned and looked at Alfgeir. The big warrior looked frightfully old all of a sudden: old and grey, like a piece of cloth that had been bashed on the washing stones too many times. He must have been awake all night, making sure the dead were where the dead should be, but his voice still sounded strong.

'I'll take the cold and the hunger, I think,' he said.

The big man smiled at that. 'Good. I prefer soldiers who want to stay alive. The other kind don't last too long.'

The shame and the guilt from the night before broke free inside Mouthpiece and smashed against his ribs, a beast in a bony cage. He had to bite his back teeth not to lose control of his emotions, but there was no judgment to be felt from Alfgeir; he just stood there, quietly looming, looking at the night's work.

As the feelings faded away, Mouthpiece stood a little straighter. He glanced over at the bodies. 'We've lost good men,' he said.

'Yes,' Alfgeir said.

'More of ours than Forkbeard's.'

'Yes,' Alfgeir said.

Something caught Mouthpiece's eye. 'Are they – theirs? Or ours?' The corpses he'd noticed looked distinctly different. Jolawer's men were discernible by their rag-tag battle gear, while Forkbeard's men all had good weapons and battered clothes. But four of them were different: dressed from head to toe in black, with neither shields nor armour, though all of them had knife-belts.

Mouthpiece realised he'd been waiting for an answer for a while. He turned and looked up at Alfgeir Bjorne.

'Where's Thormund?' the big man said.

The taste of relief was suddenly sour. 'Still sleeping,' Mouthpiece muttered.

'When he wakes up, tell him to come see me,' Alfgeir said.

The temptation to tell Alfgeir Bjorne everything was strong: how Thormund had knocked him down, how he'd fight in the shield-wall next time, how it hadn't been his fault and the old man was a coward who ran and hid – but he didn't. Thormund was perhaps his only friend in the world and it wouldn't be honourable to throw him at Alfgeir's mercy.

Mouthpiece forced the words out with all the conviction he could manage. 'Thormund fought bravely last night.'

'I know,' Alfgeir said with a wink, gesturing at the four men in black, 'and so do they. Bastards snuck up on me in the dark – they had me, too. Knocked the axe out of my hand. Then they dropped, one by one, and fast.'

Mouthpiece stared. 'Did— Did—?'

Alfgeir smiled. 'I know his handiwork. He's older now, but they used to tell some proper stories about Thormund the Cutter back in the day. Ask him to come see me when he wakes up. I want to thank him, and tell the king.'

Nodding mutely, Mouthpiece turned and walked away. The events of last night started replaying, but this time in a different order. Had Thormund known? So why hadn't he *told* him? They could have gone together! But Alfgeir Bjorne had spoken to him like an equal, like someone who was at least as dangerous as Thormund. 'The Cutter'. Mouthpiece snorted. What a stupid name. Maybe he could learn to work the cudgel and earn a name? Skull-splitter, maybe? The Cutter and the Skullsplitter: you'd write songs about them, wouldn't you?

The morning light brought a spring in his step and this time Mouthpiece was more alert. He picked out the old man's tent from a distance. The old horse thief hadn't moved since this morning.

'Thormund,' Mouthpiece said softly, 'wake up. Alfgeir Bjorne wants to talk to you.' The old man didn't budge and Mouthpiece rolled his eyes. It wasn't *that* hard to get up, surely. 'Thormund,' he said again, this time more insistent, but the back remained turned and Thormund didn't move. 'The boot it is, then,' Mouthpiece muttered. Closing the distance, he nudged the old man with his toe. 'Wake up, hero,' he said.

Thormund's body was stiff as a board and cold to the touch.

Mouthpiece felt for the words but they wouldn't come. Instead he sank down to his knees in the snow and put his hand slowly, gingerly, on Thormund's shoulder. The old man's face was grey and colourless. 'Thormund – come on. *Wake up.*' But he didn't wake up. Mouthpiece really didn't want to touch him; trying to pull the blanket off him didn't work; it was stuck. Angry now, the young man pulled hard and Thormund's body followed for a moment, but then it fell back, followed by the sound of wet cloth ripping, ripping again and then once more.

Mouthpiece stood there, struck dumb, holding a blanket with three big holes in it. Only now did he notice the blood in the footsteps leading from the battlefield to the tent. Thormund's body lay on the ground, the bloodstained blanket covering what looked like stab wounds. There was an odd look on the old man's face, quietly noble in death. It was something resembling a smile.

Distraught, Mouthpiece scrabbled to his feet and walked off in search of Alfgeir Bjorne to give him the news.

'We must reconsider,' King Jolawer Scot said.

Forkbeard looked bored. 'Wait,' he said, and when Jolawer looked like he was about to start speaking again, he added, 'for the others. We need to talk about this.'

'But we are talking!' Jolawer said. 'You and I decide – and I say we must go north.'

'Wait for the others,' Forkbeard repeated.

Jolawer didn't have to wait long. Sigrid appeared, striding through the snow, her long fur cloak swirling around her legs. Erik Hakonsson, the Earl of the North, followed her, two of his chieftains trailing behind him. Alfgeir Bjorne and Prince Karle came over from the direction of the Swedes' camp, along with the messenger, Thorkell the Tall.

'We were attacked last night,' Forkbeard said, addressing the circle. 'We lost good men. Have any of you seen anything like it before?'

'Yes.' Erik Hakonsson's face betrayed no emotion. 'This has been happening all over the North: farmers and their animals get *twisted*. More and more of them belong to Hel.'

'So the North is the source of this?' Jolawer said.

Erik Hakonsson shrugged. 'I don't know,' he said.

Jolawer turned to Forkbeard. 'We *must* go. There's something going on up there; we have to follow Sven and Sigurd.'

Face carefully composed, Forkbeard looked back at him, then at Erik. One by one, he scanned the faces of the circle of commanders. When he spoke, the answer was simple. 'No.'

'Bu—'

'Not yet.'

'When, then?' Jolawer blurted out.

Forkbeard nodded to the commanders to signal the end of the meeting. 'Soon,' he said as he walked off. Sigrid and Thorkell the Tall fell in line after him.

'Believe me when I say there is little I would rather do than go back and retake my father's home,' Erik said. 'But we have to stop Olav Tryggvason. He is the real danger.' Erik and his men walked away without even glancing back at the three men left standing.

'They're wrong,' Jolawer muttered. 'This is *all* wrong. Sigurd and Sven were right.'

'Maybe,' Prince Karle said, 'and maybe not. But we're safe with the biggest army ever assembled. We'll take on King Olav and then we can go and save the North.'

Jolawer looked away from his advisors, over the two camps and to the line of sour, stinking smoke coming from the carcases. 'If there's anything left to save,' he said to no one.

Mouthpiece walked alone in the trek line and a handful of days passed through him like wind through the trees. After finding Thormund he'd gone numb. He didn't feel bored, happy, cold or hungry. He didn't want to talk to anyone, and no one wanted to talk to him. He just wandered along, following the broad back of the man ahead of him, whoever he was, one foot in front of the other.

'Look!' someone behind him called out, and the noise that followed his call made it absolutely clear what the man had seen.

A seagull – two, in fact, no, three, all circling and shrieking into the sky.

The word travelled up and down the line with lightning speed: it's the *sea. The sea.*

Mouthpiece tried to shake himself out of his slumber. The trek was finally over! He turned to tell Thormund that he'd been right . . . but the old man wasn't there. 'Well, fuck you then,' Mouthpiece hissed into his beard.

The line moved a half-step faster now, the men reacting like horses on the home stretch. The ground below them rose gently, not enough to be a climb but enough to compact the snow and make it even more slippery. The leaders of the line reached the crest of the hill and stopped, but the momentum of the line didn't, so the warriors spilled to the sides, lining the crest. A wordless cry of celebration went out as the first hundred men disappeared from view, and five hundred yards to the left, snatches of shouted voices and commands echoed across from Forkbeard's side. Curiosity put a spring in the step of the men around Mouthpiece and he had to push himself to keep up. Higher and higher the ground rose, until all of a sudden he could almost see over the edge. Only a few steps more, then—

Mouthpiece stopped at the crest of the hill and looked down.

Row upon row of longships sat on the beach, snowed under, but still formidable in their shape and size – not to mention the sheer number of them. He counted quickly and estimated that there'd be about eighty ships. This must be Forkbeard's landing place, where he'd ferried his army over. Jolawer Scot's men ran towards the ones closest to them, and over on their side Forkbeard's men did the same.

Mouthpiece ignored the curses of the men behind him. He just stood still, staring at the beach. 'Shit,' he muttered. 'It's really happening.' Below, men made small by the distance were already swarming over the ships, hard at work, preparing them for launch.

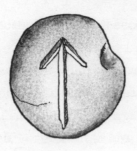

TRONDHEIM, NORTH NORWAY
LATE DECEMBER, AD 996

The morning sun climbed cautiously over the horizon. *Yeah, you watch out,* Valgard thought as he yawned in response, levering himself out of the throne where he'd slept and wincing in anticipation – but the pain didn't come. He looked down at his feet. Last night's blood had sunk into the wood, painting it the colour of rusted swords. Parallel lines led out of the blotches where Ormar and Jori had dragged the two dead chieftains by the shoulders and thrown them on the pile with the useless, broken ones.

He looked around appreciatively: Hakon Jarl's hall was a husk. Everything that could be broken had been in last night's orgy of violence. The heavy trolls had crashed through the sea of humanity, tossing men aside like a child's discarded dolls, smashing skulls and snapping bones. He'd scolded them for that – he couldn't reuse the ones with broken heads; experience had shown him they might not need brains, for once they'd changed they obeyed him without question, but apparently they did need their skulls intact to function. The blue-skinned giants had listened to his rebuke, but he had no sense that his words had meant anything to them.

Still, a new dawn and a new day; things to do, people to see.

Blinking, Valgard picked his way slowly through the rubble and towards the smashed doors where milky light was seeping through the gap.

They stood in rows, silent and massive, marshalled by Botolf, Ormslev and Skeggi, easily filling the square in front of the long-house and disappearing behind the huts. Everywhere he looked he saw blue-tinged skin, and men in the middle of a slow, agonising change. He'd counted them before he went to sleep last night, then he'd counted again.

Nine hundred and twelve.

'We have work to do,' Valgard said. The trolls stared at him. 'You're not going to be needing big speeches, are you?' he added. 'Fine by me. We're going to the pile.'

The trolls shuffled out of the way as he walked past. Moving through the blue-skinned warriors he could sense in each a little bit of himself, a grain of strength. Every time he recited the words Loki had told him, every time a human being became a warrior carved from frost and belief in the old gods, he grew stronger. His body had more or less stopped bothering him, all the old aches and pains now just a fading memory, and he walked tall among his silent army.

As he rounded the corner the stench of the pile hit him. The cold might have dulled the worst of it but there was no denying all those bodies gave a lot of death to the wind. When the trolls, led by Botolf and Skeggi, had hit the village outside the longhouse they'd caught a lot of men sleeping. Some had died hard; others had run, disappearing into the snow, but the smartest ones had sprinted down to the harbour and thrown themselves onto ships, launching without supplies or suitable clothes . . . they'd be cold and miserable and dying somewhere out at sea now. So not much of an escape.

Valgard told the trolls to gather up all the bodies they could find, but they'd been too effective: the pile of corpses was at least a hundred feet high.

'I thought we should set fire to them,' Valgard said conversationally, but no one replied. 'Oh, but you're right,' he continued, 'the weight of them and the cold will make it impossible.' He paced, frowning. 'We need a lot of . . .' He paused and chuckled. 'We need firewood. Botolf?' The big troll stayed silent. 'Tear down the long-house.' He allowed the thought to trickle out of his mind and take root in the trolls, and they started attacking the longhouse with their bare hands, ignoring the snow cascading off the roof. They started kicking relentlessly at the walls until the timbers started snapping and then passed the broken bits of wood from hand to hand to hand. A ring of wood soon formed around the pile of corpses.

'Very good,' Valgard said, and reached for the fire-steel in his belt. He shoved a starter bundle of dry moss in between two bits that looked likely to take and struck until the shower of sparks ignited them.

The flames caught almost instantly, biting into the wood and licking the exposed flesh of a dead Viking. The tongues of fire hissed when the man's frozen fingers thawed, and when the fat in his skin melted and dripped down, the red flame lurched and leaped, turning white-hot in spots. Thick tendrils of smoke drifted towards the sky and the scent of grilled meat gradually overpowered the smell of rotting flesh. The fire, insistent and hungry, travelled from log to log until the corpses were ringed by flame and shimmering air, and still the trolls flung more wood onto the pile.

Stop

Around him, all activity ceased as the trolls turned mutely towards the pyre. The heat coming off it was building, melting the snow around as flames caught clothing and hair, liquefying flesh and turning timber to ash.

In the sudden quiet, Valgard reached out with his mind. He could feel them like fog on his skin – but they needed *more*.

'Wood!' he shouted, gesturing wildly, and his silent army went for the furniture, adding broken benches and long tables, whatever else was left, throwing everything onto the voracious flames. The bodies in the pile were changing in colour, warping and twisting like worms trying to squirm off the hook. They looked almost alive, Valgard thought. Well, almost.

They were coming closer now: careful, cunning and *hungry*. He could feel the scent of battle and death drawing them in.

'MORE TIMBER!!'

Behind him, a troll bellowed and Valgard turned just in time to see Ormslev balancing the massive logs that formed the doors from Hakon's great hall, the muscles cording in his neck as he held them high above his head. The huge troll pushed through the crowd, planted the end of the twenty-foot-long door by the foot of the flames and pushed, and the big slab of timber rose, then toppled over and crashed into the burning bodies, sending a cloud of ash spiralling into the air. Something collapsed in the middle of the pile and flames rose even higher, caressing the doors, then they latched on and the conflagration billowed and roared.

Ignoring the blast of heat that had made the trolls step back, Valgard looked up towards the crest of the hill above Trondheim.

There he was: the wolf.

Come to me

All of you

Moments later, the hill was dark with shapes all heading towards the pyre.

The flames had died down soon enough and Valgard used boat hooks to drag enough corpses from the fire to bait the wolves and lure them in close. 'We probably could have picked up wolves on the way, you know,' he said to Botolf, 'but I figured this was faster. And besides, burning things is fun.' Behind him the last rays of light shone on a mound of bones, white against the black of charred corpses.

Turning the wolves had been both easier and harder than creating the trolls: their minds were simpler, but the hunger was much, much worse. Every time he tried it had threatened to draw him in, and every time it had cost him a lot to pull away.

'So now we rest,' he said to the ever-silent Botolf. 'And tomorrow we march.'

The only answer was the sound of the wind and the crackling of logs on the still-smouldering pyre. Valgard fell asleep, contented and safe.

The slap that awakened him stung his cheek and a hand grabbed the material at his throat and hauled him up roughly. The man was tall – far taller than him – and terribly strong.

You're going too far, mortal.

The voice filled his head and echoed inside his entire being.

'I didn't mean to,' Valgard said, hating himself for sounding meek.

Didn't mean to.

The voice dripped with contempt and Valgard, suddenly terrified, looked up at the face of the man who held him up by his shift. Smooth-skinned and clean-shaven, Loki the Trickster God stared at him with undisguised hatred.

You are drunk on power, mortal, and you thirst for far more than you can drink.

Raising an army?

And then what?

Around them, Trondheim looked like a reflection in a lake. 'We could march on Bifrost,' Valgard said. 'You told me to.'

Don't you dare, Loki growled. *Don't you fucking DARE tell me what I may have said!* The grip around his throat strengthened and Valgard felt his heart pounding in his chest. *I saved you. I made you. You are my creature and you will do what I tell you to.*

'I deserve this!' Valgard croaked.

Loki looked at him and laughed. Then the God of Mischief spat in his face.

Everything went black. Then there was a spark. And another, and another. Like burning thatch, something in Valgard melted away and he could feel a great uncoiling, the snapping of a bone cage.

In the clearing in the forest, the birds fled the trees. The pregnant silence was broken by a faint hissing, a few bubbles on the surface of the pond – and then Valgard broke free. For the first time in his life he was *whole*, powerful. He pushed himself thrashing out into the world, all of him, curving fangs and long neck and slabs of meat layered in powerful muscle over a sleek body. Four stubby legs with slasher's claws gripped the ground, pushing him forward. The forest faded away and suddenly he was in Trondheim, towering over Loki, shrugging off his grip as if he were a child.

Please—

And that was the last thing Loki said. Then Valgard's jaws closed on his midsection and snapped him in two.

The feeling was . . . *strange*.

The world tasted like an indrawn breath. He had a moment to stand, new-formed, a bull-monster on four legs with a long, muscular neck and a dragon's head – and then the soul of a god flooded into him and Valgard lost his mind.

Feast at a table . . . raucous laughter . . . red-faced shame . . . angry words . . . the taste of the air in a wooded grove . . . a blind god . . .

shrieks of terror . . . the feel of cold water on scales . . . cold chains on wrists . . . pain . . .

So much pain

Valgard's body morphed again, compressing and pushing in on itself as it reclaimed its human form. Trondheim appeared around him and the man in front of him slowly let go and lowered his hands. The man he'd thought of as Loki was no longer god-like: he was still tall, still handsome, but he was no longer terrifying.

He looked at Valgard, and his eyes spoke of great weariness. 'Thank you,' he said.

Thank me? Why thank me?

Loki looked at him and smiled.

WHY THANK ME?

As Valgard reached out for him, Loki dissolved into air, slipping through his fingers.

It felt less like waking up and more like coming back from somewhere. The first thing that hit him was the feel – no, the *taste* of the air. It had a bit of everything on it, strands and tendrils stretching out into the whole world and scents that made him feel like he could sense everything, everywhere, every creature, living and dead.

Then he opened his eyes and he *saw*.

He saw the trolls, suddenly wary of him, moving away like beaten dogs, except for Botolf, who dropped into a clumsy bow. He saw the wolves, heads down, ears down, as reaction spread through their pack.

'That's right,' he said. His voice sounded strange in his head – smoother, somehow, more resonant. He looked over his assembled army and couldn't help but smile; the change had taken hold of the men now and they were growing before his very eyes. The memory of what they'd once been pulled at them, stretched them, forced them to rise and become what they could be. 'I *do* deserve this.'

He stretched and rolled his shoulders, felt his fingertips and ran his hand through his long, lustrous hair. The power swelled in him, begging for mischief. 'This is nice and all,' he said to his silent audience, 'but I think we can do better.'

He closed his eyes and thought of a sound he wanted to exist in the world and a moment later hundreds of throats joined with a chorus of howling wolves.

'LOKI!'

Valgard smiled and turned to the South. 'That's more like it. Let's go.'

STENVIK, WEST NORWAY
LATE DECEMBER, AD 996

The clouds had cleared, a weak sun had crawled from its hiding place and the work groups had assembled. The men were eager to get to do something – *anything* – and the old man was proving to be a competent taskmaster. Finn was ashamed to admit it but he was all too happy to leave King Olav alone for a little while, and not at all disappointed to have handed over charge of the ship-building. From the moment they'd landed the king had been very wound up over something or other, and he'd got into the habit of looking over his shoulder all the time and praying at least twice as much as he did before – obviously something had happened in Trondheim, but who knew what? Finn knew he owed King Olav a lot, but it was beginning to feel a little like suddenly living with a caged wolf. He'd started feeling very poorly too, and had been keeping to his chambers; that had started about the time Finn had bumped into Fjolnir, so the king had not yet met his ship-builder.

Finn looked down at the work party from his vantage point up on the wall. They scurried around the white-haired figure who'd set up shop just above a slope down to the water. He heard Fjolnir barking, 'Over there!' and pointing as a burly raider swung the timber he carried around and inched away from the water-line. He moved ten feet, then twenty, then thirty, as the old man kept bellowing, 'Further!'

They'd salvaged a load of burned planks from the old town and a team had been sent to hew down nearby trees – the old man had told them to grab the first ones they saw, for now at least. 'Stop!' he shouted, and said something more; his voice carried on the wind but Finn couldn't make out the words.

Then he cried, 'No, that's just right.' He turned, looking up, and Finn raised his hand to confirm, although, from down here, the framework they were building looked nonsensical, with odd struts sticking out all over the place with no sort of obvious connection.

'We're done,' Fjolnir shouted from below. 'Time to go!'

Finn rushed down the steps and out through the south gate. When he got there, Fjolnir had already rounded up a working team and outfitted them with ropes. 'I asked Finn for the strongest men he had and he gave me you lot,' he said to the hefty warriors with a cheeky grin, 'so we'll just have to make do with what you ladies can carry.' The men smiled back and Finn felt a pang of envy. He had to work for every moment the men allowed him to lead them and it galled him to see men like Fjolnir, who did it effortlessly. 'Right – let's go while we have the light,' Fjolnir said.

They followed the northern road into the forest, and Finn had to suppress a wince wherever he saw broken branches or nicks in the timbers; every shadow held a memory of the raiders from Stenvik ducking and weaving through their home turf, leading their pursuers into the darkness. An awful lot of his men had gone into the forests around Stenvik, blades at the ready.

Few of them had come back.

And somewhere in this forest were graves for two grey-haired fighters: graves that he felt certain would be as empty as eye-sockets on a corpse.

But with every step the ominous forest became less of a worry, for the white-hair up front not only appeared to know exactly where he was going, but looked like he was actually enjoying being out there. 'Right, boys, time to get our feet wet,' he announced from the front just as he extracted a foot with a wet slurp.

The men grunted unhappily, but they still followed him out into the bog, trying to choose their footing carefully. Everyone knew stories of unlucky travellers sucked down to their deaths, trapped by one careless step.

Up ahead, Fjolnir was walking like a farmer in his own yard. 'Watch out left,' he shouted a moment before one of the men shouted in alarm as the ground sank under his foot. The men on either side grabbed him and yanked him up; he was covered up to mid-thigh in bracken and stinking bog-slime.

'Happens in a moment, boys,' Fjolnir warned them, then he held up his hand and slowed down, and it looked to Finn for all the world as if he was feeling for something with his feet. 'And . . . there we are!' he shouted. 'All eyes on me!' Moving quickly, he walked to one side. 'These spots here' – he gestured to his left – 'and here' – some quick steps to the right – 'are safe. Come on.' He gestured peremptorily and the men moved cautiously into a wide line separated from each other by a space the width of three men. 'There's a bank here – feel for it with your feet.'

Finn watched from the back as fourteen hardened warriors poked their toes into the marshland like children testing the water.

'Now it's time to get our hands wet,' the old man said with a hint of relish in his voice. He bent down and plunged his hands into the bog, then turned to the next man in line and snapped, 'Grab this!'

Confused, the man pushed his hands into the bog and Finn saw the muscles in his arms bunching; he'd definitely found something. Fjolnir was striding along the line of men, and it looked like he was measuring with his feet. Then about forty feet further along the line, he stopped and dropped to his knees.

He looked at the kneeling warrior. 'Ready?'

The man nodded.

'HEAVE!'

The two men strained, and very slowly, they pulled their arms out of the bog. Their hands clutched thick, slimy tendrils – no, ropes. As they pulled, the ground between them shuddered – and slowly but surely, a pair of long, water-slick planks rose with them.

'There you go!' Fjolnir shouted over his shoulder at Finn. 'There's your ship!' Without prompting, the other warriors started rooting around, shouting commands at each other, and Finn backed up and watched as hewn timber was pulled out of its dank, smelly storage. Within moments a handoff line had formed and soon the timber was being stacked up on the bank of the marsh.

'I talked to some of Sigurd's shipwrights up in Trondheim,' Fjolnir said, appearing suddenly at Finn's side, and he had to bite down hard to hide how jumpy he was. 'They told me they kept the wood they didn't use in the bog so the cold and the sun didn't get to it.'

'Wise,' Finn said, 'but what about the measurements? Will it be enough?'

'We'll find a way to stretch it,' the old man said, grinning, as the timber stack beside Finn grew steadily.

The first men left with planks and returned with the rest of the boat crew. Finn found himself drifting along, half-dazed, with Fjolnir in the lead shouting commands, suggestions and well-judged abuse at the men, who answered in kind, punctuated with blasts of raucous laughter.

An idea snuck into his head. *We might just do this.*

Down on the beach, hammers struck and axes sliced. Fjolnir was everywhere at once, instructing and encouraging, and under his watchful eye the wood quickly took on shape. He'd brought a carpenter with him, a thick-necked sort with a hammer and a shock of blond hair who kept himself to himself. Finn was enjoying looking down at them, scurrying around like ants by the water.

Einar Tambarskelf's voice broke his gaze. 'Well met!'

'Well met,' Finn replied.

The young man took the steps two at a time and stood beside him. 'He wants to know how it's going,' he said.

'See for yourself,' Finn replied.

Einar looked down towards the beach, muttered something unintelligible and made the sign of the cross. 'It's . . .'

'Yes it is,' Finn said. 'And it's coming on quickly.' He looked for Fjolnir to point him out, but the white-hair was nowhere to be seen.

'It certainly is,' Einar said. 'He'll be pleased.'

'How is he?'

'Not well,' he admitted. 'Fever. Confusing dreams. Keeps talking about a grey man of some sort – we're hoping it'll clear soon, but to be honest we can do little but feed him broth and hope.'

Finn spat over the edge of the wall. 'Our Lord will guard him,' he said.

'He will,' Einar said. He clasped Finn's hand and left.

'Broth and hope,' Finn muttered. 'That's a fucking way to win a kingdom.'

Below, Fjolnir emerged from behind the rising gunwales of the ship and raised his hand in salute. Finn saluted him back.

Then he looked again: the old man appeared to be giving him some kind of signal: one hand raised, fist clenched, three fingers extended.

Three days.

The longhouse smelled of sickness and Finn found himself wanting to knock out a wall just to get some air in. However, broth and hope seemed to have worked on the king because his health was definitely improving.

'Is this the honest truth, Finn?' he said, eyes wide open and a grin forming. 'You're not just telling me what I want to hear?'

'No,' Finn said. 'I – *we've* – worked as hard as we could, for the glory of the Lord' – he crossed himself– 'and we believe we'll be ready to launch her tomorrow.'

The king stared at him for a moment, then he barked a harsh laugh and slapped his thigh so hard it made Finn wince. 'Tomorrow! Finn Trueheart, you are a soldier of the Lord and your place in heaven is most certainly assured! And the sail?'

'I started them on the sail two days ago. It too will be ready tomorrow.'

The king frowned. 'Three days? How many people are sewing?'

This time it was Finn's time to grin. 'Two hundred,' he said. The look on King Olav's face was almost enough to make him laugh. 'I have seen the fate of those who displease you, my Lord,' he said.

The king grinned. 'I shall go out tomorrow and watch the launch,' he said. 'And if everything is going as you say it is, I need you to do another thing for now.'

*

Dawn crept over the eastern treeline and filled the world with grey. Finn yawned, worked his jaw to get the stiffness out, rolled his shoulders and looked down on the work.

Laid out in a line stretching to the east and west of Stenvik Pier were the raiding ships, loaded with men and ready to go: thirty-nine ships in all, sixty men to a ship. The only space left on the coastline was to the west of the pier, a gap roughly the width of five ships, crossed with logs laid side by side, running parallel to the waterline.

'Finn!' The king's voice rang out from below.

'Up here!' the big soldier shouted, looking down upon his king's face. It was gaunt and drawn, but lit from inside.

'I'm coming up!' If the illness had weakened him, he made a good show of hiding it. Quick, sure steps took him up to the edge of the stairway. 'Is it ready?'

Finn looked down at the beach. 'Yes, it is.'

King Olav took the final two steps with his eyes closed. When he opened them his lips parted slightly and he drew a deep breath. There was silence, then a faint hiss as he exhaled slowly. 'She's beautiful,' he whispered.

Finn still couldn't bring himself to call it a 'ship'; it was a monster, plain and simple, half again as long as the biggest drake he'd ever seen and nearly twice as wide. Each of the fifty-six benches had space for four rowers. They'd had to walk for a day to find a tree old enough for the mast; he could wrap his arms around it, but his fingers didn't meet at the other side. The sheer weight of the thing meant that they'd had to reinforce the struts that held it in place after the first set had snapped in three places.

It was terrible in its beauty.

'*This* is how we show them,' King Olav said beside him. '*This* will make them understand. We have used words. We have used actions. But this – this *display* – this is what they'll understand. They will fear the *Long Wyrm*.'

Fear, Finn thought. *That sounds about right.*

The ground underneath King Olav's feet gave him strength, energy and a lift in his step. The West Gate tunnel smelled of cold air and damp stone; it filled him with life. At this moment it was the smell of strength, of full lungs and wind in the sails, and he held on to it. The light at the end was the white of sun through clouds. Through the stone arch lay the support of a thousand men, the mightiest warship ever built and a clear mission to go and spread the Word of the Lord. He pushed away any thought of what might lie in the North and stepped through.

Finn watched the king exit the tunnel. The roar of the men carried over the wall but quickly died down as the king's voice rang out. Finn didn't need to hear the words any more; he knew that song by now, and how it would light a fire in the men's eyes; he knew how they swelled every time they felt King Olav's fervour.

'He's good, isn't he,' Fjolnir said at his side. The carpenter was behind him, scowling beneath thick red eyebrows.

'For God's sake, man,' Finn growled, dagger half out of his belt. 'How are you still alive, the way you sneak up on people?'

Fjolnir just smiled. 'I make noise when I need to,' he said.

'The *Long Wyrm* is a beautiful ship,' Finn said.

'That she is,' Fjolnir said. 'She will take you where you need to go.'

'What do you mean – *you*?' Finn said.

The old man smiled again. It was a lopsided thing, his face, as if his head were permanently cocked in amusement.

A surge of annoyance took Finn, and he had to exhale to stop himself from punching the smirk off the whitebeard's face. 'We're launching – right now.'

'Of course, of course,' Fjolnir said; 'of course we are. You go on ahead now,' he added. 'I just need to go and see to some things.'

Finn looked around, and suddenly the walls in Stenvik felt taller. His chest pulled in so hard that he could feel his heart crash into his ribs.

'The sea,' the old man said next to him, 'the open sea. Can you imagine the delights? The freedom?'

Going down to the ship became the most important thing in Finn's world and he turned and walked at speed towards the West Gate tunnel. 'Don't be late!' he said over his shoulder to the old man. 'You've got very little time.'

'I know,' Fjolnir said. 'I know.'

The cold stone in the tunnel seemed to suck up the sounds from outside and Finn felt like he was underwater. Something pushed him away from Stenvik; there was no going back now. He had to get to the *Long Wyrm*.

The light from outside touched his feet and traced a line up his body – and just like that, he was out and a weight lifted off his chest. The king, standing by the mast of the *Long Wyrm*, was dwarfed by its size. On the beach, two thousand men and more were lined up, at least five deep, captains and crew, all of them staring at the king.

'—and they will be judged!' King Olav concluded triumphantly.

The roar was deafening: every one of those men was raring to go, to get out of their walled prison.

'Men – to your ships!' the king roared, and the group on the beach exploded into focused activity, all except for one crew which remained still on the beach, surrounding the line of logs that led to the water.

The king turned to Finn. 'All yours,' he muttered, a smirk on his face. Moving swiftly, he put a foot down on a strut and leapt over the side and into the *Long Wyrm*, disappearing from sight for a second.

Finn heard some indistinct muttering, but he pushed it out of his mind. Instead, he cleared his throat. '*Right*, you lousy little fuckers!' He had to stop himself from smiling. He'd hand-picked two hundred of the hardest fighters and the strongest rowers from the pool of thousands, and the bulging arms and wide shoulders before him suggested he'd picked right. He'd need them all, too. They'd estimated that the beast weighed nearly three times as much as a regular ship.

'As we rehearsed. First shift left, second shift right!'

On command, the men split into two even groups and lined up on either side of the ship. Finn looked around nervously. Where the hell was Fjolnir? Too late, too late. He could feel King Olav's expectations through the hull of the ship.

'Back supports – off!' he shouted.

Two gruff voices replied, 'Back supports off!' and behind him, wooden struts clattered to the ground.

'Middle supports – off!' More wood fell. He could hear the shouts going up and down the line as the men leaned into the ship, holding her steady, effectively balancing on a plank no more than the width of his hand. These men had all launched ships before – but none that could crush a whole crew if they tipped over. Finn could feel himself sweating despite the cold. 'Front supports – away!' Behind him, the grunting intensified as the men strained together to keep the ship balanced.

Finn drew a deep breath. This would be the most important command he ever gave. 'Now – push!'

A deep-throated growl rose from the throats of two hundred men. Feet dug into the cold ground and the ship inched forward.

'PUSH!'

The growls turned to roars. Another inch. And another.

'*PUSH!*'

The keel of the ship scraped onto the first log and the vibra-tion travelled through the ship, giving power to tired legs. The men were screaming at each other now, cursing up a blue streak, growling like bears, and the ship moved. The next log even rolled a little before the weight of the ship pushed it into the ground, but it was enough to get contact with the next, and the next. The men picked up speed, stepping faster. Muscles bunched and the roar was a continuous thing now, like a giant beast claiming its territory. Faster and faster the *Long Wyrm* went, heading towards the water. As Finn watched, a man lost his footing, but the man next to him delivered a rib-cracking elbow that was hard enough to send the man spinning away from the rush of bodies and the scraping keel. *One way to save a life*, Finn thought.

And then suddenly there were only five logs left, then three – and then the cheer went up as the *Long Wyrm* touched water for the first time and went knifing through the wavelets lapping at the beach, righting herself as the weight settled and the men waded in after, whooping and cheering with that final push.

And then the *Long Wyrm* sat there and Finn understood the sheer *scale* of her. The Stenvik raiding ships next to her looked like a child's toy boats. At the stern stood King Olav, proud as a father, back ramrod-straight, looking back at the town and the men climbing over the sides, his face etched in triumph.

'Well,' Finn muttered to himself. He looked around, but Fjolnir was still nowhere to be seen. Down below, the last of the *Wyrm*'s crew were wading in after the ship and the first of the oars were coming out, holding the massive keel steady just off the shallows. 'At least *I* won't be late.'

The cold water shocked him, but he kept on wading; his big, calloused hands grabbed the freshly treated side and Finn True-heart clambered onto the *Long Wyrm*. Every single person in Stenvik was up on the walls, watching, and every one of them would tell their children and their children's children about this moment, he realised. He was part of history.

'PULL!' King Olav's voice was thick with emotion.

Finn could feel the *whoosh* as the massive sail came up and the cheer that followed them from the shore. The huge black cross on the white linen would be seen from miles away, just what the king had wanted. *Let them see,* he'd said. *Let them see, and think, and wonder how they will be judged.* His eyes had suggested that there would be a remarkably similar outcome to most judgings.

'The king wants to see you,' Einar said at his shoulder and Finn glanced towards the bow where the king stood. He'd turned the moment the sail came up, putting Stenvik firmly behind him.

Even just walking across the ship felt odd. The central gangway was so wide he could have had at least one man on either side without squeezing. On the benches, the men were coming to terms with four-manning the oars, but they were experienced rowers who fell into rhythm soon enough. As he reached King Olav, he looked down to see the prow of the ship slicing through the water, sending a fine spray skywards. The cold caught the droplets and the faint, weak sunlight.

'Einar has told me about the building of the ship,' King Olav said. 'You've done a fantastic job.'

'For the glory of God,' Finn replied.

'I didn't know you had it in you, Finn,' King Olav said. 'When did you learn to build a ship?'

'I – um – it's strange,' he said. 'I walked into a shipwright when

I'd just left the longhouse. His name is Fjolnir. And he had a carpenter with him – stocky sort, with a hammer.'

King Olav turned and looked at Finn askance. 'Einar didn't mention anything about this,' he said.

Finn's words caught in his throat. 'Buh – but – there was a man—'

Suddenly King Olav smiled beatifically and looked at him – *through* him. 'I see. Don't worry, Finn Trueheart. I know what you're trying to do, and I can see what you've done. Hold on to your humility and your true reward will come in heaven.' Contented, the king turned away and looked towards the horizon.

Dazed by the speed and the scale of the ship, Finn had to stop himself from staring at the back of King Olav's head. He waited for any kind of answer or explanation, but the king ignored him in favour of the waves zooming past.

Eventually, all he could do was to walk back towards the mast as behind them, Stenvik turned from a fortress to a tiny dot on the beach.

Einar was waiting for him by the mast. 'The men have said many good things about your leadership, Finn,' the young man said solemnly. 'It is not my place to say, but this ship is a marvel. And you taught us how to build it.'

'But . . .' Finn started, reaching for the old man in his memory, but all he could see was a weather-beaten face with one good eye, winking at him for just a moment. Then visions flooded his head, of digging for the planks, fitting the wood just so, commanding the men, shouting at them, trading insults.

Finn looked up.

High above the massive cross two ravens drifted, looking down on them. When the birds saw him looking, they both cawed.

It sounded a lot like laughter.

THE DALES, WEST SWEDEN
LATE DECEMBER, AD 996

On the border of Svealand, far to the north, Sven cracked his shoulders and winced at the noise as joints popped back to where they used to be too many years ago to count. 'And then he said Odin told him to go to Gallows Peak,' he finished.

Sigurd closed his eyes, sighed and rubbed his temples. The small fire crackled between them as the final thin sticks caught fire. 'Do you believe him?'

'Yes,' Sven said without hesitation. 'He's a good liar, but he's not that good.'

'Trust you to know,' Sigurd said with the ghost of a smirk.

'Hmph,' Sven snorted in mock annoyance.

'But it does suggest that we're doing the right thing,' Sigurd continued.

'It does,' Sven said.

'We'll sleep on it, then chart our course.'

'The mountains?' Sven said.

'Yes.'

Sven looked Sigurd up and down. 'You knew, didn't you?' he said.

'No,' Sigurd said, 'I didn't.' The old chieftain looked into the darkness as if trying to remember something. 'But I suspected we wouldn't get to Trondheim. And who knows?' he added. 'Maybe Gallows Peak will be nice this time of year.'

Sven snorted again. 'As if,' he said, crawling into his blankets under his lean-to. 'Tomorrow?'

'Tomorrow,' Sigurd said, watching as his sworn brother fell asleep as easily as he ever did.

When Sigurd Aegisson finally went to his own tent, the embers were long dead.

The men of Stenvik had taken to living like a herd of particularly stubborn, murderous goats, Audun thought. Men their age shouldn't be able to get through this much cold and wet, but Sigurd Aegisson's warriors just set their shoulders and marched on.

'How are you faring?' Sven said, appearing beside him. The old rogue didn't appear to be in the least bothered by the calf-deep snow; he clutched a sturdy walking stick as he went.

'Good enough,' Audun said. 'Not my favourite thing, the outdoors.'

'Waste of a good smith,' Sven said.

Audun remembered his smithy in Stenvik and had to suppress a sigh. If nothing else, that smelly old hovel had been warm. He couldn't rightly remember any more what being warm and dry felt like. 'Thank you,' he said.

They walked together in companionable silence for a while.

'Shame Thormund decided to go with the kings,' Audun said at last. When the words were out there, he realised that he meant it too. The old horse thief had been a source of life in their camp.

'Hm,' Sven said. 'Thormund didn't decide to stay.'

'Oh?' Audun said.

'No, we told him to.'

'What?' Audun's eyebrows knotted as he tried to work out what Sven meant. 'Why?'

'Because Jolawer Scot is in danger. Alfgeir Bjorne looks after the king and Thormund watches over Alfgeir,' Sven said. 'I'll be a son of a mongrel bitch if Forkbeard doesn't try to get to the old bear at least once. If they try to out-sneak Thormund and succeed, they can have as much of the South as they can hold. But rest assured, we will make it difficult for them.' The old rogue's jaw was set in determination but his eyes sparkled with mischief.

'I see,' Audun said.

'My namesake with the fancy beard always has a plan, the bastard,' Sven said. 'And since we can't be there to piss in his porridge we'll do it from afar.'

Audun couldn't help but smile. Sven's chatter was excellent for helping the time pass. 'So which way are we going?'

'Straight to Gallows Peak,' Sven said.

The muscles in Audun's throat froze up and his heart leapt in his chest. He twisted to look at Sven, who was suddenly nowhere near as cheerful.

Instead, the old man looked intently at Audun, studying every muscle in his face. 'He came to you too, didn't he?' Sven said quietly.

Audun's veins pulsed and he fought to hold back the waves of fury. Words would not come out, so he nodded.

'Ulfar tried to persuade us to go, but the boy can't lie to people he likes when it matters, which is a good thing. I squeezed him and he told me.'

'He says we have to. Valgard's power is growing.'

Sven shrugged. 'You're no weakling yourself,' he said. 'I'm worried, though,' he added, shooting a conspiratorial glance forward. 'Sigurd said he might run away because he was scared.'

Audun couldn't stop his eyebrows from rising. 'Really?'

Sven nodded. 'It's the truth. I swear it – no, I can't do this any more,' he said, smirking. 'Of course it fucking isn't. Most rocks have more give in them than Sigurd Aegisson. We're going to Gallows Peak and when we get there we'll most likely be cold, wet and hungry, and I don't think we'll be in any mood to show our nicest side to whatever's there. Now keep walking and stop all this chatter. It wastes your energy.'

With that, Sven stomped off towards the head of the line.

Audun watched him go, wondering exactly *what* was in store for them at Gallows Peak.

Days passed, snow fell and around them the country changed: the trees grew longer and thinner and the hills rose higher, their slopes steeper. The weather changed, too. The grey clouds drifted away and for two days the sun shone, but not enough to warm the air.

Finally, mid-morning on the fourth day after the decision, Sven and Sigurd stopped on the crest of a hill.

'There they are,' Sigurd said after a while.

'Can't hide anything from you,' Sven replied.

'You know what?' Sigurd said, and when Sven shrugged and grunted, he said, 'I've never actually seen them.'

'Well, now you have,' Sven said.

Behind them, the line of men trudged up the hill and, as one, the men all came to an abrupt halt. A soft wave of murmured curses followed the chieftains' conversation.

At the far end of the line, Audun elbowed Ulfar gently.

'Wake up.'

'Whuh—?' Ulfar mumbled, head down and feet still moving.

'Look,' Audun whispered.

Ulfar looked up and blinked. Then he squeezed his eyes shut, blinked again and stared. 'Oh . . . crap,' he said.

In the distance the world rose *up* in a jagged edge that reached up to the sky like the fangs of a silent, screaming beast.

'Gallows Peak,' Audun muttered. 'It's massive.'

Ulfar gazed at the mountains, transfixed. The range stretched away from them in both directions for as far as the eye could see. A frozen river snaked out of the hills and disappeared into the encroaching forest, but closer to the slopes the trees thinned out.

'That's the Peak!' Sven shouted, voice loud in the still air. 'That's where we're going!'

No one replied. They just stared.

'We're here to do a job,' Sigurd said. 'We'll do it over there.' He pointed towards the mountains. 'It may be the worst pile of shit I've ever walked into, and that's saying quite a lot. This is your last chance to turn away.' The chieftain of Stenvik surveyed his men for the last time before he started picking his way down the hill.

Ulfar looked at the warriors around them as they set off again, stumbling through the snow with faces set in grim determination. Not a single one of them had even contemplated the thought of turning back. 'If Valgard's there we'll give him a hard time,' he said.

'And if he's not?' Audun said.

'Let's not think about that just yet,' Ulfar said, feeling for the next step in the snow. 'Let's just hope we're on a path to glory.'

'The path to glory is wet and cold,' Audun muttered as he followed in Ulfar's footsteps for the front of the line.

In the distance, Gallows Peak itself looked like the rocks had been ripped out of the ground by an angry god. Lesser mountains, gorges, hills and valleys spilled off it like ripples in the land.

'No wonder no one goes here,' Ulfar said. 'It's not a kind country.'

'The mountain men I've met are neither soft nor fat,' Sigurd agreed. 'Tough bastards, though.'

'True,' Sven said.

The path they'd chosen led through a valley, following the bank of a solidly frozen river. About fifty yards on either side the treeline started, thickening as it reached the foot of the hills maybe two hundred yards further away. The thick cover of the trees sloped sharply away on both sides, which meant the ridges disappeared from view. It was easy going, giving cover from the worst of the wind and leading them straight towards the base of the mountain range.

But when they were a good five hundred yards in, Sigurd reached slowly over his shoulder and unhooked the big axe. 'Something's wrong,' he said, turning back and looking towards the end of the line.

Sven turned too, and looked at the single file behind them, stretching back almost as far as he could see. 'Shit,' he said, turning on the spot to follow Sigurd. 'Go back,' he said to the man behind him. 'Blades.'

Blood thumped in Ulfar's ears. The forest around him suddenly felt full of hidden, silent threats, but he still couldn't find anything that might suggest what Sigurd had spotted. Ahead of him a wave of movement swept down the line and within moments every man was holding a weapon of some sort. Sigurd led the line that was quickly doubling back on itself, delivering a steady stream of commands in a quiet voice as he passed each fighter. When they were halfway down Ulfar saw that Audun's rearguard had closed the gap.

'What's going on?' the smith said when they met.

'I don't know. Sigurd's got a gut feeling. I've not seen or heard anything.'

'Birds,' Audun said, his voice dark. 'There are no birds – forest like this, there should be at least a handful of little bite-sized ones, but there's nothing here.'

Ulfar sighed and looked to the skies. 'Fine. We get it. Just, you know. Bring it on and get it over with.'

Almost like a reply the first branch rustled somewhere above their heads and to the left, then the second – and the third and soon the whisper in the trees was everywhere, punctuated only by the sharp snapping of twigs.

'SHIELD-WALL!' Sven shouted. 'THEY'RE ON THE RIDGES!'

The men of Stenvik moved together, forming two lines of twenty men standing back to back, their shields together in the middle of the path, fifteen yards from the treeline. Behind the shield-bearers there were blade-carriers, lined up and ready to punch through the wall.

Heart hammering in his chest, Ulfar took up a place behind two of the heavier greybeards, his own sword at the ready. One of them looked at him and winked. 'We'll hold 'em, you stick 'em,' he said.

Ulfar smiled weakly in return and wished he could find his courage somewhere.

'There,' someone snapped, pointing at the trees as snow cascaded down, rising back up in a puff of white where the enemy passed. 'They're coming down the hillside.'

'HOLD YOUR GROUND,' Sven barked. 'WE'LL GIVE 'EM A RUN-UP – IT'S ONLY FAIR!'

This brought chuckles from the men.

'STENVIK!' one of them cried and 'STENVIK!' the cry came back. When the noise died down Ulfar listened for the battle-cry of their opponents, but there was nothing to hear, just that damned rustling. The treeline suddenly felt awfully close.

'How many do you estimate?' Ulfar whispered to Sven, who was moving about between the two lines like a house builder, filling the cracks.

'Enough of 'em,' Sven snapped back. 'Quit your counting, boy. It's a bad habit. There'll be fewer if you kill some. We'll stick 'em and make them bl . . .' The old rogue's voice trailed off and Ulfar followed his gaze over the heads of the shield-bearers to the treeline thirty yards away.

The creature that walked out of the woods was at least seven and a half feet tall. The clothes of a normal-sized man hung in shreds on its bulky body, exposing blue-tinted skin. Long, muscular arms hung down by its sides and one massive hand clutched a club as thick as a man's thigh.

'You told me the mountain men were rough, but I didn't expect that,' Ulfar said.

'That's not a man any more,' Sven said quietly, without taking his eyes off the enemy. 'That's a troll.'

Just as he'd said it another five trolls emerged from the forest. They watched as their leader pointed straight at the shield-wall and without any more warning the huge blue-skin sprinted towards them, his club raised. After a moment's shock he was met by the raised shields and battle roars of the men of Stenvik, who waited with spears poised until they could smell him. Then, like the fingers on a deadly hand moving all together, five thick spears launched, flew and sank into the troll's torso with force.

The spears didn't even slow it down. The warrior in the centre of the shield-wall disappeared in a fine mist of blood as the troll's club came down on him, smashing through to the ground.

The giant blue-skin bellowed, grabbed the spears impaling it in a meaty fist and ripped them out of its chest.

'DROP SHIELDS AND KEEP MOVING!' Sigurd screamed. 'DROP SHIELDS!! MOVE!!'

But the trolls were upon them, and in an instant Ulfar's world turned to screams, blood and chaos. He caught only a glimpse of Audun, fumbling to pull something out of his bag, before he was shouldered out of the way just as a massive troll club swept past at head-height, fast enough to smash through everything in its path.

'Move!' Sven hissed in his ear before darting away again. Something fizzled at the back of his brain, a small spark of lightning; a familiar voice spoke to him and he *saw*. The trolls had a rhythm to them: swing, pull back; swing, pull back. All he had to do was move with the rhythm, and—

Like a dancer, Ulfar tiptoed backwards in the snow out of the arc of another troll's club. All around him the Stenvik men had broken their lines and were goading the trolls into individual stand-offs, ten men or more to each troll. Sprawled bodies lay all about but none of the blue giants were down yet.

Ulfar stepped into the reach of the troll he was facing and his blade darted out past the big beast's knee.

'Aim for the heart!' the warrior next to him screamed.

'No,' Ulfar hissed between gritted teeth as he slapped the edge up against the troll's calf muscle and pulled for all he was worth. The edge of the blade sliced into the hard meat and the tension did the rest. When the troll pushed off to prepare for the next swing, the muscle split and the big creature sank down on one knee.

'Down you go,' Ulfar snarled, and that almost cost him his life as the club came barrelling past at rib-height on the backswing.

'CUT THEM!' he screamed as the men of Stenvik fell on the crippled troll. 'SLICE THEIR LEGS!'

'WOLVES!' Sven screamed back.

Through the chaos of fighters Ulfar could just about see in the distance grey, four-legged shapes running down the hill towards them. 'Oh, so that's how you want it to be?' he snarled, wiping the blade on his tunic.

A roar went up to his right and Ulfar glanced towards the source of the sound just in time to see a thick-bodied troll *break* and disappear behind Stenvik fighters. There was the sound of dull thuds. Oddly, the hardened Viking warriors all appeared to be inching away. Then the sight-line cleared and Audun rose from the pile of meat and bones that had been a blue-skinned monster just moments ago, holding his hammers and wearing a big belt that Ulfar didn't recognise.

The smith glanced at him and flashed a lightning smile.

'TO ME!' Ulfar shouted, wading through the snow to meet the wolves.

Behind him, Sigurd cried 'STENVIK!' and a deep-throated roar followed.

Ulfar glanced back quickly: more trolls were down. Twenty or so warriors of Stenvik followed him to meet their new foes: slavering beasts on four legs with murder in their eyes.

Audun charged through the snow ahead of them, looking like a man among boys. 'COME ON!' he roared.

Ulfar's war-grin froze.

There was more movement behind the wolves: men, moving swiftly – ten, twenty – no, more. It was getting harder to see snow among the trees.

The wolves reached the hard-packed snow out in the open and sped up, launching themselves at the warriors in a blind fury. Reacting before he could think, Ulfar struck with his blade, slicing into dirt- and blood-caked fur. A quick side-step got him away from the reach of snarling teeth, but the wolf was fast too, spinning around the moment it landed, and pain exploded in his calf as jaws locked down on the muscle. Screaming in pain, Ulfar twisted, slicing downwards with a blow that would have felled any normal animal, but the madness in the beast's eyes only intensified. A dark shape zoomed into Ulfar's field of vision and smashed into the wolf's head, inches away from Ulfar's kneecap. A hammer. The grip on his calf slackened immediately as the animal went still. Ten yards away, Audun nodded at him, then turned and set about with his remaining hammer.

Suddenly alone in the middle of the battle, Ulfar had a moment to look around. The biggest of the trolls was still standing, surrounded by Sigurd, Sven and a handful of Stenvik fighters. Battles between man and wolf raged all around the clearing, while Audun charged through the fray, freeing wolves from their curse through the medium of a hammer to the brain, but he couldn't be everywhere and far too many Stenvik fighters were already lying unmoving, face-down in the snow. There was movement everywhere on the hillside now, shades of man and wolf among the trees.

'FALL BACK TO SIGURD!' Ulfar screamed. 'GATHER UP!'

'ULFAR!' Sven shouted at the top of his voice.

That half-turn of the head saved most of Ulfar's face.

The wolf's jaws bore down on the side of his head – scalp, ear and eye – as the beast in mid-leap collided with him. He staggered under the hot breath, the smell and the fury of the growl, and Ulfar heard himself howl to match the wolf's madness as he felt the meat of his cheek tearing away. His arm felt like someone else's as it twisted to get the point of his sword under the animal's rib-cage and drove it up, hard, through the heart and into the brain, and immediately the animal was dead weight on him, the teeth scraping down his face, peeling off what it hadn't got already. Hot blood streamed down to his neck, thickening fast in the cold air. The noises of battle flowed back to him through the numbing pain and he staggered towards Sven, Sigurd and the troll. 'FALL BACK!' he screamed, but all that came out was a hoarse whisper.

Half the world was black. Bodies appeared around him out of nowhere: friends.

Strong arms dragged him through the snow, towards the small

knot of Stenvik men in the middle. As he slid to the ground in a safe spot, Ulfar saw Audun charge ahead of the warriors and into the group surrounding the big troll. Time slowed as the blacksmith pushed past the blades and hurled himself straight at the blue-skin; he threw his arms open and enveloped the troll's thick midsection in a bear-hug.

The big troll got two bone-crunching blows in on Audun's back before its spine broke. Moments later Stenvik blades made quick work of ensuring it stayed down.

Cold on the wound: snow.

'How are you holding up, son?'

'Fucking fine,' Ulfar wheezed. 'There's more coming. How many dead?'

'Too many,' Sigurd growled.

Ulfar saw some and sensed others; it looked like they'd lost nearly one man in four. There was an odd noise . . . retching? A cold memory settled in Ulfar's spine and he rose up on his elbow, searching.

A couple of yards away Audun was doubled over, coughing up bile and blood, clawing at the belt, which looked to be strapped very tight around his middle.

'Sometimes,' Sven said between gritted teeth, 'sometimes I *really* hate my life.'

Tearing his eye off Audun, Ulfar tried to find what Sven was looking at.

Rough-looking fighters, at least two hundred of them, had formed up in wide lines on both sides of the survivors. Wolves stood by their side, their yellow eyes trained on Sigurd's men.

A gap formed in the lines.

Another ten trolls stepped in on either side.

KATTEGAT, DENMARK
LATE DECEMBER, AD 996

The cold night air stung King Olav's face and tingled in his nostrils. They'd left the smell of salt along with most of their ships out at sea and reefed their sails halfway up the river. He turned and looked back at the body of the *Long Wyrm*. Half of his crew were manning the oars, pulling softly and almost silently. It was hard work, but the heavy ship had kept its momentum well. The rest of the men crouched in the shadows of the *Wyrm* as it glided upriver, black among the snow-covered trees. He watched the big warriors as they grinned to each other, adjusted their straps and holds, checked their mail shirts and helmets, tested their weapons.

It was the ship he'd been on his whole life, raiding the coast of Britain, praying to the old gods: this was his past and his present at once. *But this time it's different,* he thought. *This time it's for a worthy cause.*

As squat house-shapes appeared up ahead, ugly and dark against the new-fallen snow, a familiar shape approached through the shadows and Finn touched his arm and in a low voice asked, 'Do you want us to take the riverbank here?'

'Yes,' King Olav replied. 'We'll hit it first: ten ships behind us; the others go past the village and beach there.'

Finn nodded and walked towards the man at the rudder, stepping nimbly in the dark, and moments later the king could feel the ship shift in the water, leaning in towards the bank on the left. At a softly whistled command from the captain the oars on the left hand side rose from the water.

After the gentle sweep up the river, the landing was quick. The *Long Wyrm* crushed branches and flattened the mud bank with its weight as thirty warriors leapt over the side and ran towards the first of the huts. Behind them the ten designated longboats unloaded their deadly cargo, one by one, and the other half of the raiding force sailed past the village to do the same from the other side.

King Olav Tryggvason ran at the front, Finn on his right, blood thumping in his ears. It had happened only moments ago, but for some reason he couldn't remember the leap from the bow; all he could recall were times long past, and another man with the same face, rejoicing in the speed and the power of his body. He looked ahead and took aim at a house close to the centre. In the distance, a wolf howled and a thrill went through him. Here he was, at the head of his own pack, about to make the heathens pay for their sins. He knew that once he'd gone in, with Finn at his back, his men would pick their own houses to attack. The inhabitants of this sad, nameless town would never know what'd hit them, and their false gods would be nowhere near to protect them. Somewhere inside King Olav, fury unravelled and everything came together to light his inner fire: the events of Trondheim, the scheming jarls, the meeting in the forest . . .

When he got to the door, he kicked it so hard it flew off the hinges.

The other men got back to the *Long Wyrm* eventually, flaring torches illuminating teeth flashing in bearded grins.

King Olav searched out Finn in the crowd and beckoned him over. 'What did we get?'

'Not much,' Finn said. 'A handful of silver. A couple of useable swords, axes and spears. Some furs.'

'Good,' King Olav said.

'Yes,' Finn muttered.

The king's anger flared again. 'Do you have something you wish to say, Finn?' he snapped.

'I . . . saw the men.' King Olav didn't reply so the big warrior continued, 'I saw the men take what they wanted. They struck down unarmed villagers – peasants. And they . . . some of them . . . they took women and hurt them,' he continued.

'These are Svear,' King Olav snapped, 'and mixed-blood Danes. They worship *false gods* – they deserve no better! This is the will of Christ. We are on the path, and anything that stands in our way must be eliminated. Do you understand?'

Face half in shadow, Finn made no sound.

'Do. You. Understand?'

'Yes,' Finn said, almost inaudibly.

'Good,' the king said, turning away. 'Get the men on the boats. Let's leave this place and go and bring the word of the Lord to somewhere else.' With that King Olav stepped back and disappeared into the darkness beneath the carved bow.

The waves hissed at the side of the ship, powerless to stop it. Under wind, the *Long Wyrm* was a real sight to behold: the mast creaked with the force of the sail pulling them forward, and Finn had to be vigilant at all times to make sure they didn't outpace the rest of their fleet. In the distance he could make out the stocky frame of Gunnar, captaining the *Njordur's Mercy*. No mean ship itself, yet the lean raider still had no chance of keeping up with the *Long Wyrm* at speed. *This is a ship that could cross oceans*, Finn thought, *and battle with the gods themselves*. Not for the first time, he thought back on the old shipwright, though try as he might, he couldn't quite see him in his mind; there was just a vague sense of someone who had been there, teaching and directing – but none of the men remembered anything about him. There was just this feeling of *belonging*, of doing something right . . .

'We're almost there.' Einar's voice brought Finn back to the ship, back to the water. The young man had just appeared next to him and was now calmly nocking his bow.

Unlike their previous target, this village was big, a local trading centre, according to one of Gunnar's men. At least thirty houses sprawled along the coast and up the hillside, organised loosely around what looked like a central market square. This time they didn't have the cover of night and in the distance they could see the villagers running back and forth, half of them forming into a group of sorts and the other half disappearing up into the hills.

'Women and children,' Einar said, still not looking. 'We'll have a fight here.'

Around them, the men were readying for battle. Young, strong warriors pulled on leather-padded shifts that offered a good range of movement; older warriors who had survived a few fights went without fail for the discomfort and weight of chainmail shirts.

Finn almost jumped as Einar's bow sang next to him. 'What'd you do that for?' he said, but Einar didn't answer; he just calmly nocked another arrow. Finn looked around, trying to spot the first shaft, but he couldn't see it. The bow sang again just as the group of peasants in the distance scattered; in the middle, one of them dropped to the ground like a sack of potatoes.

After a third shot, Einar put his bow back down. 'That should give them something to worry about,' he said, voice level.

'SAILS!' The command went up from the captain and behind Finn and Einar teams of strong-armed sailors pulled on the thick ropes, slowly raising the lower beam. The sail flapped and snapped in the wind, but the tension went out of it very quickly.

'OARS UP!'

Two hundred and fifty yards away the peasants had gathered back into a group positively bristling with pitchforks, spears and other makeshift weapons. Einar sent an arrow flying their way, but this time they were ready; a shout went out and the group dispersed, reforming as soon as they thought it safe.

Two hundred yards.

The *Long Wyrm* still had quite a lot of momentum.

'OARS DOWN!' the captain shouted, and, 'HOLD!'

Sixty pairs of muscular forearms strained against the pull as the blades went down into the water and pushed against the waves, turning the *Long Wyrm* from sleek serpent to bristling hedgehog.

One hundred and fifty yards.

Far behind them, another fifteen ships pulled level and headed towards the shore. Flames burst into life amongst the defenders as torches were lit, unnaturally bright in the sunshine.

A hundred yards.

Ninety.

Eighty.

Finn felt the keel shift under him as the *Long Wyrm* leaned to port and headed away from the village's makeshift pier, leaving the defenders wrong-footed, looking flustered by the change.

Fifty.

Einar's bow sang three more times, and on shore, three men more dropped dead. Spurred into action, the peasants ran towards the place where the *Long Wyrm* would have to land. The ground split underneath the sheer weight as King Olav's flagship ran aground and a host of screaming warriors leapt ashore and met the defenders head-on.

The Svear fought like cornered animals, but they were no match for the king and his men. Olav was moving among them, deflecting blows off his shield, shattering faces with powerful swings of his sword, until soon even the battle-crazed Svear were falling over themselves to retreat away from the bloodthirsty man with the crown.

By the time Gunnar's ship was close enough for shouting, the battle was over. Six villagers knelt in the middle of a ring of bloodied warriors. The gentle sound of the water mixed with the moans of the dying.

King Olav could still taste the blood-lust in his mouth. His arm hurt where one lucky farmer had got in a solid blow with a cudgel and his right hand ached from clutching the hilt of his sword, but there was none of the rage left in him. He just wanted to get back onboard the *Wyrm* and be away.

'What do you want us to do?' Finn said.

King Olav looked at him. 'You? Get aboard the *Long Wyrm* and prepare for departure. But first, send Gunnar over.'

The big warrior walked off without a word. A short while later, Gunnar approached.

King Olav looked him in the eyes. 'Send a message,' he said. 'Loot and burn the village.'

'What about them?' Gunnar said, glancing at the villagers in the circle.

King Olav shrugged. 'We will do unto others as they intended to do unto us,' he said, looking to the skies. 'And leave the selection to the Lord.'

With Gunnar at his shoulder, King Olav stepped into the ring and reached for the hilt of his sword.

'PULL, YOU BASTARDS!' Finn roared at the rowers. Even with twice thirty men under oars, the going was slow when the wind died down. The best path to Rus lay through the Sound, through a cluster of islands as close to the coast of Svealand as it was to Danemark, but they found out soon enough that no one had ever tried to take a ship like the *Wyrm* through. The moment they were within shouting distance of land the wind died down and suddenly the weight and the stability were working against them.

'I SAID PULL!' Finn screamed, but it was all for nothing. By the time they were close enough to count the branches on the first island they had slowed down to a crawl. Their fleet had overtaken them, ship by ship, and Finn was pretty certain he'd seen the rowers on the other raiding boats give it an extra bit of power just to make sure the *Long Wyrm* was humbled. Some of them had even had the nerve to shout insults at them, calling them fat nursemaids out for a swim and all manner of other, less complimentary terms.

Behind them, the strait seemed to narrow as soon as they were in. Thick woodland covered the sightlines and Finn felt his chest tighten. It reminded him all too much of the tunnel under the wall in Stenvik.

Einar Tambarskelf vaulted up from his bench to loud curses from his oar-mate. 'To arms!' he shouted.

Finn shot a quick glance behind them. They were the last ship in the fleet and there was no threat whatsoever behind them. The next ship was three hundred yards ahead.

'SILENCE!' King Olav roared. 'Sit DOWN!'

Einar froze. 'My King, we must get free of this place!' he shouted. Up ahead someone shouted back, but the words got lost.

'Sit. Down,' King Olav snarled from the other end of the ship. 'And everyone else.'

There was no mistaking it this time: another shout from the front, and then screams.

The first sleek raiding ship slid out from an almost entirely tree-covered bay two hundred yards up ahead to their left, silent and purposeful, and quickly followed by another – and another. As three more joined it from the right Finn swivelled and looked behind them to see a row of ships, at least ten wide, had suddenly appeared, some five hundred yards off their stern, blocking the exit.

In between the trees on both sides, shadows moved. Shadows with blades.

They were trapped.

'ROW, YOU BASTARDS,' King Olav screamed, 'as hard as you can! Give me speed! Hit their line!'

Up ahead, past the line of enemy ships, they could hear the first, sharp noises of metal on metal skipping across the sea like flat stones on a lake. The ships in front of them were crawling with activity and Finn noted with a heavy feeling in his stomach that ropes were flying across, being thrown fast and hard by experienced hands. Whoever had them trapped knew their work.

The first thing they heard was a single word.

'HEAVE!'

The enemy ships *shifted* to the side as many strong hands pulled them close together.

'Einar!' King Olav shouted.

The young man was up like a flash, bow in hand. He moved so fast that he tripped on the bench and stumbled – and just avoided an arrow that flew past him at head-height and buried itself deep in the mast.

A tall man in white stood at the front of the middle boat, holding an impressive-looking longbow. Without any sort of urgency, he nocked another arrow.

And just like that, the spell was broken. 'COVER!' King Olav shouted, and as quick hands grabbed the side-mounted shields one man caught the second arrow in his shield. The man next to him struggled and spasmed silently as the third took him in the throat. He rose and toppled over the side.

An arrow whistled past Finn's head, missing by inches.

'Finn! Up front!' King Olav shouted, and pointed to where a handful of men led by Einar Tambarskelf had started firing back. They were crouching behind shield-carriers at the bow, and by the time Finn got there the king had shifted the two rowers on the front benches and was busy hacking at the benches with an axe.

'What do you want, my Lord?' Finn asked.

'Quickly – hack the benches! First three pairs.'

'Why?'

The king's head snapped to the side. 'Just *DO IT*,' he growled. 'Now.' He craned his neck to look back at the rowers. 'FASTER, YOU BASTARDS! WE *HAVE* TO PUSH THROUGH! DO IT FOR OUR LORD!'

Finn dropped to his knees behind the cover of the shields and started working to break the benches free of their bases while the king was issuing orders, all the while pointing and shouting. One man rose to run back towards the mast and immediately hurtled forward, pushed by an arrow punching into his spine.

'OVERBOARD!' King Olav shouted and three men immediately leapt towards the fallen man, dragged him to the side and tipped him over.

'Faster with the benches or we're all dead!' he cried, and Finn glanced up: over the edge of the shields he could now see the masts of the other ships. A scream went up from the stern; a screaming rower clutched his shoulder where the arrow had sunk deep into muscle and bone. Finn redoubled his efforts, and smiled when the wood finally gave way and the bench came loose. He yanked it out and thrust it into the waiting hands of the rower waiting there, crouched by his side, ready to shift the planks. Up ahead, the king was bent over some kind of construction, pulling on a rope.

The noise of battle was doubling and redoubling as raw-throated screams melded together with the echo of breaking timber and the clash of steel on steel.

'Don't stop!' King Olav shouted, 'More! ROW FASTER!' Then, grunting, he lifted the thing he'd been bent over: he'd lashed the benches together to form the biggest shield Finn had ever seen. It was almost five feet high and the moment it rose, three arrows thudded into it.

'We need another!' King Olav roared and Finn glanced to the side as the forests glided past, then looked up ahead. They were no more than eighty yards from the line of ships, and now he could make out individual fighters. The man in white was there, as was a big, broad-shouldered man next to him, and next to him in turn was a beanpole of a man.

'QUICKLY!' King Olav screamed, his own knife flashing as he cut rope and tied planks.

Hidden behind the big shield, Finn and another four rowers hacked away at the next set of benches. He didn't see the signal from their enemies, but he heard it: the first clang of hilt on shield boss, spreading out like a wave, growing and swelling until it was almost unbearable.

'Fall back!' the king growled as he finished roping up the final plank. Then, hefting it, he took a couple of experimental steps backwards. 'Shield-wall!'

The press of heavy bodies created a solid wall across the *Long Wyrm*, just ahead of the mast. Behind them, the rowers still pulled.

Thirty yards.

Finn finally stood up, his knees creaking and back aching, and looked across the ever-decreasing gap to the ships ahead of them, which had been lashed together and beams placed across their bows to form a solid fighting platform. The men on it were in constant movement; arms, blades, wild eyes, bared teeth.

There was one point of stillness: a man of average build, clear-eyed and calm, surveying the scene that was unfolding before him. Thick beard, woven into two braids.

As Finn watched, the man drew a deep breath and shouted, 'SPEARS!'

Mouthpiece held onto the mast as hard as he could. Forkbeard had split their force in three, setting Jolawer to command the vanguard and Erik to run the rearguard. How he'd ended up on Karle's boat he could not fathom; that had to be his bad luck. They had been hunkered down, silent as the night, since the news had travelled south: King Olav was burning villages as he went towards Rus. The instructions had come down days before: they'd form a line that would cut King Olav off from his fleet, which would be engaged by Jolawer up front. Following Forkbeard's commands, the men had loaded ropes, hewn down trees a hundred yards or more from the coastline and prepared to close the trap, waiting for just the right moment.

When they'd seen the Norse fleet a shiver of excitement had run through them. This was it: this was going to be the biggest sea battle in anyone's memory.

Being part of history did not make Mouthpiece happy at all, he was discovering. The two spear-throwers next to him suddenly rose, clutching their thick, fire-hardened missiles, as Forkbeard's voice rang out.

'SPEARS!' he cried, and a path cleared through the throng as the throwers ran to the bow and launched their missiles towards the *Long Wyrm*.

Forkbeard's ships looked like toys next to that bloody thing. *It's too big*, Mouthpiece thought. His insides suddenly felt like cold water. It would crush them. Someone yelled at him to move and pushed him into the mast and the pain shook him out of his bemused state. Mouthpiece stepped gingerly away from the safety of the thick timber.

'HOLD ON!' someone screamed, and moments later his world juddered and shook as the *Long Wyrm* crashed into the ship in the centre. The whole of Forkbeard's fleet shifted with the impact and Mouthpiece watched as a wave of men lost their footing, tumbling over in a flurry of limbs. The momentum of the big ship carried it halfway through the line, but there it ground to a halt, timbers groaning against timbers. Someone screamed on the *Long Wyrm*; halfway down the ship they'd raised *huge* shields bristling with all manner of blades, shielding the rowers who were furiously trying to push the ship through Forkbeard's cordon.

Screaming filled Mouthpiece's ears and it took him a moment to realise that it was his voice. On the inside he felt calm, but on the outside he was finding his feet on the rocking ships, leaping from his own boat to the next, shouting words that meant little to him. He vaulted over the edge of the *Long Wyrm* and found himself beside Alfgeir Bjorne. The big warrior took one look at him, nudged him hard in the ribs with his elbow, then raised his shield and advanced towards the mast of the huge ship, which was too large for Mouthpiece to fathom. The stumps standing up where the benches had been hacked off looked like broken bones and the sides groaned where the Wyrm was locked in a death-dance with the ships around it, but it was truly majestic: a ship fit for a king.

Mouthpiece squeezed in between Alfgeir and his handful of men as they advanced on the shield-wall, quickly closing the distance. He was rapidly losing his urge to fight.

There was a moment where no one made a move.

Then a spear shot out from the side of one of the shields and retreated just as quickly. Alfgeir Bjorne roared, took a quick step forward and gave the shield closest to him a swift – and very hard – kick with his heel. The men behind the shields shouted back and that was it: battle was joined.

Next to Mouthpiece the press suddenly softened as the man on his left slumped down, silently coughing up black blood. Fear washed over him then and he started laying about him with his cudgel, slapping away swords and spears as they swung towards him, all the while squeezing his eyes shut and screaming as he smashed away at the shields, putting all he had into each blow.

Steel clashed against steel just next to his ear, and Mouthpiece opened his eyes in shock just as he saw Alfgeir Bjorne's axe swoop past his head and a broken spear-head skitter to the deck at his feet.

'Keep your fucking eyes open,' the big warrior grunted.

Behind them a commotion rose over even the battle noises. Mouthpiece hesitated for only a moment, but his nose and mouth exploded in pain and he stumbled backwards, hitting a rower's bench with the back of his leg. His feet lost touch with the deck and for a moment everything was spinning upside down.

Then there was nothing but black.

Finn adjusted the shield. Getting smashed in the mouth was the least that annoying little shit with the cudgel deserved.

'Gunnar is coming! He's falling on Forkbeard's back!' King Olav shouted, and the men in the shield-wall pushed harder. They had downed two and it was going well on Finn's side but King Olav's men were struggling with a grizzled old bear of a man who was laying about him with a hand-axe and a shield.

'Hold this,' Finn growled at the man next to him and yanked the man's arm into the shield-strap. Then he pushed to the side and grabbed an oar. Lifting it like a giant club, Finn found the balance of the thing and raised it high enough to clear the shield. He slammed it down towards the big fighter, but the man's shield came up just in time to deflect the oar. He was a wily old greybeard; he didn't leave the opening Finn had hoped for but instead responded to the challenge by deftly taking two steps backwards, moving out of blade range.

'Die, you bastard!' Finn roared.

The man looked up at him and grinned. 'Make me!'

Blades flashed on King Olav's side and two of the man's comrades fell, leaving the big warrior the only one of the attackers left standing.

Finn grabbed a shield, drew his sword and pushed past the shield-wall. He bashed the hilt into the boss once for luck, then charged at the big man.

'I am Alfgeir Bjorne, son of Asvald, son of Eyvind,' the warrior growled at him. 'And it will be my pleasure to kill you.'

'In the eyes of the lord you will be weighed,' Finn said, stepping in and sweeping the blade upwards in a powerful swing. The scrape as the old man just managed to get his shield in was music to his ears.

Alfgeir kept his balance and stepped backwards over a bench, but Finn pressed the attack. 'You will be measured!' Voice rising, he hacked downwards with a most satisfying vibration as his sword smashed into the shield. His shield arm was up and ready to push through with a straight left, but the old man's shoulder wasn't there any more. Instead, Finn found himself having to pull his own leg backwards to avoid a murderous axe blow coming in at groin height. 'And you will be found wanting!' Finn bellowed now, sweeping his sword downwards. He caught Alfgeir's axe on the blade and swept it to the right.

The old man looked him straight in the eyes and grinned. 'Is that what the king whispers to you at night?' he said. Then the shield blocked out Finn's vision and a sharp pain pierced his right cheek. A red haze coloured his eye as, stumbling backwards, he sensed more than saw Alfgeir close in for the kill.

But then the old man stopped in his tracks, strong arms grabbed Finn's shoulders and under his arms and he felt himself pulled in behind the shield-wall just as Alfgeir Bjorne collapsed onto the deck, three arrows sunk deep in his broad back.

Standing in the stern of a ship maybe eighty yards away, the man in white nocked another arrow. Next to him, Forkbeard turned away and looked towards their stern.

A sudden quiet settled over Finn's end of the *Long Wyrm*. His forehead throbbed something horrible and he could feel the blood running down his cheek and into his beard, clotting and pulling at the skin.

'Einar! Get rid of their archer!' King Olav shouted.

'He's gone,' Einar said. 'He walked off to the other end.'

'Put down the shields and lose the dead weight!' the king shouted, and a handful of men darted past the dropped shields and grabbed bodies.

Finn just heard the splashes as the corpses dropped overboard, then he heard Einar Tambarskelf's bow, singing just above him.

'Turn around!' the young man shouted.

'Oh for the sake of all that's holy,' King Olav muttered. 'Rowers – to arms! Pass the shields down to the stern!'

Finn staggered to his feet and tried to make sense of what was happening. There were ships all around their stern. He shook his head to clear the fog of pain and regretted it immediately.

The *Long Wyrm* was rocking as screaming fighters leaped across the cold seas and landed on their deck. Foremost of them was a tall, fierce warrior, swinging his double-bladed battleaxe freely. Anywhere he moved, men collapsed.

'FINN!' King Olav shouted and Finn turned, squeezed his one good eye shut and opened it again to see a force slowly advancing from the bow. At the fore was a skinny man at least a head taller than the others who was wielding an oversized shield and the longest spear Finn had ever seen. One of Einar's arrows caught the man next to him in the shoulder; the injured man was quickly pulled out of the front line and another immediately took his place. 'Einar! Take him out!' The sound of snapping wood was painful and sharp. 'What was that?' King Olav shouted.

'The sound of Norway, breaking in your hands,' Einar said, his voice leaden. Finn glanced at the young archer. Arms at his side, bow by his feet. No tension to the string. Two halves to the bow.

King Olav turned to Finn. The king suddenly looked older, as if a flame within him had gone out. 'They will kill us if they catch us, Finn,' he said. 'If we go, there is a chance our men will lay down their weapons and be spared.'

Finn tried, but the words wouldn't come.

'Surrender.' The voice was clear and carried remarkably well across the swell of the sea, the cracking of the timbers and the sounds of pain coming from the stern. Forkbeard walked down the centre of the *Long Wyrm* behind his men like a farmer surveying his field. 'Surrender, King Olav, and we will spare the remainder of your men. We will also swear to leave Christians to practice their faith.'

King Olav calmly put down his sword, but he kept his shield up. He looked across the *Long Wyrm* at Forkbeard. 'There will be no truce. There will be no surrender. You and yours will burn: you will burn in hell.' Then he took two quick steps to the side and leaped overboard.

King Jolawer Scot gritted his teeth, but did not speak. Instead, he waited for Forkbeard to finish his story. 'What happened then?'

'We fished out his second-in-command,' Forkbeard said.

'But no sign of Olav?'

'No.' Beside Forkbeard, Karle shook his head sadly.

Jolawer looked at Erik and his men, sitting and quietly talking. Forkbeard and Karle had dropped their armour and weapons by the fire and pulled him over to talk. 'Why not?'

Forkbeard smiled. 'Finn – his man – put the shield over his head to protect from spears, but Olav Tryggvason, the crafty bastard, grabbed his and gripped it between his knees.' When Jolawer frowned, he added, 'To sink faster.'

'And you didn't find the body?'

'No,' Forkbeard said. 'I told you. There were about thirty ships there. But the sea's freezing. He's dead.'

'I wish I could believe that.'

'And I wish I could have been there to stop Alfgeir, but he just went straight for them,' Forkbeard said. 'There was nothing I could do.'

Karle hung his head.

Jolawer Scot looked away then, grief almost overtaking him, and he saw Sigrid approach from the lengthening shadows. Unusually, she stopped a good thirty yards away. 'Sweyn—?' she said hesitantly.

Forkbeard motioned for her to come closer. 'What?' he said.

'We've had travellers,' she said. 'Norsemen.'

'And?'

She glanced at Jolawer, but Forkbeard waved for her to continue talking. 'We are all together in this,' he said.

'It appears,' Sigrid said hesitantly, 'that a force far bigger and stronger than Olav Tryggvason's army is sweeping down from the North.'

Forkbeard listened, but did not react. 'Where are they going?'

'Gallows Peak.'

'Hm,' he said. 'So be it.'

'What do you mean by that?' Jolawer said, his voice rising.

'I am not going to risk the lives of countless men over winter to go chasing stories,' Forkbeard said quietly. 'We'll see what's what come spring.'

'You are a coward and a liar,' Jolawer snapped.

Sweyn Forkbeard froze for a single moment, then he turned and looked at Jolawer. 'You know what? You bore me. So I think we'll end this alliance now.'

He raised his voice. 'YOU TAKE THAT BACK!'

By the fire, Erik and his men rose.

'How DARE you say that about our Norse friends?' The knife was in Forkbeard's hand in the blink of an eye. 'You fight for King Olav, don't you?' His voice sounded flushed with indignation; the glint in his eye told a completely different story. Erik and his men were moving towards Jolawer now, hands on hilts.

Jolawer looked at Karle, and the cold hatred in his cousin's smile hit him like a gust of winter wind.

Only at the last moment did he notice a solitary figure waddling towards the Norsemen. The light at the man's back cast his face in shadow. 'Erik Hakonsson!' The voice carried surprisingly well. 'I've poisoned the rations of the filthy Danes, just like you ordered.'

A moment of doubt clouded Forkbeard's face.

'Who in Thor's name are you?' Erik snarled. 'And why are you shouting such nonsense?'

'Come now! Yesterday you told me to mix shadowroot in with their mead and cut their grain with ground-up horseshit. Don't tell me you've forgotten?'

'Who is this man, Erik?' Forkbeard said.

'Never seen him before!' Erik shouted.

'Yes, you have!' the man shouted back. 'Are you calling me a liar?' The man's path to the Norsemen lay past Jolawer; as he came closer, Jolawer could make out the man's misshapen jaw and hastily bandaged head. 'Karle killed Alfgeir. I was on the boat and I saw it happen,' the man muttered out of the side of his mouth. 'I'll set them on each other. Run!'

Jolawer blinked, then shook his head. He watched as the man's hand moved slowly to an old club hanging from his belt.

When he'd passed, Jolawer's eyes met Karle's again. The prince stared at him, scowling.

'For Forkbeard!' the mysterious man screamed, launching himself at Erik Hakonsson's men, swinging his club wildly.

'Get him!' Forkbeard screamed. 'He's *nothing* to do with me!'

The club connected with an arm and a skull, then froze in midair as Erik Hakonsson's axe buried itself in the head of a warrior who had answered to the name of Mouthpiece.

'Is that the best you can do, Forkbeard?' Erik snarled as he pulled the axe free.

'He had *nothing* to do with me, Erik,' Forkbeard said. 'Nothing at all – I promise you! I've seen you fight – if I did want to kill you

I'd send some of the thousands of men I have waiting at my command over there.'

Erik eyed Forkbeard and said nothing as he wiped the axe blade,
very slowly.

'Bastard,' Karle said.

Forkbeard looked at the spot where Jolawer Scott had been
standing, but the young king was gone.

Ulfar could feel the blood clotting in the ripped skin where the wolf's teeth had torn his face to shreds. *I should be screaming,* he thought, then, *No. I should be dead.* Instead, all he had was a dull pulse in what remained of his cheek, along with one blind eye. He ignored it and looked down at Audun. The blacksmith was lying at his feet in the snow, doubled over, blood-coloured spittle cooling in his beard, the broad belt by his side.

Then Ulfar looked up, and wished he hadn't.

Surrounding the men of Stenvik were faces, staring at them – nothing like an army; mostly peasants in rags, men and women both, clutching a variety of weapons – but there was something common to them all. Common, and wrong. The way they stood, the way they moved: there was no *spark* in their eyes.

Nothing human, Ulfar thought. *They just look . . . empty.* Empty and stiff, like hastily made clay figures. And there were a lot of them, too; Ulfar estimated around two hundred and fifty, perhaps more. Add to that one wolf to every five men – and then the trolls, of course: twenty of those, some bigger than others, but all of them taller and broader than the largest of the Stenvik fighters.

Ulfar looked at his travelling companions and brothers in arms.

Some were wounded, others dead; they were all old and tired. His eye met Sven's.

'Well, son,' the whitebeard said conversationally, 'we sailed for a good long while, but I think this might be the shore.'

Beside him, Sigurd Aegisson smiled. 'Sven, my friend – I've never told you this, but—'

The grizzled chieftain's hand went up to intercept Sven's answer. 'You don't half complain like an old woman sometimes.' He hefted his axe, turned to face the trolls and took one step forward. For a moment there was quiet in the circle.

'Who wants a go?' Sigurd Aegisson growled.

Nobody moved, although one by one the wolves started sniffing the air. 'I SAID—' Sigurd's voice trailed off as the circle broke without a word. The trolls, moving together, stepped past the broken and wounded men of Stenvik without a second glance and lined up alongside humans and wolves, facing south.

The Stenvik raiders looked at each other, puzzled.

'Is this a new strategy?' Oskarl, standing behind Sven, mused. 'Are we supposed to run away now?'

'Shut up,' Sven hissed. 'Let me *think*. We just—'

A woman's voice rang out, incredibly loud, and cut him off. *'RIGHT, YOU GOAT-FACED BLUE-SKINNED GRANNY-FUCKERS. LET'S SEE WHAT YOU GOT!'*

The trolls formed a line. The dead-eyed humans and wolves followed them, moving mindlessly.

'Looks like you scared them off,' Sven said to Sigurd.

Sigurd looked puzzled. He looked down at his axe. 'That's never happened before,' he said.

'The woods!' Oskarl shouted. 'Look!' He pointed, and they all turned as a lone warrior emerged from the trees to the south. Then two more figures stepped out and stood next to him. They might have been half his width, and neither reached his shoulders, but they still radiated menace. Behind them a group of men moved into position, slow and measured, spreading out in a battle line about two hundred yards away.

Sven looked around. 'Who the hell is that? Anyone we know?'

'Hold on,' Sigurd said. 'It— No . . .'

'What?'

'Nothing. For a moment I just thought—'

At that moment the trolls burst into action, charging the new enemy in a wave of death and destruction, followed by the humans and howling wolves.

'We need to move – NOW!' Sven barked, turning towards the fallen men. 'Pick up what you can and go – we've got a couple of moments to get to higher ground! Help the wounded!' He rushed to the nearest man on the ground and tried to pull him up. 'Come on, move it!

'Sven?' Sigurd said. He hadn't moved.

The old rogue wasn't listening; he just kept shouting, 'What's wrong with you all? *MOVE!*'

'Sven!' Sigurd snapped.

'*WHAT?*' Sven growled, whirling to face his chieftain.

'We're not running from the trolls,' Sigurd said.

That stopped him. 'Why—?'

Sigurd pointed to the clearing. 'Because they're all dead.'

Ulfar was vaguely aware of Sven's mouth moving, but he didn't hear a word; he couldn't take his eyes off the fighters, who had moved like water, flowing past and through the trolls, lopping off limbs as easily as branches on old, dead trees. The battle, such as it was, had been over in moments. Ulfar saw the trolls knock maybe five of the fighters down, but at least three of those were getting back up. One of the new arrivals didn't move, mostly because half of his head was missing; the rest were chasing and hacking down the peasants, with what, from where they were standing, looked like very little effort. The wolves had run off. 'Smart puppies,' Ulfar muttered.

'Look at them,' Sigurd said. 'The only crew that fights like that . . .' his voice trailed off.

Sven finally managed to form words. 'You're right. Screw me sideways with a pine tree,' he muttered. 'I can't decide if we're saved or dead.'

'What do we do?' Ulfar said.

'I think that's pretty clear,' Sven said, glancing at Sigurd. 'We can't run, so we'll go greet their leader and hope he hasn't found out.'

'Found out what?' Ulfar said.

'That I killed his father,' Sigurd said.

'It's never easy with you two, is it?' Ulfar said.

'Nope,' Sven said.

'Right,' Ulfar said. 'Well then. Let's try and get our warriors up and standing, shall we?' With that he bent down and hooked an arm under Audun's shoulder. 'Come on, big man. Up you get.' He felt the full weight of the blacksmith through his arms and legs and grunted. 'We need to get you eating less. You weigh as much as an ox.'

Audun mumbled something incomprehensible.

'What?'

'. . . blood . . .'

His forehead and cheek throbbed with the effort of lifting him. 'Yes. I know. The beast bit off half my face. Should've asked it to take a bite out of your arse instead. Might've made it easier to get you to your feet.'

'Maybe . . .' A rattling cough shook the blacksmith as he got one knee under himself.

Ulfar frowned. 'Are you . . . laughing?'

'. . . you promised her you'd marry her?'

'Fuck off,' Ulfar said, smiling.

Another cough, followed by a smirk as Audun rose, clutching his stomach with his left hand. 'Ugh,' he managed.

'Is it that bad?' Ulfar managed.

'The belt rips my insides,' Audun muttered. 'I can lift a mountain with it, but the bloody thing kills me.'

'Right. If you could just look mean for a little while longer, maybe pretend that you're not dying, that would be very good for our immediate health and future,' Ulfar said under his breath. 'We've got visitors.'

Audun looked up and across the frozen river to the force now advancing on them. He closed his eyes, then looked again. 'It's . . . Helga,' he muttered.

'What?' Ulfar hissed.

He mumbled, 'The woman I stayed with? On the farm? She's there.'

Ulfar took a deep breath, pushed all his questions aside and looked once more at the warriors approaching the men of Stenvik. There was no doubt who was in charge – the man in the middle carried an axe Ulfar doubted he'd even be able to lift, let alone swing. On his right was a short, wiry woman with spiky hair, lean and mean. On his left was a boy of maybe thirteen years who wore a nobleman's sword and had an unmistakeable family resemblance to the leader. Behind them was a woman, clad in travellers' clothes but moving gracefully, with the confidence born of certainty and the bearing of a queen. The weak light caught on strands of silver interwoven in her braid of smooth dark hair. Behind and around her was a group of the hardest bastards Ulfar could remember seeing.

'I hope you mean the tall one,' Ulfar said.

Audun elbowed him just as Sigurd and Sven stepped out in front of the men of Stenvik. In comparison with this group, Sigurd Aegisson's men looked like what they were: old, and grey, and tired.

'Well met, Skadvald, son of Skargrim,' Sigurd said.

'Well met, Sigurd Aegisson,' the big man replied.

'You've saved our lives,' Sigurd said.

Skadvald looked around. 'This is true,' he said.

'And you are no doubt aware that I am responsible for the death of your father,' Sigurd said.

Ulfar looked up in horror. Sigurd had just dropped it in there, like he'd been asking for an extra chicken at market to go with the three he'd bought already. All around him old hands drifted slowly in the direction of blades, preparing to defend to the last, hoping to maybe take one or two with them to Valhalla.

'My father should have left raiding to younger men,' Skadvald said, matter-of-factly.

'And listened to better advice,' the woman next to him snarled. 'There was no dishonour in it, Sigurd Aegisson. But if I ever get my hands on that bitch—'

'The woman in the boat?' Ulfar's stomach dropped as he realised the voice behind the words had actually been his own. He felt the eyes of both groups on him and wished that just for once he could have refrained from speaking, just for a moment.

The short woman looked as if she'd happily spend a long time killing him. 'Yes. Do you know her?'

'We killed her,' Ulfar said.

'Really?' The short woman's face lit up in genuine joy.

'We had to,' Ulfar said, ignoring the heat of Sven's glare. 'She was wielding the powers of Loki.' The smile disappeared off the short woman's face as quickly as it had come, and her mouth clammed shut.

'This is why we need to talk,' Skadvald said. 'I am told that the dark powers walk here. We will need to work together.'

'How?' Sigurd said. 'We can't give them half the fight that you just did.'

The teenager standing next to the big man smirked. He was almost vibrating with energy.

'I believe you will,' the big man said. 'But first, let's bind our wounds and clean our blades.'

'Start a fire,' Sven said to the men next to him.

'No!' the big man said quickly. 'No fire.'

Out of the corner of his eye Ulfar caught the tall, dark-haired woman hiding a smile.

Skadvald's men helped drag the corpses of the hacked-up trolls to one side. The trolls had taken nearly a quarter of Sigurd's men; the fallen needed to be properly laid out and sent off.

Oskarl stood beside Ulfar, watching as Sven knelt by the bodies. The old man moved slowly, stopping by each one, then he leaned over and muttered a few quiet words, things that needed to be kept and carried to Valhalla.

'It's a bad business,' the Eastman said.

'That it is,' Ulfar said.

'I reckon there'll be more of this before we're done.'

'Probably.'

They stood in silence for a while, until Oskarl spoke again. 'How's your friend?'

'His health improved rather quickly when our visitors arrived,' Ulfar said, unable to hide the smirk.

'Good. He's a hard one.'

Ulfar chortled.

'What? We'll need him to hammer our enemies.'

'Oh, nothing,' Ulfar said, grinning as much as his bandage would allow. 'You're absolutely right.'

The ceremonies ended and a group of men set to breaking the frozen earth for graves. Sven motioned for Ulfar, Audun and Oskarl to come over.

'Right. Sigurd's over there' – he motioned to where the chieftain sat on a fallen log – 'and we're going over and we're going to listen to what Skadvald and his lot have to say. What do you do?'

'Stand in the back and look dangerous?' Audun offered.

'That's exactly right,' Sven said. 'I'll make men of you puppies yet. Come on!'

Shuffling over, Ulfar took a good look at Sigurd Aegisson. The old man looked like there was nothing left of him but skin, bone and stubbornness. His axe lay across his legs and he was deep in thought. Sven approached and sat down at his right-hand side without a word. Audun, Ulfar and Oskarl crossed the log and took up position behind the two old men.

Skadvald did not wait long; he walked towards the log with a party of three and sat down in the snow, apparently untroubled by the wet and the cold.

'This is Thora,' he said, looking at the short-haired woman. 'She sailed with my father.' Sigurd and Sven gave her a warrior's salute and she sneered in return. *Not showing teeth is probably as close as she gets to politeness*, Ulfar thought.

'My son, Ognvald,' Skadvald said.

Ognvald looked at the men on the log and smiled, and Ulfar made a mental note to stay either behind or far away from the young man next time there was killing to be done.

'And this is Helga,' Skadvald finished.

The tall woman bowed her head. Ulfar caught the slightest glance at Audun when she looked up and he couldn't help but smirk. The blacksmith looked less like a fearsome warrior and more like a nervous boy.

'I am afraid I can confirm what you may feel you know,' she said. 'Valgard is here, and he is not alone.'

'What does he plan to do?'

'He's going after Bifrost.'

'*What*—?' Sigurd's jaw dropped, and Sven looked equally lost. 'He's—'

'—looking for the bridge to Valhalla. That's right,' Helga said. 'What's worse, I think he'll find it.'

'How?' Sven said.

'Loki will show him the way,' Ulfar said.

'But he's not a god!' Sigurd protested. 'Only the gods can call down the Rainbow Bridge.'

'I'm afraid he will find a way,' Helga said. 'He will force the gods to come and fight him, and you know what happens when the gods spill blood on Earth. In the East, Jormungandr will rise. In the West, Fenrir will walk the earth.'

'Ragnarok,' Sven muttered. 'The end of the world as we know it.'

'How do we stop him?' Audun was hoarse, but determined.

'Glad you asked,' Thora said. Her smile was anything but reassuring.

Skadvald pulled up the sleeve of his tunic. A row of runes had been carved into his forearm, neatly and with precision. They were too small for Ulfar to read at a distance, but he could feel the power radiating off the symbols. 'Helga will carve you with runes that draw out your inner strength,' the big Viking said. 'She's done all of us.'

'It's filthy magic,' Thora said, 'but it works. And I figure—'

'—they're cheating, so why shouldn't we?' Sven said.

Thora smirked at him. 'Indeed.'

'Then that is what must happen,' Sigurd said after a couple of moments. 'How are you for supplies?'

'We've got enough,' Thora said.

'Good.' Sigurd turned to Helga. 'How long will it take to carve runes on my saggy old goats?'

'Depends. Longer if they kick,' she said.

Slowly, smiles were spreading around their little circle. 'We'll make sure we don't send you two cranky ones in a row,' Sigurd said. He turned to Skadvald. 'Rest, runes, move?'

'Sounds good,' the big Viking said.

The smell of burning flesh was hard to shake. Helga sat, straight-backed, on the log where Sigurd and Sven had held their council earlier. The Stenvik warrior sitting opposite held his arm out, clutching a spear with the other. When the tip of Helga's red-hot knife touched his skin he breathed hard and clutched the shaft in his other hand, but he did not cry out. Thjodolf was one of their oldest walking brothers; he was wiry and bent, and he looked determined to sit through the trial in silence.

Ulfar, standing next in line, tried hard not to think about what it would feel like. By now he could deal with pain in battle, but waiting to be slowly burned? Not the easiest thing to do.

'There. That's it,' Helga said. Thjodolf looked at her, blinking away the tears of pain and wiping his eyes with a wizened hand.

'But I don't feel any different,' he said.

Helga smiled at him. 'Just . . . wait.'

'What do you mean *wait*? My arm hurts like hell because you burned it and I'm not going to just sit here and—' The words abruptly stopped as Thjodolf's jaw dropped. 'Aah . . .' He sighed. Then, as if discovering it for the first time, he stretched out his left arm and rolled his neck, waiting for the aches and pains of an old body to tell him to stop.

They didn't.

A radiant smile took over the old man's face. He looked at Helga, then at his arm, then back at her. A twinkle appeared in his eye and lifted his eyebrow.

Helga laughed. 'Go on, old-timer, off with you. Go and cause some trouble.'

Thjodolf grinned and rose gracefully from the log, saluting Helga as he left.

'Next,' she said.

Ulfar walked towards the log, feeling the tension build in his chest. He sat down opposite Helga, watching as she cleaned her knife and put it down next to her small fire; the most Skadvald had allowed them, and only on the condition that Helga stay by it at all times. Ulfar watched as her hands worked, every movement assured and confident. Her and Audun? Yes, he could see that – but his friend had done well there. He was so distracted by her that when she looked up she caught him staring.

Despite the cold, Ulfar's cheeks flushed. 'Um . . . hello,' he stammered.

'Hello,' she said. 'You're him, aren't you?'

'I think most people are,' he said. 'Well, most men. Women are her, obviously.'

Helga smiled. 'You're Ulfar.'

'Yes,' Ulfar said.

'In which case,' she said, putting her knife back onto the fire to heat, 'I can't help you.' Ulfar frowned, but she just looked at him levelly. 'Yours is a different path.'

'What? So – you're not going to . . .' Ulfar searched for the words, but they wouldn't come.

'No,' Helga said.

'Uh, well – goodbye?' Ulfar said.

'Goodbye for now, Ulfar Thormodsson,' Helga said.

'Did I—? Did Audun tell you my name?' Ulfar said, but Helga's attention had turned back to the fire and the set of her shoulders suggested that there would be no more conversation on this subject.

Ulfar rose awkwardly, feeling the twinge in his wound, and left. Over his shoulder he could hear Helga's soft voice.

'Next.'

Thora was bent over a travel pack tightening straps when Sven approached. 'What do you want?' she snapped without looking at him.

'Nothing,' Sven said.

'That's good,' Thora said, twisting the rope brutally.

'Why's that?' Sven said.

'Because nothing's what you're getting,' Thora said.

Sven chuckled. 'If you fight half as well as you talk we'll' – his left arm shot down and their daggers met with a soft *clink*, inches away from the big vein in Sven's groin – 'be just fine.'

A soft flick of the wrist and the slim woman's dagger disappeared up the sleeve of her tunic. 'I like you, Hairy,' Thora said as she rose and hefted the travel pack.

'And why is *that*?' Sven said, grinning.

'Because you're a cheeky old git and you're not even half as friendly as you pretend to be.'

Sven was openly smiling now. 'You're a cranky bitch yourself and you're too fast by half.'

Thora grinned at him. 'Don't you forget it. Now fuck off out of my way. We've got some things to kill.' With that she marched off, leaving Sven grinning and scratching his head.

'Cheeky old git. Well – I suppose that's not too far off,' he said as he walked towards the group of Stenvik men, rubbing the freshly carved runes on his forearm.

'She says she won't give me runes,' Ulfar said.

'Really?' Audun said, turning the blade over in his hand and working the other side of the edge. 'Any reason?'

'Says she can't help me. My path is different.' Audun's sharpening strokes slowed down for a moment, but he remained silent. 'How much did you tell her about what happened to us?'

'I . . . can't remember,' Audun said.

'Oh come *on*,' Ulfar said. 'You can't have been boning her *all* the time?'

Audun looked up from his blade and Ulfar took an involuntary half-step back. 'Forgive me. I didn't mean it,' he said quickly.

Audun forced himself to breathe. He unclenched his jaw and looked away from Ulfar. At last he said, 'We didn't.'

'*Really?*' Ulfar said.

'Yes,' Audun said.

'Not once?'

'No.'

'Man. You should have—' Audun looked up again. 'Fine. Good. Not my business. I get it. But—' Ulfar made a frustrated sound. 'I don't understand. *You* go and talk to her!'

Audun stopped sharpening the sword, took a deep breath and got to his feet. He shot a final glance at Ulfar. 'I will, but on one condition.'

'What?'

'That you try to shut your mouth from time to time.'

Ulfar smiled and clapped the blacksmith on the shoulder. 'Forgive me, my friend. But it has to be said – you know that's not going to happen. Besides, you make a fine target.'

'Maybe so, but you'll get what you give,' Audun said as he walked off. When he got to where Helga was sitting, there were three men standing in front of him. Audun got a chance to stand and just watch her for a moment.

The pain of losing their time together hit him so hard that he had to close his eyes and clench his fists to find calm. He had to remind himself that he'd been forced to leave – it had been the only decision. But he'd decided that he'd never see her again – so how could she be here?

'Next.'

When he opened his eyes he thought he could see her quickly looking away and his heartbeat quickened as the colour rose in his cheeks. *Snow*, he thought. *Cold, wet and unpleasant snow. Slush. Shards of ice. Nothing warm or inviting. Oh, Fenrir take it all.*

'Next.'

Audun swallowed. He tried to find peace in watching the rune-knife gliding smoothly over the exposed forearm but his gaze kept going to her hand, then up to her shoulder and the nape of her neck, a sliver of white skin exposed under raven-black hair . . .

Stop it! He almost punched himself out of frustration.

'Next.'

The man ahead of him moved away and suddenly there was only distance between them. The warrior, a burly greybeard named Askell, sat down and pulled up his sleeve, exposing a meaty forearm that had slightly gone to fat. Helga smiled and handed him a wrist-thick branch to hold on to with his other hand. They exchanged a few words and then she removed her knife from the fire again. Askell did not flinch when the hot metal touched his skin and Audun watched, spellbound, as the sizzling point of the knife did its dance. When it lifted, the air between the point and Askell's forearm shimmered. The old man sat stock-still for a moment.

Then he closed his eyes gently and pulverised the branch in his grip.

'Oh my,' Helga said. 'You must have been quite a handful in your younger days.'

Askell opened his eyes. 'Still am,' he rumbled. 'Thank you,' he added quietly before rising.

'Next.'

Audun drew a deep breath and sat down in front of her.

Helga looked at him and for a moment there were only the two of them in the world.

'Well met,' she said.

'I thought I'd never see you again,' Audun said.

'Why did you leave?'

'I had to. Trouble finds me, and I didn't want to bring it to you.'

Helga smiled then. 'Well, we're both in trouble now.'

Audun found that he couldn't hold back a smile. 'You're right there.'

'I won't draw runes on you. Or Ulfar. I don't know what would happen, but it feels wrong.'

'I know. We're both . . . *different*, I think.'

Helga nodded, reached out and touched his forearm. 'I don't know what'll happen when we find Valgard and whatever he has with him, but it will not be a happy gathering.'

'I know,' Audun said. 'Trouble finds me.'

'Maybe it's the other way around,' Helga said.

'Get up, you old farts!' Thora's voice rang out. 'We're moving!'

Audun put his hand over Helga's and squeezed once, silently. Then he stood up, walked towards the men of Stenvik and did not look back.

Helga watched him go, breathing deeply. Then she set to carving slivers of wood out of the tree she sat on, gritting her teeth in determination.

'I have to say,' Ulfar said, wheezing, 'the old boys look a lot less old.'

'This is what they must have been forty years ago,' Audun said.

Ahead of them the men of Stenvik were keeping up a punishing pace alongside Skadvald's raiders. They'd left the clearing and moved up through the valley, which had begun sloping sharply upwards. A day ago Sigurd and Sven had been looking decidedly faint; now the incline didn't slow them at all. Around them the woods thinned out, the big pines giving way to spindly little trees.

Gallows Peak rose in the distance, a monument to the impossible.

'They sound happy, though,' Ulfar said.

'You're not wrong,' Audun huffed, stumbling on the snow-covered scree. The men had undeniably changed after being carved with Helga's runes, and now a couple of them had had to be shushed when they started up a rowdy marching song. 'We're doing better, I think.'

'Oh,' Ulfar said, 'I wish you hadn't said that.'

Up ahead, a line was forming at the top of the hill: the raiders of Stenvik and their new-found friends were watching something. None of them were moving.

'Hurry up,' Ulfar said, scrambling up the hill as fast as he could.

The silence rolled down to meet them, thick with despair.

Audun and Ulfar got to the top, squeezed in beside the warriors and looked down into the valley on the other side of the ridge.

For a while no one spoke.

Then Sven turned to Helga.

'We're going to need more runes.'

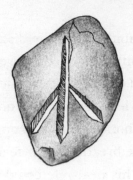

THE MOUNTAINS OF THE NORTH, SWEDEN
LATE DECEMBER, AD 996

Ten feet from their toes the snowy ground dropped away and the landscape opened up, tree-covered valleys and gently sloping hills stretching into the misty distance. Audun and Ulfar stared down at the view below and tried to understand what they were looking at.

'What are they?' Skadvald asked after a while.

'Many,' Oskarl said from the back.

'What?' The big Viking snapped.

'Many. They are many,' the Eastman replied, oblivious to the filthy looks he was getting. 'That means there's a lot of 'em,' he added.

'He's not wrong,' Sigurd said. 'I think we'll be meeting with Valgard rather sooner than anyone really wants.'

The tide of bodies washing in from the North covered almost the entire width of the valley below, and it reached back three times as far. The column was irregular, but even at that distance they could see that it was moving steadily forward. Small groups kept peeling off to go and scout the terrain; others would rejoin, flowing across from other valleys.

'Are those *all* trolls?' Ognvald said, trying to pretend his voice wasn't trembling ever so slightly.

'No,' Sven said, squinting into the distance, 'it looks like the trolls are front and centre. There're some quick-moving things on the flanks . . . wolves? I don't know,' he said. 'I just don't know. It's too far away. That's at least ten miles, if not more.'

'Fucking fuckers,' Thora muttered to no one in particular.

Ulfar drew a quick breath as the feeling swept him away. Stars sparkled inside his head. He could taste metallic cold on the tip of his tongue and he felt something – pressure, maybe – nudge him in the back. 'We have to get to the base of Bifrost,' he said. '*Now*. We have to get to Bifrost before they do – we have to go now.'

'We don't know where it is,' Sigurd said.

'But you do, don't you?' Helga said.

A circle of silence spread around her and Ulfar could feel their eyes on him. 'Yes,' he said, words inching out of his mouth. 'Yes, I think so.'

'You *think* so?' Ognvald started, but Ulfar had already turned to the west and started walking. 'Hey! Ass! Explain yourself!' the boy shouted after him, to no effect.

Audun cast an eye on the assembled crew of raiders, then turned and followed Ulfar.

'Oh, for fuck's sake,' Thora said, following them.

Skadvald moved to walk after her, but Helga's hand on his forearm stopped him. 'Be careful,' she said.

'Of what?' Skadvald growled.

'I've heard stories of these mountains,' she replied.

Skadvald looked down at her, puzzled. 'How is a story going to hurt me?'

Moments later the raiders were all headed west, further into the mountains.

*

The dark army disappeared out of sight as soon as the raiders crested the next hill. A heath stretched out before them, sweeping fields of white topped with black rock peaks the height of a man. Ulfar had found the energy to keep up with the old men some-where and now he inched towards the head of the line, with Sigurd and Sven flanking him. Behind him the heavily armed Vikings waded through the snow, silent but determined.

'Where to now?' Skadvald said.

Ulfar closed his eyes. He could sense the pull of the bridge. 'That way,' he said, pointing to their left, to a snow-covered valley.

'We're not going up?' Ognvald said. 'You have no idea, do you? The gods live above us – everyone knows this.'

'It's still that way,' Ulfar said. He couldn't quite bring himself to look the boy in the eye, because the kid was right; he didn't know. He wasn't certain in any way he could put words to. But something told him to go left, so that was where he must go.

Valley, hill, another heath . . .

Audun could sense their tempers rising. They needed something to do, something to turn their anger towards. The kid was suffering the worst; Ognvald was nearly frothing at the mouth, charging off the line, stomping into the snow, kicking drifts and snorting in fury. His father shouted at him from time to time, but it didn't make much difference; the boy was like an angry bullock.

The wind was vicious up here, and they could even see patches of bare ground. Husks of yellow straw clutched at the earth in sullen defiance, pushed this way and that by the elements, and jagged edges of rock breached the ground like swimmers coming up for air.

Lost for anything better to do, Audun trudged along after Ulfar. He didn't quite dare look at Helga; he could control his anger now, but he wasn't sure he would be able to keep his other emotions in check. After they'd seen the dark army sweeping in from the North, there had been no time for anything more: they had to find the Rainbow Bridge. That was what Ulfar said, and that would have to be that.

Up ahead, Ognvald ripped up a fist-sized rock and launched it at a large, jagged peak in the snow about a hundred yards away.

'Missed,' a brown-haired man shouted gleefully.

'Fuck you, Ygval,' the boy shouted back. 'Didn't miss your mum, did I?'

'Neither do I – she was half bear and half wolf,' Ygval shouted back. He paused for a moment. 'Yours was much nicer.'

'Liar!' Skadvald shouted from the front. 'She was all bear and all wolf too and I've got the scratches from my belly to my knees!'

The laughter from the men only infuriated the youth. His head whipped round until he found a small boulder. He growled and dived for it, glared at Ygval and launched it at the thing into the distance with a grunting scream.

It seemed to fly for ages.

Then it connected to the rock in the snow, and time slowed down.

The boulder smashed into five pieces, but the stone . . . *crumbled.* It exploded outwards, sending shards flying.

'DRAUGR!' Ygval shouted. 'To arms!'

'What did you *do?*' Helga screamed.

Ognvald didn't reply. He stared into the distance at something only he could see, his face frozen in abject terror.

A cold wind lashed at their backs, picking up strength and speed, whipping up the snowflakes on the ground – and now Audun saw them too: shapes in the air, gliding towards them.

'Ward your thoughts!' Helga screamed. 'Don't believe *anything*!'

he loved you

The voice entered Audun's head like water seeping through an old roof.

he loved you and you killed him

'Shut it,' Audun said between clenched teeth. He tried to scout out the others, but they'd disappeared behind an odd milky-white fog.

your father loved you and you killed him because of your whore mother

Audun's back convulsed and arched as the thing on the wind touched him.

and she loved you too and you threw it away because you're worthless worse than worthless you are harmful

The feeling of being probed suddenly stopped, as if the thoughts had pushed up against something they couldn't penetrate: something at the core of him.

'I am not,' Audun said. 'They deserved to die.'

you do

'Maybe,' he said, 'maybe I do. But you already did – and when I go, I won't be stuck in a hole.' He could taste the rage on the air as the draugr sought a way in.

your rage will destroy you

'Yes, it will,' Audun said, and found to his surprise that he meant it. 'I don't mind.'

The draugr screamed in frustration, the sound grating on Audun's spine.

let me in

let me in let me in let me in

Audun looked at the swirling form in the snow. 'No.'

he will kill you all even you and the other one you're going to suffer you'll suffer you'll—

A speck of light appeared in the centre of the draugr. The flame spread in a circle, burning upwards and down, outlining the stretched and torn figure of a human in flames.

A maniacal cackle echoed in Audun's head.

suffer suffer suffer suffer suffer

The milky fog around him dissolved and he found himself staring into Helga's eyes.

He was about to speak when she grabbed his head with both hands, pulled him in and kissed him, her fingers moving in his hair, heat blossoming in his face and travelling with astonishing speed to the rest of his body.

When she broke contact, moments and ages later, they both caught their breath like divers. A moment, then he caught her eyes again. They twinkled, and her mouth twitched in a barely suppressed grin.

'Had to see if you were alive,' she said.

'*Mm*,' Audun said, utterly unable to form words.

'Take these,' she said, pulling his hand out, palm up, and placing two slivers of wood in it. 'They get hot. Find the draugr and stab them.' The runes in the wood glowed faintly.

Audun looked around. The first man he saw was Sven, and he pushed off immediately.

The old man held a rock in his hand, the jagged edge pointing towards his face. Charging through the chaos, Audun leaped and caught Sven by the elbow, pulling hard and struggling as the old raider's arm moved with determination to hit himself in the head. Audun's hand closed around the slivers and he struck out towards the shimmering form in front of Sven.

When the wood hit the draugr, the sizzle in the palm of his hand almost made Audun drop the weapon. The flame sprung into life where the point met the form in the air and a flickering, orange circle spread quickly to fill out a human shape. The draugr's piercing scream set Audun's teeth on edge but he held the flaming splinter still, gritting his teeth as the hairs were singed off the back of his hand.

Sven came out of the trance and coughed violently. 'Bastard,' he hissed. 'Bastard.' Tears streaked down the old man's face.

Lost for words, Audun gave him a quick, hard embrace and ran off to help the next warrior.

'Seven,' Sigurd said.

'And nine of mine,' Skadvald said.

They stood to one side, watching as the men methodically went about stabbing into the ground, dislodging enough frozen soil to bury the dead. Some of the men had killed themselves with blades. Others had simply ceased to live.

'And Ognvald?'

Skadvald paused. 'He's . . . troubled,' he said eventually. 'I've taken his blade away for now.'

Sigurd looked Skadvald straight in the eyes. 'I look forward to fighting an enemy I can see,' he said.

Skadvald didn't reply. He didn't have to.

Thirty yards away, Helga walked amongst the bodies. 'There was a battle here,' she whispered.

Sven walked beside her. 'So there was,' he said. 'Must have been a while ago, too. I couldn't help but notice—'

'—that the draugr weren't all of the same size.'

'Exactly.'

Helga stopped and looked at Sven. 'Don't worry too much about it. They were old souls, and whatever they met is long gone. Now I'll need you to leave.'

'Why?' Sven looked ahead. 'Oh.'

Curled up in the snow ahead of them, Thora suddenly looked

very small, shivering and moving her mouth silently as she rocked back and forth.

Helga's fingers found the cord tied around her waist and searched until they found a small pouch. A pinch of herbs travelled to her mouth, where she rolled them around on her tongue, grimacing all the while. Moments later she had a smooth, round green pellet in her fingers.

'You won't like me for this, *sister*,' Helga whispered.

Then she jumped on the prone woman, pinning her arms beneath her own knees. A moment's shock, then Thora started screaming and bucking – but it was too late. Helga's free hand shovelled snow over the smaller woman's head and sought out her nose, pinching it shut. As Thora's mouth opened once more to shriek, Helga dropped the pellet in and threw a half-hand of snow in after it, then pushed off and rose, red-cheeked with effort as Thora started to cough.

A heavy hand landed on her shoulder and yanked her around. 'What have you done to her?' Skadvald said. 'Undo it – now. Or I'll break you.'

'Let her go,' Audun said, stepping towards them both.

'Back off,' Skadvald growled, grabbing Helga's shoulder harder.

'No,' Audun said, calmly unhooking the hammer from his belt.

Helga gently placed her hand on Skadvald's, then she drew a deep breath and pressed her thumb down, *hard*. The big raider screamed in pain as his hand slid off her shoulder, forcing his body to follow.

Helga *twisted* and suddenly Skadvald was on the ground.

A coarse laugh broke the stunned silence. They all turned to see Thora, sitting bolt-upright in the snow, a fierce gleam in her eyes.

'You're alive,' Skadvald said.

Thora ignored him. Her focus was on Helga as she clambered to her feet. 'No one has done that to me and lived.'

Helga grinned. 'I take it you never had an older sister?'

'I should kill you, you know,' Thora said.

'You should,' Helga said. 'Broth first.'

Thora grinned.

The two women walked off side by side, leaving Audun and Skadvald standing like puzzled oxen, staring at each other and trying hard to figure out what had just happened.

The heath slowly changed to hill, and the hill to mountainside. All around Ulfar, raiders clambered up the steep incline with varying levels of grace.

'They can fuck this mountain with a boar tusk,' Oskarl grumbled. 'And not one of the nice smooth ones.'

'Stop your complaining, you big girl,' Sven said up ahead. 'It's always grumbles and moans with you Eastmen.'

'We just like to describe the world like it is,' Oskarl said. 'That way no one gets disappointed.'

'How do you not just kill each other *all* the time?' Ulfar said.

'Sometimes we do,' Oskarl said.

Below them, the landscape stretched out until the colours blended into soft curves of white on grey on white. Ulfar had seen most of the men cast a glance in the last bit of climb, and then resolutely look forward.

The dark army was there, behind them and drawing closer. They'd caught glimpses of it from time to time, but now they were starting to feel its presence, like heavy clouds before thunder.

'WATCH OUT!!' The scream was raw, immediate, and without thinking, Ulfar threw himself to the ground and felt the mass of the boulder whoosh past. A dull crunch followed by screaming suggested that someone further down hadn't been so lucky.

'*Giants!*'

Ulfar glanced up and cursed: two massive silhouettes were out-lined against the grey-white sky, and one was holding a boulder the size of a grown horse. Moments later the giants vanished behind the onrushing rock. Ulfar pressed his head against the cold ground and winced as it shook with the impact.

When he looked up again with his one good eye, three shapes were moving, scurrying up the hill with speed towards the giants. Their screams, high-pitched and inhuman, drifted down towards the cowering raiders.

Sven.

Thora.

Ognvald.

One of the giants bellowed something deep and incomprehen-sible, grabbing the other's arm and pointing. Moments later, the two huge figures stepped back from the edge.

Thora reached the top of the hill and launched herself after them. A rock the width of her torso shot through the air where she'd been moments before, missing Sven's head by inches as the old raider and Ognvald reached the top of the hill side by side and disappeared.

For a moment there was absolute silence. Then a sharp northern wind carried a bellowing roar from beyond the edge.

'COME ON!' Sigurd screamed, and all over the hillside, the raiders scrambled to their feet, rushing to follow them.

The first thing that struck them was the smell: a musky animal stench, only ten times stronger. Then blood.

A lot of blood.

The next thing was the upturned foot of a giant, lying on its back.

Skadvald roared and charged past the foot, which reached up to mid-chest.

No one followed.

None of the men had seen a giant before, but they'd all seen their share of dead bodies – and this one was as dead as they got.

About twenty yards further on, they saw the body of the other one. Skadvald stopped in his tracks and stared.

Ognvald, Thora and Sven stood around it, panting and grinning maniacally at each other. Thora and Ognvald carried a dagger each, and Sven held one in each hand. Thora tried to say something, but all that came out of her was a strangled chortle.

The raiders gathered around them in a half-circle. No one was in any rush to step any closer to them than strictly necessary. Sticky giant blood cooled as it pooled around the feet of the three.

After a moment, Thora found her voice. 'I needed that,' she said.

'Mm,' Sven said.

Ognvald just grinned. Then he turned to his father. 'I'd like my sword back,' he said. Skadvald looked at his blood-soaked son, standing next to the corpse of a giant, holding what was for all intents and purposes a skinning knife. Then he reached for his belt and silently unhooked a sword, passing it over hilt-first.

'Thank you,' the boy said, sheathing the sword at his side. Then, almost as if he was noticing them for the first time, he looked at the assembled raiders. 'So. Are we going to the top of the mountain or what?'

Without any big speeches, the group started up again. Audun pulled on Ulfar's sleeve as they walked past the dead giants.

'Look,' he said under his breath.

The bodies of the big creatures were covered in knife wounds, stabs, slashes and gouges. They'd both been hamstrung and one of them, which might have been male, wasn't any more.

Ulfar's eyes opened wide as he took in the pure fury of the onslaught. 'Looks like they've been done over by a pack of wolverines,' he muttered.

Audun looked up ahead at the forms of Sven, Thora and Ognvald. 'I don't think I'd bet on a pack of wolverines against those three,' he said. 'Remind me to be on their side when the thunder comes.'

'I don't think you'll have to wait too long for that,' the lanky Swede replied.

They walked on in silence, leaving the dead giants behind them in a halo of cold blood.

A moment was all it took.

The climb ranged from the steep to the nearly-vertical and then back again, rising all the time. When the sight-lines opened down to where they'd come from, forests of trees they knew to be six times the height of a man and at least a day's walk to get through were nothing but a smudge in the white. Ulfar led the way, stumbling onto cracks and crevices that made up a path of sorts, always leading upwards, until the ground evened out and they reached a plateau roughly circular, four hundred yards across.

And then, in that moment, he knew.

'It's here,' he said to Sigurd.

The old raider stopped and looked around as Skadvald walked past them. 'Here?' he said.

'Here,' Ulfar said.

Sven looked around at the blue-black snow-capped stones. 'It's less colourful than I'd imagined,' he said.

'What are you talking about?' Skadvald said, turning away from the far edge and stepping towards them.

'He says the Rainbow Bridge is here,' Sigurd said.

'Makes sense,' Skadvald said.

'Really?' Sigurd said.

'Well,' Skadvald said, grinning as he unhooked the axe from his back, 'they seem to think so.'

He looked at the far edge of the plateau as Sigurd and Sven glanced at each other.

'You go first,' Sven said.

Sigurd rolled his eyes and walked towards the far edge. He stood there for a moment, then walked back towards Skadvald and unhooked his own axe, limbering up, rolling his shoulders.

'Oh fine,' Sven said. 'I'll bite.'

He walked towards the edge of the plateau. Slowly the landscape came into view, far away valleys stretching towards him, hills and lesser peaks rising to meet his eye.

Then the deep valley below and the two-mile slope that led up to their plateau.

And the mass of bodies ascending, human and troll.

'Oh fuck,' Sven said.

The raiders of Stenvik and Skadvald's men prepared for battle like they'd done all of their lives: all around the plateau practised hands checked armour straps, reinforced leather strips on sword hilts and pushed padding into helmets where needed. Some of the men joked around, while others looked inward, staying silent.

Ulfar watched as Old Thjodolf crept up to the edge and looked down. It looked like he was measuring something, index finger moving against his thumb. Then he went back to the packs and unwound a bundle of spears, arranging them carefully by thickness and jabbing them on the ground in a line leading from the edge. The spear on the far end was longer and thicker than the others.

Sven was talking to Askell, a big hulk of a man, pointing towards barrel-sized boulders strewn about the big plateau. Behind big Askell, a handful of men of similar shape all hung on the old raider's every word.

In his own world, Sigurd took two steps back then two steps forward, swinging his axe in ever-widening and quickening arcs. With every swing another year dropped off the chieftain.

'This is it, isn't it,' Helga said at his shoulder.

Ulfar made an effort and managed not to jump. 'Yes. I think so.'

'How is your wound?'

'Still can't see out of the eye,' Ulfar said, 'but there's no pain, which I should be thankful for. Healed over quick. I'll be useless in the fight.'

'Oh, I don't think so,' Helga said. She thought for a moment. 'Would you believe me if I said I still don't know why I'm here?'

Ulfar smiled. 'Oh, I would. I don't.'

Helga touched his arm. 'I think you know more than you realise.'

With that she left him and walked over to Skadvald.

'I'm pretty sure I don't,' he mumbled. 'I don't even know where—' His jaw snapped shut and a sensation burned its way up and down his spine. Lips pursed, he closed his eyes.

He *did* know. He knew exactly where they needed to be.

When he opened his eyes again his body had relaxed. 'Sven. Sven. *Where is Sven?*' Pushing past warriors, he found the greybeard standing next to Sigurd. 'We need to twist the position of the men to the left.'

Sven turned and looked at him. 'Why?'

Ulfar squeezed his eyes shut and held his forehead with one hand, trying to keep the thought still. 'It's going to be ... *important.*' When he opened his eyes again, he saw the trace of a glance between Sven and his chieftain.

Sigurd shrugged. 'Fine. I'll go and tell Skadvald.'

'Thank you,' Ulfar blurted out. 'I—'

The voice swallowed up Ulfar's words.

'RIGHT: WAVE GOODBYE TO YOUR COCKS, YOU GOAT-BOTH-ERING PUS-FACES – THEY'RE COMING!' Thora moved back from the edge.

'Rocks!' Sven screamed as behind him, Skadvald roared orders to his own men, who shifted their planned lines of battle towards Ulfar's indicated position.

Carrying boulders the size of sheep, Askell and another six muscle-bound men staggered to the front and dropped their cargo over the edge. From far below, roars carried up on the wind. Ulfar saw Sigurd move to the edge and peer over, then quickly catch Sven's eye.

'Throwers!' Skadvald shouted. Ten of his men and another ten of the Stenvik raiders, led by old Thjodolf, ran towards the edge and launched spears down towards the unseen army.

'Hand-axes and spears!' Sigurd shouted, retreating from the edge. 'Keep your eyes and ears open!' A group of rune-carved warriors armed with shields and axes took up position in a loose half-circle facing the edge. Spearmen stood behind them, both hands on their weapons, ready to stab over their shoulders. When the first wolf came bounding up the slope, Sigurd shouted again.

'STEP ASIDE!'

As the warriors in the middle of the half-circle created an opening wide enough for three carts side by side, Sven and a handful of his chosen men started wailing and banging weapons on shields. The wolves flowed through the gap and into the middle of the plateau, charging at the source of the noise, a tide of grey fur and sharp teeth.

'CLOSE!' As the last of the wolves streamed past, the axemen formed their circle again – and not a moment too soon. The trolls reached the top of the slope and went straight for the nearest humans. There were four of them; ugly bastards, too, swinging clubs and crudely broken tree branches.

Ulfar watched as the mobile fighters quickly split up, two to a troll, giving them moving targets while the spearmen jabbed, aiming for knees and hips. The trolls bellowed, then in a blink of an eye stepped close into what looked almost like a formation.

Another three trolls came running up the slope, followed by a handful of ragged humans with spears.

'Humans first!' Skadvald shouted.

The spear-wielders followed his advice mercilessly and within moments throats were split and guts were spilled as the thick, pointed missiles found their targets, with force. The corpses fell where they stood and Ulfar watched as a troll angrily kicked one of them out of the way. Blood spilled in the snow and mixed with the sight of wolves losing their shapes, breaking in half under the ferocious assault of an attack team led by Sven and young Ognvald.

'Bad choice of prey,' Ulfar muttered.

But the enemies kept on pushing up from the slope and what had been four trolls a moment ago were now eight, and a good twenty ragged people clustered around them. Slowly the mass advanced, with more bodies appearing by the edge.

'STEP BACK!' Skadvald shouted, and the axe-men were only too happy to oblige. Old Thjodolf, stepping backwards, sure-footed, yanked a spear from the ground and threw it hard into the group of enemies, then moved to the next one before the first spear had even connected. A cheer went up from the men as the first spear hit a troll dead in the eye socket, shattering its face, but many hands grabbed the lifeless body and shifted it out of the way almost instantly.

The point where the slope rounded off onto the plateau had disappeared under a line of trolls and humans that stretched out, forty yards to either side. There were more than thirty trolls now, and they were advancing in precise formation, as one, step by step.

In response, the raiders had drifted into a line of their own, facing the dark army. The gap was fifty yards wide and closing.

At the front Ulfar saw Sigurd glance back at him, then draw a deep breath. 'Fall back to Ulfar when the time comes!' he shouted. Then he turned to face the trolls, slapped the handle of the axe and let out a fearsome roar.

'He is a good man, Sigurd Aegisson.'

Ulfar spun around so fast that he almost fell over. The sword was in his hand before he realised he'd reached for it. Only after he'd regained his balance and focused his eye on the source of the voice did he realise that Audun had somehow come to stand beside him and a fine white mist was lapping at their calves.

Here, in the mountains, as high up in the world as anyone could go, he seemed somehow more substantial.

Odin stood before them, tall and proud, grey and white like a mountain. Next to him stood a muscle-bound man, slightly shorter. There was a tangible sense of mass about him: broad chest, long arms, blacksmith's hands. A big hammer in his belt.

Thor.

'There is a problem,' Odin said.

'Really?' Ulfar said, casting his eye over his shoulder. He could see the fighting men in a haze. 'You are truly all-knowing.'

Thor's nostrils flared but he kept still, though with some amount of effort. 'Shut up,' he growled.

'Loki has chosen Valgard to take his place,' Odin said, 'and he is working hard to bring about the destruction of the world.'

Ulfar looked at Audun, then back at Odin. 'You're going to say what you want to say, so could you make it quick? We have to go and kill an army of trolls.'

'No, you don't,' Odin said.

Ulfar sighed. 'Fine. We don't. What is the master stroke that I've missed?'

'Your friends are mighty and strong. I am happy to see Helga Finnsdottir's hand in this.'

Ulfar smirked and glanced at Audun, who glared back at him.

'But even if you slay all the trolls, Valgard will quite easily defeat all of you.'

Ulfar searched for a witty comment, but he couldn't think of anything. 'What can we do?'

'Belief is a powerful thing,' Odin said. 'Did you hear many of the men shout my name before they went into battle?'

'... hm,' Audun said. 'No.'

'My powers are fading,' Odin said. 'They don't believe in me because they don't feel they have to, and if they don't have to they won't believe in me.'

'So what is there to do?' Ulfar said. 'Are we troll-food?'

'They don't eat,' Thor said. 'Don't be stupid.'

Shocked by the familiar tone, Ulfar looked at the blacksmith. Then he looked at Audun, standing next to him.

Then Ulfar understood what needed to happen. '... Oh,' was all he managed.

Odin looked at him then, a twinkle in one eye. He raised his finger. Ulfar strained against it, but his sword rose as if it had its own will. The All-Father placed the point at his heart – and stepped forward.

Ulfar screamed, frozen in place, staring at the sword handle where it met the sternum of the All-Father.

Odin coughed and whispered, 'Don't fight him on the ground. When the gods do battle in the realms of man, the gates of Hel will open and that will be too much even for you.'

Ulfar had a moment to break Odin's gaze. To his side, Thor held a hammer handle-first to Audun. The Norse blacksmith grabbed it and swung.

When Ulfar opened his eyes, all worlds rushed in to meet him.

The plateau was a cauldron of battle. A hundred and twelve men were left standing, Sigurd and Sven among them, but there were a hundred and seventy trolls and more coming: a flood of them.

'Too many,' he said. 'Need to even this out.'

He turned to the nearest Stenvik man. Too close by far. The raiders had pulled back and left a score of dead men and trolls lying between the two armies.

'Spear,' he said.

The grizzled raider took one look at him and scampered away, looking frantically for a spear.

At Ulfar's side, Audun rooted in his backpack.

'Ah! There we go.' He pulled out a broad leather belt.

Ulfar looked at his friend. The old blacksmith's hammer in his belt had been replaced. The new hammer looked a lot more substantial. A square head inlaid with runes all round sat on top of a handle reinforced with leather straps for grip.

'Nice hammer,' Ulfar said.

'Thank you,' Audun said. He took a deep breath, fastened the belt around his waist and almost *inflated*, becoming more solid than his surroundings.

The raider re-appeared and wordlessly handed Ulfar a thick spear. Words came unbidden, muttered incantations that seeped into the wood, then Ulfar pulled his arm back and sent the spear flying.

The missile arced over the fighting forces and cleared the heads of the onrushing trolls by a wide margin.

'You missed,' Audun said.

Ulfar just smiled.

Skadvald's men and the raiders of Stenvik shouted in surprise as the snow trembled beneath their feet. Where the spear had passed figures emerged out of the ground, pushing troll and human alike out of the way.

'Einherjar?' Audun said.

'Hey – if he is allowed to cheat then so am I,' Ulfar said.

The moment they were on their feet the big warriors, armed and armoured and almost of a size with the trolls, laid into the nearest of the dark army's soldiers. The newcomers came in all sizes – some were dressed like mercenaries; others wore big furs and wielded heavy clubs – but they all had one thing in common: they had been sent to Valhalla for their valour in battle. Bodies fell around them, but wherever one dropped, two came to fill his place.

Ulfar glanced towards the far end of the plateau. Almost half of it was filled with dark bodies now, all twisted inwards towards the distraction of the risen Einherjar, pressing in towards them, suffocating them with numbers. With one careful eye on the spectacle, the raiders of Stenvik were inching backwards to a position by Audun and Ulfar.

'About time you two showed up,' Sven said.

Ulfar looked at the old man. He looked tired, but there was a twinkle in his eye. 'What can I say? Sometimes it takes a while to figure things out.'

Sigurd snorted at that. 'Well, now you have, and here you are.'

Skadvald, Ognvald and Thora approached, as did Helga.

'So what do we do now?' the big raiding captain said.

They glanced over at their soldiers, less than a hundred of them now left standing. As they looked at the line of trolls and dead-eyed humans, the line of the dark army turned to look at them. They stepped forward.

Audun looked at Ulfar and unhooked the hammer from his belt. Then the two of them stepped forward, between the chieftains and the trolls.

'We're going *that* way,' Ulfar said, gesturing over his shoulder with a thumb at the advancing army. 'And if you don't join in we *will* have all the fun.'

With that, they set off at a run. Ulfar drew his sword just in time to feel a rush of air as something flew past his head and pulverised the chest of the first troll. The hammer was a blur as it returned to Audun's hand.

'Nice!' Ulfar shouted. Within range now, he swung at a thick blue leg; the sword passed clean through the knee joint and the troll toppled over.

A many-throated roar went up behind them, and Ulfar didn't need to look to know that was Sigurd and Sven, charging into battle.

Thora was behind them, grinning fiercely.

On either side of her were Skadvald and Ognvald, father and son, armed with axe and sword.

And then the trolls were upon them. This close they were even bigger, the smallest of them at least a head taller than Ulfar. He looked at their muscles and their blood-crusted clubs and felt a curious absence of fear.

It's almost like a dance, he thought as he bent under a swing, came up so close to a troll he could smell it as he sliced up under the armpit, severing the cords that powered the arm. The big beast roared at him, but a savage kick broke its kneecap and it collapsed in a useless heap.

Ulfar was moving, grabbing a spear that was thrust at him and yanking, feeling the satisfying transfer of weight as the wielder lost his footing in the snow. A knee to the nose sent bone into his brain and ended his life instantly. The tall Norseman spun the spear in his hand, leaned to the side almost lazily and thrust the point of the weapon up under the chin of a charging troll.

Almost like a dance, he thought again. Then he glanced to his side and couldn't help but grin. *Well, for me at least.*

On his right Audun pushed with the flat of his left hand, trying to pull his fist clear of a troll's ribcage. His right flashed out to the side just in time to catch the returning Mjölnir, which was slick with blood. Behind him lay a straight trail of carcases with smashed weapons and pulped joints, suggesting that Audun had considered an approach that meant sidestepping and found it to be bothersome.

On the flanks Sigurd and Sven fought as a pair, forming a whirling cloud of blades that moved in perfect harmony, slicing every bit of flesh that came close. Skadvald moved without hurrying, timing every blow to hit where it should. Beside him Ognvald and Thora hacked at anything they could get at, moving almost too fast for the human eye.

But am I human?

Ulfar smashed the bridge of an onrushing attacker's nose with the pommel of his sword.

Have I been, since Stenvik?

The man dropped like a stone and was ground into the snow by a troll stepping into the breach.

Was I ever?

Slowly, ever so slowly, the line of Valgard's army inched backwards, trying to absorb the furious attackers.

'I'VE TAKEN A SHIT THAT WAS MORE CHALLENGING THAN THIS!' Ognvald screamed at the top of his lungs, legs wrapped around the waist of a troll and knives going snick-snick into its neck, searching for the – *yes, there!* – spine. The troll's legs buckled and Ognvald pushed off, landing on his feet. 'SEE? THERE'S NOTHING TO—'

Ulfar smelled the death on the air moments before he felt the wind on his neck and heard the beating of the wings. He dispatched his opponent with a fierce slash and stepped backwards, picking his way past the bodies of fallen men.

As one, the trolls stopped fighting and stepped back, a line of silent, sullen faces.

Ognvald's face had turned a deepening shade of red. Behind him, the dark shape of a raven descending melted into human form and landed smoothly on the plateau. Skadvald shattered the skull of the troll next to him and rushed towards the boy, who had fallen to the ground, blood seeping out of his nose.

'I'm afraid I must disappoint,' Valgard said, dusting an imaginary speck off his rich, purple cloak. 'Your son is dead. He just doesn't know it yet.' Quick as a flash he spun and grabbed Thora's knife hand by the wrist. She had been silent and quick – but not quick enough.

'I like you,' he said, smiling. They stood toe to toe, almost like tentative lovers. 'You've got a bit of enterprise. But I'm afraid you might have' – she screamed as he snapped the bones in her hand – 'issues.'

Thora's scream was cut short as Valgard's free hand swept up in a smooth arc and he spun her around so she hit the ground face-first, a spray of arterial blood from her cut throat painting a line in the snow that ended under her body. With a smooth movement he eased the sliver of wood back into the folds of his tunic.

The plateau had fallen silent.

Valgard's dark army, quiet and malicious, filled over half of the area. In a corner a handful of beaten and battered soldiers huddled, staring at the gathering in the open space.

Sven stepped out in front of Valgard. 'Kill me.'

For a fraction of a moment, Valgard was confused. 'Stay out of this, old man,' he hissed.

'Shut up, whelp, and do as you're told. You need to kill me.' Sven's voice was cold. He looked Valgard straight in the eye and very deliberately moved into a relaxed fighting stance.

'I said—'

'Because twenty-five years ago I clearly made a mistake, and now I'm going to correct it.' The words hung in the air between them – and then Sven moved.

Almost too quickly for Ulfar's eye he flicked his left hand, just so, and sent a blade flying towards Valgard's face. The moment the knife was airborne and in the tall man's field of vision Sven followed, pushing off like a cat, swiping at Valgard's stomach.

Like a tree in a storm Valgard swayed out of the way of the onrushing blades. His hand shot out and plucked the flying knife from the air by the hilt. A quick step put him to the side of the old fighter. He buried the knife in the old man's spine, just below the neck. The momentum of Sven's lunge carried him forward, but when he hit the ground the body was already dead.

'Bastard,' Ulfar said.

'I could have made that last a *LOT* longer!' Valgard screamed, looking down at Sven. Then, with visible effort, he regained control. 'It's regrettable. But if I'd inflicted on him only a small part of the pains of my childhood, he'd've been screaming for a month.'

He looked at Skadvald and Sigurd. 'If you touch your weapons you will die too. What I've got planned will be a lot more fun if you stay around. I am only here for them.' He turned to look at Audun and Ulfar. 'And they do not get the option to—'

The sheer weight of Oskarl's shoulder crashing into Valgard's ribs pushed the air out of him. The Eastman's big, meaty hand shot up and grabbed the collapsing form of the tall man by the hair on his neck. 'You talk—' Oskarl grunted, smashing the top of his head into Valgard's face, '—way—' and again. Blood gushed. '—way—' and again, and bones cracked. '—too much.'

As he twisted Valgard's body to the ground, Oskarl's head snapped up to see Audun and Ulfar staring at him, open-mouthed.

'RUN.'

The breath caught in Ulfar's throat. This was how it'd have to be. He looked to the skies. The clouds cleared.

He didn't dare think about what would happen if this didn't work.

The rays of the midday sun found the plateau.

Oskarl screamed as Valgard's fingers dug into his flesh, tearing their way into the muscle, but he still held on, smashing Valgard's head into anything he could find.

Multi-coloured light washed over the assembled warriors as a rainbow touched the place where Audun and Ulfar were standing.

Behind them, the trolls stepped back even further.

Audun looked at Ulfar then. 'Are we—?'

'Yes,' Ulfar said, 'yes, we are. Only a god can call down Bifrost.'

Oskarl's last sound blended into a roar and then disappeared.

Valgard rose from the snow. He looked stretched, like a beast that had shed its skin.

Ulfar stepped onto the light. It felt oddly solid under his feet. He watched Audun step to the side and grab Helga.

Something passed between them, quickly.

Then Audun followed, and Helga was with him. He took a few steps, walking tentatively at first, but then moving quicker.

Helga's scream cut him to the core. He turned and saw her, standing at the foot of the Rainbow Bridge, one foot on the ground, one foot raised. Their eyes met and she put her foot down on the bridge of light again and this time he *heard* the sizzle. Her face contorted in agony and she screamed again as she pulled her foot off. She mouthed something to him, just a short sentence, and shook her head.

They could see sadness in her eyes before she staggered away, limping.

Audun looked at Ulfar.

'I am sorry, friend,' Ulfar said.

Audun drew a deep breath and exhaled slowly, hands forming into fists as he moved further up the bridge, closer to Ulfar.

Valgard, eyes blazing, strode towards the foot of the rainbow and looked up at them. 'And what do you think this will do? Are you going to run away?'

Ulfar smiled and looked over his shoulder as he kept walking up the bridge. 'Us? Run away? Oh, we wouldn't do that. That would be the act of a—' He turned, savoured the insult, then threw it at Valgard with all the venom he could muster, '—coward.'

Roaring, Valgard sprinted towards them; his quick, sure steps took him up onto the bridge, closing the distance – and then Audun's fist caught him square in the mouth and he stumbled backwards, sprawling like a new-born lamb. Then he fell.

Lying on his back on the Rainbow Bridge, Valgard smirked as he wiped blue blood off with the back of his hand. 'And now you get what you deserve,' he snarled. A thought flashed across his face and below, the troll army started moving towards the foot of the bridge. 'You've shed blood. We'll overwhelm you where you stand and this ridiculous realm of man will be overrun by the glorious beasts of Hel.'

Audun shot Ulfar a glance and received a smirk in return.

Infuriated, Valgard pushed himself up to his elbows. 'The Wyrm of Midgard will rise!' His voice rose, becoming shrill. 'Fenrir will walk free!' He got up and faced Audun and Ulfar. 'And you – *you will die.*'

Behind him the width of the Rainbow Bridge was filling up with soldiers of all sizes and shapes.

'Would you like us to take a few steps back, maybe?' Ulfar said, smiling as he stepped slowly backwards up the bridge. 'Give you some room?'

'I don't care!' Valgard said, eyes ablaze. 'You will be trampled where you stand, you bastard.'

Audun smiled as well. 'And then what?'

'RAGNAROK!' Valgard shouted, and as one, his soldiers roared.

'Because . . . ?' Ulfar said.

Doubt flashed across Valgard's face. 'You – you *hit* me! And I *bled*!'

'And . . . ?' Audun said.

Behind him, the trolls were pushing each other to get to the front. A tall skinny one lost its balance and fell over the side.

Ulfar watched it fall. 'One . . . two . . . three . . .'

The troll hit the ground with a dull crunch.

'When the gods shed blood in the realm of man, the gates of Hel will open,' Valgard said, his voice wooden.

Ulfar rolled his shoulders experimentally, as if trying out a new weapon. His smile was wide and honest. 'That is, by and large, correct. But we are no longer in the realm of man. And that means that we can do exactly as we please, my son. And there is one thing that would please us greatly right now.'

He drew his sword.

The hammer flew.

Battle was joined.

Epilogue

CONSTANTINOPLE, THE OTTOMAN EMPIRE
AD 1034

The steps of the palace, still warm from the midday sun, were empty save for two guards. They were both young, and from a distance they could have been mistaken for brothers – tall, blond and bearded, broad in the shoulder and lean in the waist. They carried big axes in their belts; mean-looking things with long hafts and nicked blades. They were the Emperor's Guard, the finest and most loyal warriors, the feared and loathed Varangians.

They were also bored nearly to death.

Ufrith, taller by a thumb's width and two summers older, turned to Bjarki. 'My grandfather was there, you know,' he said.

'I know,' Bjarki replied.

'He fought alongside them,' Ufrith continued. 'He saw them do battle with the armies of Loki and Hel. Audun and Ulfar, they called themselves then, but everyone knew it was *them*.'

'And then—'

Ulfrith carried on, ignoring the interruption. '—just as they charged Loki and the trolls singlehanded, all the soldiers from Valhalla came running down. They fought on the bridge for half a day and apparently, the old man said, it took another four days just to throw all the corpses off the mountain.'

An old man in rags shuffled up to the steps. He walked with a limp, but his back was still straight. Without sparing him a glance,

Ufrith stepped out of the shadows and barred the way to the doors. 'They saved the world from Ragnarok, which would have made Loki the supreme of all gods,' he said.

'I know,' Bjarki said.

'And the way of the North was preserved, thanks to Odin and Thor.'

'Thou shalt not worship false gods,' the old man muttered, fumbling for a sword that was no longer there.

'What?' Ufrith said, noticing the visitor for the first time.

'Nothing,' the old man said, turning away. White hair with a few remaining streaks of blond hung down past his shoulders, but his chin was still clean-shaven.

Olav Tryggvason touched the wooden crucifix tucked into his shift and walked off into the shadows.

THE END

Acknowledgements

And then there were three.

I could say I had all this planned out. I might say there was never any doubt, and from there it would be a short step to saying that it is so hard being a writer, doing all of this stuff by yourself.

But I won't, because none of that is particularly true.

Thanks go to the formidable Jo Fletcher, Nicola Budd and Andrew Turner for their tireless pursuit of excellence on all fronts. The books look gorgeous, and thanks to their joined efforts, are 35% better, and because this is a percentage, it is therefore science and fact.

I would like to thank Nick Bain. I would not like to expound on just how much he has taught me about writing and how hard he continues to kick my various body parts when I present him with sub-par stuff.

To the staff, students and families of Southbank International School – thank you all for waves and waves of support, encouragement and belief. I love you all and will miss you dearly.

Further thanks go to the tireless Jane Magnet, endless fount of kind words. Madam, you are an inspiration.

Whenever I do anything, my family always deserves thanks and a whole heap of credit. Mum, Dad and Árni – you rock. Thanks also go to my adopted auntie Geraldine.

And lastly – to Morag, my wife. Without her I'd be less of a marauding Viking and more of an odd, fluffy man, adrift in a barrel somewhere. I am so, so proud of you.